天符經

一始無始一析三極無盡本

天一一地一二人一三一積十鉅無匱化三

天二三地二三人二三大三合六生七八九

運三四成環五七一妙衍萬往萬來

用變不動本本心本太陽昂明人中天地一

一終無終一

Heaven Within

Heaven Within

The Key
Bridging the Millenniums

Tammy and George Klembith

Bell Rock Development Co.

Bell Rock Development Co.
1404 W. Southern Ave. Mesa, AZ 85202

Printed in South Korea

ISBN : 0-9658848-9-9
LC   : 99-63494

Divine Mind Is the Eternal Light, Looking toward celestial Light
Human Bears Heaven and Earth, and the three make One
One is the End of all, and No Ending has the One

- Scripture of Heavenly Code-

ACKNOWLEDGMENTS

We wish to express our sincere love and gratitude to Grand Master Lee for his inspiration, wisdom and guidance -- and for taking us by the hand on the path of lessons we were clearly meant to travel.

Much appreciation to our wonderful editor, Dana Henninger.

Sometimes there are reasons for things beyond our own limited comprehension. Many obstacles, including language barriers and cultural differences, were overcome to achieve the creation of this book. We believe the message contained within has a higher purpose than we, as mere mortals, can grasp at this time. And so we give you Kari's story, portions of which were inspired by incidents in Grand Master Lee's life.

Many blessings, love and light to all. We are humbled, grateful and honored to have been a part of this unique collaboration.

PREFACE

EVERYONE CAN EXPERIENCE
HEAVEN WITHIN

Inspired by real life events, *Heaven Within* elaborately details the unlikely odyssey of Kari Beacon, an ordinary woman who undergoes a radical spiritual transformation.

From the magical red rocks of Sedona to a tiny, isolated village in South Korea, Kari follows the same path traversed by sages of the past. It is a journey fraught with many obstacles, culminating in an ascension into another realm of reality where Kari receives her divine mission.

Heaven Within dramatizes this journey from Kari's initial inspiration to the profound bliss she eventually discovers. While she is fortunate enough to have wonderful spiritual mentors, Kari also makes her share of sacrifices along the way - fasting, isolation, discipline and the painstaking removal of her stubborn, multi-layered ego. Each time Kari steps away from the confines of civilization, she goes deeper inside herself and discovers what all sages know: the answers are within.

Heaven Within

Prologue

Moments before he heard the unmistakable sound of a rotor blade cracking, Joe Beeber spotted an eagle, in all its grandeur, gliding past the bubble-like windshield of his helicopter. The blazing sun glinted off the eagle's wings, and as Joe watched the majestic bird soar over Bear Mountain in Sedona, Arizona, he smiled to himself. Things were good in his life: an upcoming marriage combined with a business that was finally showing a profit, had provided Joe with an inner sense of peace. That serenity was instantly decimated when the rotor blade abruptly snapped and Joe's helicopter began to spin out-of-control.

Joe's first thought was the safety of his sole passenger: a middle-aged photographer named Gil Danton. Turning to Gil, he shouted, "Hang on. I'm gonna try to land!"

"What?" Gil replied, but the gyrating movements of

the helicopter had already triggered an instant state of panic in him. While clutching his camera tightly in his
trembling hands, Gil struggled to suppress thoughts of an
imminent death. His own. But it was virtually impossible
when the helicopter suddenly took a one-hundred-and-
eighty degree turn, swinging sharply into the rocky
canyon wall. The cacophonous sounds of the craft rattling
against the red rocks momentarily numbed Gil's mind.
Frantically searching for something, anything to hold onto,
Gil looked directly ahead; with dispiriting reality, he knew
that his fate lay in the pilot's hands.

For the first time since he began flying solo, Joe had
lost complete control. Nothing had prepared him for this.
Unnerved, he futilely attempted to maneuver the chopper
away from the rocks. Finally, the movement of the helicopter stopped in mid-air. One of the working blades had
somehow wedged itself inside a crevice. The craft lurched
but remained in place, precariously hovering approximately two hundred feet above the terrain.

Joe glanced out the window and motioned to Gil.

"Look for a place to jump!"

"What?" Gil could hardly decipher what Joe was
shouting. Instead, he followed Joe's frantic gesticulations
which indicated a ledge directly outside.

"You're kidding," Gil thought out loud, before his
survival instincts sprang into gear. Suddenly, it was as if
every cell in his body were screaming in unanimity,
begging him to summon up the necessary courage.
Unsnapping his seat belt, Gil slid open the side door.
Fighting to maintain his balance in the midst of turbulent

vibrations that waylaid any chance of equilibrium, Gil stared at the rocky ledge in front of him. Terrified, yet still clutching his camera under his arm, Gil leaped onto the narrow plateau only seconds before the helicopter broke loose from the crevice.

Gil peered down, watching helplessly as the chopper repeatedly smashed against the jagged rock during its perilous descent. Spiraling downward, the chopper crashed to the ground with an earth-shattering impact that echoed throughout the canyon.

Gil searched the area below until he spotted Joe slowly crawling out from the wreckage. Despite the conspicuous pain snaking through his body, Joe managed a listless wave to Gil, signaling that he was still alive. Gil waved back.

"Don't worry. I'll get help!" Gil called down to Joe, before shifting his attention to the task of getting down the mountainside.

Fortunately for Gil, several protruding ridges created a virtual staircase for him to follow. Still, Gil was wary; this was pure, untouched wilderness; there were no clear pathways. Gingerly he worked his way down, carefully avoiding protruding needles from the ever-present cactus clusters. Around fifty feet above ground level, Gil vaulted down to a huge rocky ledge. As he stopped his motion and caught his breath, Gil noticed that the ledge curved upwards towards an imposing cave entrance that seemed to be guarded by several trees partially blocking its mouth.

Engulfed by mountainsides of whispering ponderosa pines, Gil felt as if a voice from within was ordering him

to investigate. Following these overbearing, but not uncomfortable instincts, Gil dropped to his knees and crawled
inside one of nature's sculpted rooms. Sunlight filtered
through the branches of the trees and reflected off the
inner walls, partially illuminating the cavern. Gil was
awestruck by what he saw: Distinct symbols were deeply
engraved in the rock. He reached up and ran his finger
across a portion of the elaborate etching. Mesmerized, his
curiosity aroused, Gil began snapping pictures. He was so
caught up in the moment that he finished the remainder of
his roll before responding to the reverberating sounds of a
helicopter approaching.

Gil quickly walked out to the ledge and observed a
rescue chopper descending towards the crash site. He
concluded that Joe had managed to radio for help before
impact. Relieved, Gil briskly made his way down, his
mind still reeling with images from the cave.

* * * *

After getting his photographs developed, Gil spent
hours staring at the pictures of the ancient symbols. He
assumed they were Native American in origin but he was
perplexed; they resembled nothing he had seen before.
Now he felt compelled to know what they represented.
Instinctively, he sensed the symbols were trying to convey
a message; his frustration mounted as he tried to unravel
it.

Finally, on the advice of a neighbor, he drove up to
Northern Arizona, where he made an appointment to see
Professor Jeff Globus, a specialist in Native American

archaeology. Trying to camouflage his own passion after seeing the pictures, Globus suggested they return together to the cave so that he could personally inspect the symbols and verify their authenticity.

Wary of helicopters, Gil insisted that they drive to the base of Bear Mountain before hiking out to the cave where he had made his discovery. Together, the pair made their way through the dense, oftentimes treacherous, foliage towards the crash site. Only an isolated piece of metal casing remained, as the wreckage had since been cleared from the area. Gil pointed towards the partially hidden cave.

"Up there," he told Globus.

The Professor didn't respond. Instead, he began trekking upwards, meandering past the numerous agave that blanketed the terrain. Globus was impatient and eager to get inside the cave to see for himself.

With Gil in tow, the Professor ascended approximately fifty feet to the pronounced ledge. Seemingly puzzled, Professor Globus turned and surveyed their surroundings.

"This is most unusual," he said abruptly.

"What do you mean?" Gil asked.

"Aside from the fact that there are no actual ruins here, this area appears to be a most unlikely spot for Native Americans to have set up residence," Globus replied, before crouching beneath a tree and heading into the mouth of the cave.

The Professor carefully stood up and quickly retrieved a powerful flashlight from his canvas knapsack. After snapping it on, his jaw gaped as the light brilliantly illuminated the symbols on the wall.

"Well," Gil said. "What do you think?"

Globus motioned for Gil to remain silent as he switched on the video camera dangling by a thick nylon cord around his neck. Slowly and meticulously, Globus was careful to tape each symbol, individually zooming in for close-ups, before recording the wall in its entirety.

After completing the video, Globus began making copious notes about the symbols: their placement on the wall in proximity to the entrance, the measurements of the symbols, as well as the cave's interior dimensions. Professor Globus seemed to be in another world. Daunted by his frenzy, and starting to feel a bit useless, Gil lowered himself to the ground and crawled back outside onto the ledge. Staring up towards the sky, he noticed an eagle perched about a hundred feet above him. Its eyes seemed to gaze right at Gil. Gil stared back until the eagle lofted itself into the air, disappearing beyond the canyon walls above.

Finally, an invigorated Globus finished his work. On the hike back, he extolled Gil's discovery. Gil's interest was suddenly piqued: his ego's first instinct was to mull over the financial possibilities. But Professor Globus quickly squelched Gil's budding enthusiasm, asserting that the cave was on National Forest land and therefore, it belonged to the people.

"This is not a treasure to get rich from," Globus declared. "Hopefully, it's a find that will enlighten us all. In the end, isn't that more important?"

"I guess," replied a clearly disappointed Gil.

* * * *

Professor Globus spent weeks analyzing the symbols. He invited some colleagues from other universities to fly in and confer on his conclusions.

When he didn't hear from the Professor, Gil decided to drop in for a visit. Globus elaborately went over his findings. He told Gil that the eighty-one symbols were not uncommon - they had been discovered in several spots around the world at different times throughout history. To the best of his knowledge, they had first appeared on a Korean mountaintop over five thousand years ago. At that time they had been inscribed in Chinese characters. The Native American symbols from the Sedona cave closely corresponded to the Chinese characters found on that mountain, which bordered North Korea and China. Professor Globus felt it was safe to conclude that their meaning was identical.

"But what does it mean?" Gil asked.

Professor Globus smiled. "You could spend your entire lifetime trying to interpret something like this." he said.

"You're kidding?"

"In the end, you might end up more confused than when you started," Globus continued.

"That sounds crazy. So what's the point?" Gil questioned.

"The point is, by studying these symbols you might very well come up with the true meaning of life."

"Really?" Gil responded, suddenly intrigued.

Bell Rock

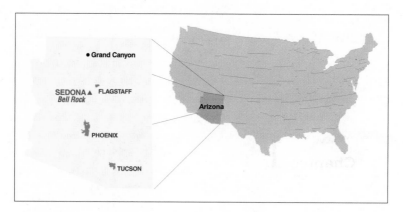

Bell Rock

Bell Rock is located in Sedona, Arizona. Two hours north of Phoenix, Sedona is a favorite haven for artists and other spiritual explorers who consider it a sacred place for inspiration and otherworldly awakening. Bell Rock is a huge red rock formation as large as a small mountain. With the shape of a giant church bell, it rises approximately 550 feet above the surrounding terrain.

It is said that Bell Rock is a vortex-- a place of powerful energy spiraling up out of the earth. People travel there from around the world to experience the strong vortex energy, which is often characterized by healing power.

Chapter 1

Kari Beacon was rarely at a loss for words. Half her days were spent in meetings where she was in charge of coddling, cajoling and convincing advertising clients that they weren't wasting their money. Kari felt she had a genuine knack for making people trust her business acumen. Now the tables had turned - across from her sat a man named Jack Streeter - and it was Kari's turn to listen. One of Los Angeles' most prestigious headhunters, Jack had spent the last hour extolling Kari's virtues, creating glorious visions of her future employment prospects. Jack guaranteed Kari that when she returned from her first vacation in two years, he would not only double her base salary, but he ensured that she would finally receive commensurate bonus compensation for her hard work.

"Wow," Kari thought to herself. Originally, when she had set up this appointment, she had few expectations.

"Well," Jack began, nestling back into his leather chair. "Are you ready to make your move?"

"Uh, of course," Kari stammered, nervously clearing her throat.

"You're like everybody else," Jack continued. "You're wondering if you're ready to be on top of the world. Hey, we all have those fears. But let me tell you something... when you walk out that door I will begin painting a scenario about you that will have the whole advertising community in heat. That's what I do best. In less than a week, I'll have everybody and their mother wanting to hire you. Once that happens, we'll set up a few choice interviews and let you decide who will sign your paychecks. We'll take the power out of their goddamn hands and put it in yours. It's going to be an early Christmas this year, Kari."

Once again Kari was speechless. At that moment the only sensation she felt was a sharp, aching pain that rippled through her stomach. The chronic pain invariably flared up in pressure situations. Kari assumed it was an ulcer but she kept putting off an appointment to see her doctor.

"So why don't you call me when you're back from vacation and we'll really get the ball rolling?"

"Sure," Kari replied. "I would like that."

Jack stood up to escort Kari out of his spacious office. He casually draped his arm around her back, lightly massaging her.

"Enjoy your vacation kid," Jack said as they reached the reception area, where a man in an ill-fitting, dark suit impatiently waited. As Jack perused his phone messages, Kari slowly walked towards the door. She glanced back one last time in Jack's direction and he smiled at her. While a part of Kari questioned his sincerity, another part realized that it was people like Jack who ran the world - people without any tangible skills except the uncanny ability to manipulate and coerce others into believing anything they said.

On her way to the elevator, Kari reached into her purse and pulled out a bottle of Pepto Bismol. She craved the soothing comfort it instantly provided, and without hesitating, swigged it right from the bottle. After pushing the elevator button, Kari studied her image in the full-length wall mirror. Maybe she had dressed too conservatively, she pondered, but that had been a premeditated move. She didn't want Jack to prejudge her by the way she looked, but in retrospect, she regretted that she hadn't appeared sexier. Hell, she was in a business that sold sex every day. What did she have to be ashamed of? Her thoughts bombarded her conscious mind until the ping of the elevator momentarily ceased their assault.

On the ride down Kari struggled to ward off her self-effacing shield by convincing herself that the meeting had gone well. Kari often felt that these internal debates were her raison d'etre. They took up an inordinate amount of her waking hours. Their unsettling confluence kept her mind in an endless state of flux.

Spotting her parked car, Kari indifferently glanced only one way before stepping out into the street. As she reached for her keys she heard an abrupt screeching sound. Panicked, Kari remained frozen in place as a Ford Explorer braked only inches away from her body.

"Are you all right, lady?" an older man hollered as he hopped out of his vehicle. Still in a daze, Kari looked all around, unaware that people were staring at her. Now trembling, she allowed the man to escort her to the side-walk. The pain in her stomach erupted again, shooting into her nerves and precipitating a throbbing headache. A chorus of car horns enhanced her discomfort as the man quickly scrambled back to his vehicle, leaving Kari alone on the concrete. After what seemed like an eternity(in reality only a minute and a half) Kari managed to cross the street. Once inside her own car, she slowly regained her composure.

On the drive home Kari tried to call her fiance, Brad, who was in San Francisco on business, but there was no answer on his cellular. Undaunted, she speed-dialed her best friend, Diane, and told her all about the meeting. Although Diane was sincerely excited about Kari's pros-pects, she tried to sway the conversation towards their trip to Sedona. They were scheduled to leave the next day. Diane knew Kari was upset because Brad wasn't accom-panying her, yet she felt Kari had made progress by agreeing to go without him. Diane's opinion of Brad diminished with each passing day, but she did her best to keep those impressions to herself. Diane tried, usually with only a modicum of success, not to judge others. Since her recent divorce, Diane had spent a good portion of her spare time indulging in a New Age lifestyle. Kari, who was more amused than repulsed, categorized her as a New Age junkie. To Kari, going to Sedona was only another spoke in Diane's spiritual wheel that continued to rattle down the road.

Twice before, both times at the inconvenient last minute, Kari had thwarted plans to accompany Diane to Sedona. Once again, Kari's instincts were demanding that she cancel this trip, but then she knew she'd be faced with the challenge of searching for another best friend. Moreover, Kari couldn't refute her overwhelming need to get away. After being informed by Diane that the airport shuttle would arrive outside her apartment building at seven o'clock the next morning, Kari switched off the car phone and turned on her CD player. The music helped alleviate her jangled nerves, momentarily. Kari soon found herself ensnared in a traffic jam which only triggered more frustration.

When she finally arrived home, Kari was still frazzled. After swallowing some Advil for her pounding headache, she quickly finished off a bottle of white wine that was on the kitchen counter. Too tired to cook, she popped a low-cal, frozen lasagna dinner into the microwave, before drawing a bath. As she was about to submerge herself in the bubbly water, the phone rang. Draping a towel around her body, Kari quickly slid down the hall to answer it.

It was Brad. Without asking about her day, he rapidly spoke about his own problems. Not only was his business partner backing out of the sale they had been working on for months, but their company was suspiciously under investigation by the Internal Revenue Service.

"Someone's trying to set us up," Brad said.

"But why?" she asked.

"Anyway, I'm going to be away longer than I thought. So you and Diane have a great vacation and I'll talk to you when you get back."

"Sure," Kari said, flabbergasted that he didn't ask how her meeting went.

"I love you, honey," he stated, before abruptly hanging up, not even allowing her to reciprocate the verbal affection.

While soaking in the tub, Kari rationalized Brad's recent, indifferent behavior. His business had always been an integral part of his life. When he had made the shocking decision to sell the company, even Brad hadn't grasped the full ramifications. Kari knew it must have troubled him, but he refused to communicate those deep-rooted feelings to her. Fortunately, she thought, their wedding was at least six months away, so Brad would have sufficient time to put his priorities in order. Except, what were those priorities? Those nagging questions, among others, kept Kari tossing and turning all night. Too often she felt as if her thoughts unrelentingly shattered her tranquility, like a harsh wind tears through tree branches on a blustery day. Finally, at around one a.m., rather than spend the entire night obsessing, Kari surrendered and swallowed some potent sleeping pills.

* * * *

Diane was her cheerful self the next morning, but Kari required a rather large cup of coffee at the airport to begin to activate her consciousness. The pills from the previous night had put her in such a deep state of slumber that she woke up more sluggish and listless than usual.

After the short flight to Phoenix, the pair rented a spacious Taurus for their two hour trek up to Sedona. Diane insisted on doing the driving which allowed Kari time to rest as they travelled through the barren desert. Kari was nodding off again, just minutes after Diane turned onto highway 179. Suddenly, Diane banged her on the shoulder.

"Look at that!" Diane exclaimed.

Kari blinked her eyes open. Immediately, her vision was assaulted by lush, green mountainsides and immense red rock formations which seemed to have materialized, as if by magic. The richness in color highly contrasted the miles of empty wasteland they had crossed. The noon sun reflected off the incredible landscape, highlighting the burnished tint of the rocks - providing a crimson backdrop that was downright picturesque.

After spotting a sign for the Bell Rock Inn, Diane swerved the vehicle off the main road and parked in one of the hotel's allocated spots. Kari emerged from the passenger side and glanced up - looming before her was a majestic, red rock mountain. She didn't understand why, but she kept staring in its direction. Diane exited the car and followed Kari's gaze.

"That's Bell Rock," Diane informed. "If you want, we could go hiking there later."

"Hiking?" Kari repeated. "I don't think so."

"What are you talking about?" Diane asked, puzzled.

"I'm here to enjoy myself, not work out. First I was thinking of getting a massage, maybe even a facial. Then I'd like to sit in a hot tub until the moon comes out."

"All right," Diane conceded. "You can relax one day, but tomorrow we're going to start really exploring this town."

"Whatever you say," Kari replied.

After checking into their room, on the recommendation of the desk clerk, Kari and Diane had lunch at a nearby Thai restaurant. Following a meal of coconut lemon grass soup and curried chicken, they drove to one of the most lavish resorts in Sedona and purchased week-long passes to use the facilities.

While Kari had a full-body massage, Diane strolled around the pool area and started flirting with a bartender named Rick, who prepared a potent strawberry daiquiri for her. She ended up divulging several personal, clearly one-sided, details from her failed marriage. When Diane started to get into the particulars of their sexual relationship, Rick did his best to change the subject. He was immensely relieved when Kari joined them.

Diane grew irate, storming away when Rick refused to make her another drink. Apologizing for her friend's unwonted deportment, Kari left a generous tip before leaving to find her. She found Diane vomiting in one of the bathroom stalls.

"It must have been that Thai food. I never eat Thai food," Diane rationalized.

"You were also never able to drink or did you suddenly forget that?" Kari scolded.

"Dammit, he put something in my drink, didn't he?" Diane began, suddenly embracing the paranoid thoughts that were percolating inside her brain. "Did you see that expose they had on Prime Time two weeks ago?"

"No, and I don't think he spiked your drink,"

Diane began rubbing her forehead. "I don't feel so good," she conceded.

"Let's get you back to the hotel so you can rest," Kari said as she helped Diane to her feet.

That night, while nursing Diane, who was suddenly stricken with a terrible case of diarrhea, Kari watched a thriller on cable. Every time she emerged from the bathroom, Kari had to fill-in the missing elements from the plot of the movie. It only made Kari acutely aware of how pointless and contrived the story really was. Finally, exhausted, her stomach stretched and empty, Diane passed out. Kari tossed a blanket over her and returned to her own bed, where, true to form, she was unable to sleep, so she continued to gaze mindlessly at the television.

When she did drift off, Kari experienced a vivid dream in which her deceased mother appeared. She often dreamed about her mother, but usually the situations were mundane and instantly forgettable. In this particular dream, her mother beckoned Kari to follow her down a hallway. As Kari continued down the hall, wearing a nightgown but no shoes, she noticed that the space grew narrower with each step. Ultimately, she reached a point where it was impossible for her to continue - her body literally couldn't squeeze through the cramped space. To compound Kari's dilemma, her mother had disappeared, and for some odd reason, Kari couldn't return in the direction from which she had come. She was trapped and became cloaked in panic. All that was visible was a thin, shimmering shaft of light which appeared directly above her. It was within that radiant glow that Kari noticed the splendid image of a golden peacock. Its feathers were pulsating like spires of vibrating light. Surrounding its luminous head was a rainbow halo which seemed to expand as it blazed into Kari's eyes. Kari experienced a loving warmth, which encircled, then embraced, her entire body. Abruptly, she woke up with a jolt. A bit shaken, Kari stayed beneath the comforting confines of her blankets until she noticed the morning sunlight peeking in from behind the blinds.

As if by rote, she slipped out of bed, quickly dressed, and went down to the hotel lobby to search for a hot cup of coffee.

* * * *

When Diane woke up she felt listless and void of any appetite. Kari suggested a jeep tour, thinking that might be relaxing, but the bumpy paths they traveled along soon took their toll on Diane. At one of the stops, beside the Seven Sacred Pools, an ancient Native American watering hole, Diane felt contrite.

"I'm really sorry about the way I've been," she told Kari.

"Hey, don't worry about it. It could have happened to anyone."

"But it happened to me. And I'm the one who insisted you come here."

"Will you relax? Didn't you hear what that tour guide was saying?"

"If he mentions vortex one more time..."

"Not about the vortexes. He was talking about the intense energy here and how it can affect our bodies,"

"Are you saying that the energy caused me to have the runs?" Diane asked.

The tour guide, a friendly man named Carl, interjected, "Runs? Who has the runs?"

"Oh my God," Diane said under her breath.

"Happens to nearly everyone who comes here. Your body needs to cleanse itself, that's all. Once you do, you'll really be able to experience Sedona. Hell, when I first moved here I spent a week in the can."

Diane smiled awkwardly at Carl.

"Soon you'll start tapping into the magnificent energy which is all around you," Carl continued, extending his arms outwards. "What about you?" Carl inquired, looking directly at Kari. "How's your body holding up?"

"Fine," Kari replied.

"Good for you. The energies here can affect you in many ways. Have you had any unusually vivid dreams?" he asked.

Kari was dumbfounded. Was he able to read her

mind? she wondered.

"Well?" he persisted.

"Actually, I did have a pretty intense dream last night."

"Yeah, you can expect a few more of those while you're here. When you're first exposed to this energy it's like lighting a firecracker in your unconscious - things will start popping. My advice is try to relax and enjoy the show," Carl said, before turning back to the others. "Alright, folks, snap a few more pictures and let's get going. There's a lot more to see."

As the tour resumed, Kari struggled to dismiss everything he had said. Yes, this was beautiful country and the red rocks were exquisite in design and color, but Kari hadn't tangibly felt the energy Carl spoke of. In fact, Kari hadn't felt anything to speak of since she had arrived.

Later, when the group stopped at a renowned vortex area, Kari once again didn't experience anything extraordinary. Perhaps it was because she wasn't allowing herself to. After the tour was over, Carl pulled Kari aside and calmly draped his arm around her shoulder.

"I don't know why, but I'm getting this feeling that you should climb to the top of Bell Rock."

"What?" Kari exclaimed.

"Look, I don't ask to get these feelings, they just come to me. I'm telling you - Bell Rock. If you didn't feel anything out there today, you will at Bell Rock," he insisted.

"What are you, a psychic on the side?"

"Something like that."

Kari stared at Carl. Why was this virtual stranger intruding on her life with these seemingly absurd suggestions?

When a curious Diane moseyed over to join them, Carl reiterated to her the need to get Kari to Bell Rock.

"He wants us to climb all the way up," Kari informed Diane. "Only if you can. You can feel the energy in many spots there, not just the top," he stated.

"Let's do it," Diane said excitedly. "This is what we came here for, isn't it?"

"But you aren't feeling well," Kari reminded her.

"Maybe a good hike is what I need. The question is, are you up for it?"

Kari meekly nodded. Her plans to spend the afternoon getting another massage and lying out by the pool had been obliterated.

* * * *

Since Diane still wasn't comfortable eating, Kari grabbed a quick chicken salad sandwich at a coffeehouse in the Tlaquepaque Village. The pair chose to sit at an outdoor table so they could watch the tourists saunter through the cobblestone streets all enclosed by unique Spanish architecture. While Kari admired the elaborately tiled fountains, an animated Diane couldn't stop talking.

"I told you this was a very special place," Diane said.

"He probably tells that to everyone. I bet he gets a kickback or something."

"There's no admission for Bell Rock," Diane scolded. "This is National Forest land. People can hike wherever they want," Diane paused, then asked, "Can I have a bite of your sandwich? I think I'm starting to feel a little better."

"Take it," Kari insisted as she handed the remainder of her lunch to Diane. "I'm going to get another cup of coffee. Would you like something else?"

"Those muffins looked great," Diane suggested.

Kari smiled, then turned and followed the flower-lined pathway leading towards the restaurant's entrance and disappeared inside.

During the drive to Bell Rock, Kari experienced her familiar stabbing pain.

"Dammit!" she exclaimed.

"What's wrong?" Diane asked.

"I left my Pepto Bismol back at the hotel."

"We can stop and get some," Diane suggested.

"No, that's okay. It'll go away, eventually."

"You really should get that checked out," Diane reprimanded. "I had an aunt who..."

"I don't want to hear it!" Kari shouted, severing her friend's sentence.

Minutes later, Diane turned off Highway 179 and stopped the car on a red dirt parking area. The pair followed the easy trail leading to the base of Bell Rock. Slowly, they made their way towards the formidable structure, which indeed possessed the uncanny resemblance to a circular bell.

As Kari gazed upwards, she couldn't help but notice the abundance of faces, both animal and human, that seemed to be etched into the crimson rock facade. She pointed them out to Diane.

"Yeah, I can see that. What I want to know is, how do we get up there?"

As they surveyed the rock formation, an older woman, probably in her mid-fifties, approached.

"I usually go up along that way," the woman informed them, pointing to a series of crevices along the right side.

"You've been up there?" Kari asked in amazement.

"I go up all the time," she answered in a friendly manner, before giving them directions.

"If she can do it, I can do it," Diane whispered under her breath.

The woman smiled. "It's not that easy," she chided, before walking away.

Kari and Diane started out with irrepressible vigor. They scaled the rounded rock along the base and headed upwards. Around halfway up, sweating, and slightly fatigued, Diane grew apprehensive.

"I knew I shouldn't have eaten the rest of your sandwich," she began.

"What's wrong?" Kari asked.

"I'm feeling queasy. Maybe it was the mayonnaise."

"Are you going to be all right?" Kari grew concerned as she looked down to face her friend.

"You go on," Diane insisted. "I'll rest here a while." Diane sat against the rock on a protruding ledge.

"Are you sure?"

"Positive. Go on. I'll catch up eventually," Diane smiled and motioned for Kari to continue upwards.

Kari hesitated, torn between the responsibility of attending to Diane's needs and a stubborn determination to make it to the top. Once Kari embarked upon something, she became obsessed; even if she wasn't enjoying herself, Kari felt the need to finish whatever she started.

With one more quick glance in Diane's direction, Kari continued to ascend the side of Bell Rock. The higher she climbed, the more perilous it became. As she wedged her sneakered feet into the narrow fissures, it dawned on her that it might have been easier had she purchased hiking boots. Like a spider, using both hands and feet, Kari carefully hugged the curves and inched farther up.

Suddenly, her foot crunched down on a loose rock. As she watched the tiny pieces fall directly beneath her, Kari struggled to get a firmer grip. The reality of what she was attempting to do jangled her nerves. Kari had never liked heights, but here she was, over one hundred feet above the ground, clinging futilely to the jagged rock. Kari was afraid to climb any higher, yet as she gazed below, she was bombarded with a staggering amount of anxiety. Her knees trembled. They seemed frozen, locked in place. She closed her eyes and tried desperately to think of something - a way out of this dire predicament - but all she could focus on was disaster. Kari was paralyzed with fear. She wanted to scream for help, but she couldn't muster up the necessary energy to activate her vocal cords. Horrific images of falling and crashing to the ground overwhelmed her. Now, unable to move either up or down, Kari remained still.

A soothing voice suddenly said, "Take my hand."

Kari opened her eyes. A gentle-looking man gazed down at her. The precarious situation didn't allow Kari to contemplate where this man had come from.

"I can't move..." she began anxiously, before focusing on her hands which were tightly-clenched around the rock.

"Look at me," the man commanded. "Now, relax for a minute. Take a deep breath and reach your hand up to mine."

Jarred back to the reality of surviving, Kari loosened the grip of her right hand.

"I can't!" she exclaimed.

"Think of the rock as your body. You are one with the rock. It won't let you fall."

Normally, Kari would instantly dismiss what this man was saying, but somehow, deep down, she knew there was no alternative. After taking a deep breath, Kari summoned up the courage to extend her right hand up towards the man. Clasping it firmly, he effortlessly pulled her onto the ledge he was standing on.

"Thank you," Kari began, but then it dawned on her that this was only a temporary solution. "How am I going to get down from here?"

"Down? You haven't made it to the top yet," the man stated. "Come... we can do this together."

"That's okay... but I think I..."

"You're almost there. Start climbing. Don't worry, I'll be right behind you." He offered his hand and said, "My name is Kim."

Kari smiled. "I'm Kari." As they shook hands, Kari gazed directly into his dark eyes - they were friendly and inviting. For some reason, Kari felt a hint of familiarity towards him, but she quickly dispelled it. He was in his mid-thirties, and possessed a quiet, genial manner; always smiling. Thin, with short-cropped, straight black hair, the man's rich, Asian complexion was tinged with a hint of red tan from sun exposure. He gestured for Kari to commence climbing.

Rejuvenated, and feeling safe in his presence, Kari made it to the top without any further delay or interruption. Once there, Kari profusely thanked Kim again. He nodded modestly and spread out his arms, indicating the magnificent view.

"Aren't you glad you continued?" he asked.

"Absolutely," Kari responded. "Except I have no idea how I'll get down."

"Don't worry about that now. Try to enjoy the experience. You're in a powerful energy spot, a vortex,"

"There's that word again," Kari said. She noticed Kim staring at her as if he were in a trance. She grew self-conscious beneath his gaze; it was almost as if he were peering inside her, to the core of her soul.

Unbeknownst to Kari, Kim was scrutinizing the perimeter of her face. After tapping into his psychic sight, Kim slowly examined her auric field. To the normal eye, the aura - the etheric field which surrounds the body - is invisible. But Kim had considerable experience in analyzing peoples' body energies. He could often decipher what was physically wrong with a person simply by noting the varied colors around their face.

What was immediately apparent to Kim was that Kari's aura colors were not bright, illuminating shades that indicated robust health. Rather, her colors were dull, muddled tones of bluish-grey and dark red. When he noticed that a harsh red distinctly encircled her lip and nose area, Kim broke his concentration.

"You have problems with your stomach?" he asked abruptly.

Kari shifted her body, nervously shuffling her feet from side to side. "How did you know?"

"I'm simply reading the energy around your body," Kim said, as he pointed directly to the location where her stomach pain originated. "That is where your pain exists?" he asked.

Kari meekly nodded.

"Your energy is low there. It's a common problem. You need more heat in the lower half of your body - your abdomen. Right now, the energy in that area is cool, like water. When your circulation is working to its full potential, the coolness will rise to the top of your head and the heat will descend."

Without touching her, Kim placed his hands around the circumference of Kari's head. "Right now, the heat is concentrated in your head which makes it impossible for your body to be in true balance or harmony."

"What?" Kari was confused.

"Do you get a lot of headaches?" he asked.

"Do migraines count?"

"Headaches and stomach problems are the direct result of an imbalance of energy," Kim stated.

"Then I guess my energy must be completely out of whack," Kari joked.

Kim walked over to a small tree growing on top of Bell Rock. He knelt beside it and pointed down into the red earth.

"This tree exists in harmony with fire and water energy. Water rises from the roots and circulates that energy upwards through evaporation. Simultaneously, fire energy from the sun enters the top of the tree and circulates down the branches, through the trunk, to the roots. It is this constant flow of energy that keeps the tree alive and healthy."

Kari nodded, her mind still reeling with where she was and the apparent stranger she was with.

"Come with me," Kim instructed.

He led her to the very edge of the rock. Then, without hesitation, he leapt approximately two feet, across to another plateau.

"Can you help me?" she asked, extending her hand. Kim shook his head. "You must do this on your own."

Kari stood there for a long time, assessing her situation. Kim remained silent, but kept a watchful eye on her. After three long minutes, Kim finally spoke. "Your fear is an illusion. The only reason you feel you can't come across is because you're telling yourself you can't."

Kari stared long and hard at the gap between the rocks. Without warning, she jumped forward onto the other side. Kim embraced her and said, "You have learned a lot today."

"Yeah, like I probably shouldn't have left the hotel this morning."

Kim smiled and said, "May I hold your hand for a minute?"

Kari studied him. While he appeared harmless, Kari

had been raised in an unbending culture of distrust, where appearances are often deliberately deceiving. Indeed, she worked in a ruthless business, where deception was the norm. Bombarding people with misleading messages makes it difficult, if not impossible, for them to recognize real truth.

"Sure, why not," Kari blurted out. In the recesses of her mind Kari knew she would need his assistance to get down from the summit.

"Close your eyes and try to relax," Kim began, while reaching for her right hand. Once again, he took a deep breath, and willed his mind into another state of consciousness, where he could readily summon the energy required.

Kari felt an instant warmth emanating from his hand, and was able to detect a rhythmic, throbbing in the center of his palm. With each passing moment, the energy grew more intense, and almost tangible to her.

"Relax," Kim repeated, as Kari struggled to ease the doubts which kept surfacing in her mind. He continued to gently hold her hand. Finally, she experienced a soothing sensation - the warmth spread throughout her body and encapsulated her like a womb. Kari began to sway, ever so slightly, as if she were floating in a comforting energy bath.

"Good," Kim said, while slowly releasing her hand. Kari opened her eyes and smiled at him. She examined her right hand which felt feverishly warm; her whole body seemed energized.

"Have you ever had acupuncture?" he asked.

"Are you talking about needles? I don't think so," Kari quickly answered.

"Needles are not necessary. I can use my fingertips to apply pressure to certain meridian points." Kim held his ten fingers up in the air.

"What do you want to do, exactly?" Kari questioned. Once again, fear had leapt to the front of the line, bypassing all other emotions, stubbornly flaunting its power.

"By touching the points that correspond to your stomach and intestines, I can attempt to alleviate your imbalance of energy."

"I'm sure you can. But why are you doing this?" Kari asked suspiciously. The moment the words were released, she wished she hadn't uttered them.

Kim touched the area around his own heart. "I want to help you. It's what I do."

Kari felt ashamed. His genuine, heartfelt response necessitated an apology. "I'm sorry," Kari quickly stated. "I'm just not used to this."

"Few people trust others. Trust comes from understanding. And even fewer people take the time to understand one another."

"You must be visiting here from a big city, too," Kari said.

Kim laughed and his eyes glistened with joy. "Would you like me to proceed?"

Kari nodded.

"Close your eyes and try to feel your whole body for a few minutes," Kim instructed, as he raised his left hand above his heart, palm side up.

Kari complied and attempted to relax. She wanted to dissolve her mind's racing thoughts, but found it impossible. One overriding question kept arising: Why was she allowing a complete stranger to work on her body on top of a mountain that she never should have climbed in the first place?

Kim placed two fingertips, his pointer and middle, from his right hand, onto the acupressure point between Kari's navel and sternum, for about twenty seconds. Kari felt warmth radiate from Kim's fingers as they lightly pressed into the particular spot. Her thoughts focused on his touch - she felt him making a slight indentation into her skin, as soothing energy began to flow within her.

After a couple of minutes, Kari's lower body began to feel considerably hotter than before; a tingling sensation, like white heat, trickled down to her feet, then shot up her legs. Simultaneously, a cool, persistent breeze wafted within her head.

Kari wasn't aware that Kim had long since removed his fingers; the energy continued to flow as if his hand remained in place. Her head felt like snow melting in springtime - a cool, fresh feeling. The rest of her was warm, and Kari felt expanded - both in mind and body. Unbeknownst to Kari, Kim had transferred his peaceful, harmonious energy to her.

Kari felt she had been released from bodily confinement. She had brief flashes of merging into the atmosphere; an uncontrollable feeling of bliss enveloped her. She experienced undiluted love for the first time in her life - not towards a person or even herself - but, pure love for all, and it was incredible. For a few brief, but impressionable moments, her mind emptied itself of all thought.

Standing across from her, Kim closed his eyes and whispered a prayer, sending gratitude to the divine source - where all his energy originated. Intuitively he sensed Kari's experience would have a lasting impression. He was honored and pleased that he had been chosen to help enlighten her.

Kari's eyes sprang open. When their gaze met Kim's, she wanted more than anything to reach out and embrace him. Instead, they exchanged loving glances - a knowingness that didn't need to be vocalized. When Kari finally turned away, she enjoyed the magnificent view.

"How do you feel?" Kim asked.

"Wonderful!" Kari responded. "I don't know how to describe what I'm feeling because I've never felt this way. It's incredible! Thank you."

"Bell Rock is a very sacred place," Kim began. "I come here often. Because of it's pyramid-like shape, it's very balanced and well-harmonized. The energy is concentrated at the top - where we are now. It's one of the best places in the world to meditate."

Kari's experience had happened with such relative ease, that her rational mind was waiting anxiously for the chance to question its authenticity. But those inquiries would have to wait. Kari was reveling in the unfamiliar, but agreeable sensations that invited her body and mind to simultaneously experience new levels of understanding.

Chapter 2

As they climbed down from the top of Bell Rock, Kari's sense of awareness was heightened. While Kim's close proximity assuaged the few lingering nerves that remained, Kari viewed her surroundings with newfound insight, acutely observing the exquisite color and texture of the sky, the trees, and the glorious red rock. By redirecting her attention, she lost track of time; before she knew it, Kim had clasped her hand and they were sidestepping down the last rounded mounds close to the base. Holding Kim's hand felt very natural to Kari, who suddenly experienced an extended deja vu - it was as if she had done this when she was a girl of ten or eleven, holding hands with a friend the same age. However, considering this was Kari's only time in Sedona, that was impossible.

Diane's glowering face pierced Kari's tranquility, like a spiked nail ruptured a smooth rubber tire - a sudden, unwanted interruption. "Where the hell have you been?" Diane shouted. "I almost left without you."

"Sorry," Kari offered. "I wish you could have been there with me."

"I wish I could have found a rest room! I ended up having to go in the bushes over there."

Smiling inside, but maintaining a compassionate facade, Kari peered over her shoulder and motioned for Kim to join them.

"Diane, I'd like you to meet someone. This is Kim... he saved my life."

"I'm sure," Diane practically snarled.

Kim stared at Diane, a smile wreathing his face. "It's a pleasure to meet you," he said.

"Why is he looking at me like that?" Diane asked.

"He's probably reading your energy," Kari volunteered.

"Well tell him not to," Diane demanded. But as she swiveled her head back towards Kim, his attention had reverted to Kari.

"Would you and your friend like to join me for some lunch?" Kim offered.

"I want to go back to the hotel," Diane emphatically stated. "I'm not having a good time and I really need to have a bathroom handy."

"If you would like to go, I can give you a ride back," Kim suggested to Kari.

Ignoring Kim, Diane's face pleaded with Kari not to

abandon her, but Kari didn't care if her actions were interpreted as selfish. She was having a good time and didn't want it to end.

"I'll just go for a little while," Kari hedged.

While unable to conceal her disappointment, Diane felt a dire need to quickly return to the comfort and convenience of her hotel room. "Do whatever you want," she said coldly, as they started walking towards the parking area.

Briskly trudging a few paces ahead, Diane ignored Kari and her new friend. Livid with anger, she felt Kari was deliberately forsaking her for some strange man she had only known for a few minutes. Compounding her frustration was her own failure to climb to the top of Bell Rock. That's why she had come to Sedona, but so far, her vacation had been an unremitting disaster. Diane kept wondering what she had done to deserve this.

After Diane drove off in the Taurus, Kari hopped into a jet black jeep with Kim.

"I must have a jeep when I'm in Sedona," he stated.

As they drove back onto highway 179, Kari confessed that Diane and she had taken a jeep tour that very morning.

"I've taken all the jeep tours," Kim added quickly.

"But now I find it more exciting to explore myself."

"It sounds like you come here a lot."

"As often as I can," Kim said. "I still remember the first time I came here from Korea," he continued. "At that time I was just beginning my own spiritual transformation. This place truly inspired me. It's a sacred location."

"So you're originally from Korea?" Kari asked.

"Oh yes."

"You speak very good English," Kari commented.

"Thank you. I've been in America for several years now so I've had a lot of practice."

"What exactly do you do?" Kari inquired.

"I just helped open a Dahn Center in Phoenix. I teach there but I also travel to other centers across the United States to assist and train other teachers."

"Excuse my ignorance, but what is a Dahn center?"

"It's a place where we teach the Dahn exercises, breathing techniques and meditations. These exercises are based on ancient teachings. They're designed to facilitate good health and spiritual growth."

"Really?" Kari asked, suddenly intrigued.

"We're in the process of opening centers all over the world. You're from Los Angeles, right?"

"How did you know?" Kari asked, but then quickly added, "From my energy, right? Nothing like Los Angeles energy!"

"We have some centers in LA. I would love for you to try the exercises."

"But it wouldn't be any fun if you weren't teaching."

"Next time I'm in Los Angeles, I will call you," Kim promised.

"I would like that. So where are we going?" Kari asked, consciously aware that they had been driving for some time.

"An area near Slide Rock - a very peaceful place. It's only another ten minutes."

Kari leaned back on the head rest and enjoyed the scenery as they proceeded uphill towards Oak Creek Canyon. An abundance of tall pine trees framed the sinuous road; marbled through their needled branches, Kari observed the lofty stone mountainsides.

Kim swung into the dirt parking lot of the Junipine Cafe and Grill, which was nestled snugly among a cluster of the resort's wooden cabins and towering trees. After climbing out of the jeep, Kari noticed what to her felt like a movie backdrop: steep rock walls overshadowed the area, rising perpendicularly towards the pristine sky. Conspicuous at the top of these imposing formations were what appeared to be delicately carved spires that closely resembled the turrets of European castles. Kim allowed Kari time to enjoy the view.

"Wow," she finally blared. "It's magnificent here."

"Let's go inside," Kim suggested. As they approached the steps leading towards a wooden deck, Kari spotted a grey squirrel scurry past her legs.

"Would you like to eat inside or out?" Kim asked.

Kari noticed that several people were smoking at the outdoor tables. "Maybe it would be nicer inside."

"Sure," Kim said, opening the door for Kari to enter.

The rustic-style dining area had cathedral ceilings with exposed wooden beams. The walls were pine-paneled throughout, causing the room to exude a certain warmth and vitality. Kari and Kim were greeted by a pleasant woman who escorted them to a round table beside a fireplace, comprised of smooth river stones and a slate mantle. A set of tall windows surrounded them on the other side.

After they ordered salads and some herbal tea, Kari noted how crowded the restaurant was. People were indulging themselves all around them. She noticed Kim quietly observing the other guests.

"People in America love their food," Kim stated.

"What's wrong with that?" Kari retorted, suddenly growing defensive.

"Are you aware of the three types of food?" Kim asked.

"You mean the three food groups - like proteins, carbohydrates and..."

"No... no... no..," Kim chided playfully. "The three types of food I'm talking about are solid, liquid and air."

The waitress carefully set the Cobb salad by Kari and the bowl of spinach leaves in front of Kim. Kari dipped an orange spice tea bag inside her clear glass mug, then twirled it around three or four times.

"Okay, solid is the salad, liquid is the tea, and air is something you're obviously going to have to explain to me because I don't think too many people are looking to order air for lunch."

Kim smiled. "Energy from food is wonderful but we need a balance. True food is love. Air represents our breath - our connection to the divine source of love and energy. Have you ever fasted?" Kim inquired.

"No. Although I could lose about ten pounds. Why, is that what you're recommending for me?" Kari asked, feeling self-conscious.

"If you fast you will completely understand. Because

when people fast they can survive on the third type of energy alone, no longer relying on the energy from solids or liquids. The food that sustains them is the air and their connection to the universe."

"You're losing me here, don't we all need the energy that comes from food? I mean, what are you trying to say? That we should all stop eating?"

"No. It's healthy to enjoy food. Food is a wonderful form of energy, but people rely too much on it, almost exclusively. That's why there are so many overweight people in society. They eat past the point of satisfying their physical hunger. Instead, they eat until they have satiated their emotional and spiritual hungers as well. Look around you," Kim suggested. Kari surreptitiously glanced at several of the other tables.

"A lot of these people don't know when to stop. Remember outside? Those individuals crave the energy that comes from their cigarettes and drinks. When people drink too much they're attempting to avoid being in touch with their true selves. Drinking is a form of escape, done by people who are impatient, afraid of giving love, and terrified of accepting it into their lives."

Suddenly, images of her father flooded the transom of Kari's mind. She recalled that he was not only overweight, but a hearty drinker with a propensity for whiskey, who grew more surly with each drink.

"It's a process of relearning, teaching our bodies and minds to act in accordance with our spirit, not just our physical instincts which crave immediate satisfaction and attention."

Kim plucked a red grape from the fruit garnish of Kari's plate and held it up.

"During my training in Korea, my teacher handed me a grape similar to this one and said, `This will be enough to satisfy your hunger.' I did not understand what he meant. I sat there for several minutes trying to comprehend how a single grape could accomplish this."

"Was it some type of trick?" Kari asked.

Kim shook his head. "I finally figured out that my teacher had concentrated a lot of energy into that grape, therefore, by eating it, I would receive all of that energy, and as a result, my hunger would be satiated." Kim popped the grape into his mouth and grinned.

"You're kidding," Kari exclaimed.

"Everything is energy - just in different forms."

As Kari continued to pick at her Cobb salad, she listened with rapt attention to Kim. Everything he said resonated within her; when he spoke about other people it was with genuine compassion, not the harsh judgmental criticism she was used to. Kari was especially excited when Kim offered to escort her outside to do more energy work. Still energized by the memory of what had occurred on top of Bell Rock, Kari couldn't wait to see what else he had up his spiritual sleeve.

While Kim was paying the bill, Kari made a quick trip to the bathroom. As she emerged, she collided with a man; his camera sharply jabbed into the side of her rib cage. Reeling from the sudden pain, she listened only halfheartedly to the man's apology, but when she peered into his eyes, Kari felt she knew him from somewhere; the odd sense of familiarity still lingered as she rejoined Kim.

What Kari wasn't privy to, was that the man, Gil Danton, experienced a similar sensation. On sight, he too felt he knew this woman from somewhere. But as she hurriedly dashed off, Gil made himself comfortable at an isolated table where he ordered a beer. He reflected back on the day when he had once again returned to the cave with the strange etchings. This time he went alone, and as he approached the cave entrance, he distinctly spotted an older Native American man hovering nearby in the brush. When he suddenly disappeared without a trace, Gil thought he might have entered the cave. Cautiously he proceeded, fully expecting to confront the man. However, when Gil arrived inside the rock enclosure there was no sign or presence of anyone.

After meditating inside for about an hour, Gil felt as if someone were trying to communicate with him. He heard a male voice whispering his name, very softly, almost inaudibly. Feeling uneasy, like he was being watched, Gil crawled back outside the cave and stood up on the ledge. Once again, Gil spotted the Native American man - this time he was about a hundred feet above him, standing erect on a circular spire. He appeared to be staring directly at Gil. Gil had the urge to wave, but before he could raise his hand, the man disappeared.

As Gil sipped his beer, he pondered his experience, wondering what the Native American man symbolized. Had he been trying to communicate some message? And why did Gil feel the constant irresistible urge to keep returning to the cave? Gil's mind remained muddled with these questions as he ordered another beer.

* * * *

Outside the restaurant, Kim led Kari down a slope to a wooded area near Oak Creek. Bubbling, rippling and murmuring sounds penetrated the air as the crystal-clear water gently caressed the rocks - now smooth from the constant flow. Kneeling down upon a metal cattle crossing directly over the rushing stream, Kim reminisced about his youth. As Kari knelt beside him he expressed how much he loved water as a child; once he embarrassed his parents by jumping, fully clothed, into a lake, just because he had the sudden urge to hug the water.

Kari noticed that Kim's eyes sparkled as he spoke.

"Sometimes, I would sit and watch the water all day long. It soothed my soul."

"Hey, if taking long, warm bubble baths counts, I like the water too."

Kari followed Kim as he strolled along the creek bank, over towards a grouping of tall pines. She noticed that he stood silent, momentarily bowing down before the trees. Kim stared intently at one trunk in particular for a long time.

"Is something wrong?" she finally asked.

"This tree looks like a tree I remember from when I was ten years old," he began. "It was winter time and a friend and I set out to gather some branches for firewood. Even though it was forbidden, my friend dared me to cut down a tree. Being foolish at that age, I succumbed to my friend's relentless taunts. Just as I lifted up the axe to cut the tree, I heard a voice bellowing inside my head. 'Please, don't cut me. I am alive. I am alive,' it pleaded. Shocked, I lowered the axe. Somehow I knew it was the voice of the tree. But my friend continued to torment me. He called me a coward and made me feel weak, so ultimately, I went ahead and cut down the tree. I wanted to prove my courage to my friend. But when my father found out, he punished me. He placed the trunk of that tree beside the doorway of the gate that led to my house, for an entire year. Every time I walked inside or out, I saw the corpse of the tree - a staunch reminder of my cruel deed. I heard the voice of that tree in my head many nights before falling asleep. I have never forgotten its sound. I have come to realize that trees are alive. I've made my peace with them - they are my friends now."

Kari didn't know how to respond. Part of her wanted to embrace Kim, but she held herself back, feeling awkward. Fortunately he took the initiative and instructed her to sit on the ground between two towering pine trees.

When Kari closed her eyes, Kim intuitively knew she had trouble relaxing. He imagined all the random and chaotic thoughts pouring into her mind, before he went to work. Using his hands, he created a swirl of energy around her head. As he began, Kari blinked her eyes open but Kim politely instructed her to keep them closed. Kari obeyed. He delicately placed his palms on her forehead, before sliding them around to her temples. Kari perceived a warmth emanating from his fingers, as energy flowed into the top of her head - it felt as if he were injecting an electric charge into her.

"Now... concentrate on your fingertips," Kim directed. "Your ten fingertips. Concentrate on the tips of your fingers. Sense them. Feel them."

Kari focused her scattered thoughts on her fingertips as Kim gently repeated the word "fingertips" like a mantra.

"Fingertips. Fingertips. Fingertips. Place your hands together in front of your chest, in a praying position."

Kari complied, still concentrating on her fingertips.

"Fingertips. Fingertips. Slowly, separate your hands. Slower. Slower. About three inches apart. Now bring them together slowly. Slowly. Don't let them touch. Separate them again, slowly, about five inches. Good. Now bring them together. Slower. Good. Feel the energy between your hands."

Kari felt as if a tiny needle had pricked some of her fingertips. It was a bizarre, sometimes uncomfortable, yet thrilling feeling. Energy seemed to shoot out from the microscopic holes in the tips of her fingers. There was a pulsing sensation, a subtle throbbing - as if each of her fingertips possessed their own rhythmic heartbeat. How unbelievably strange, yet wonderful, Kari considered.

Kim continued in a gentle tone, "Visualize your palms. Palms. Palms."

Trying to relax, Kari focused on her hands. The steady pulsing seemed to switch locations when she shifted her intense fixation. Gradually, the warmth from her fingertips spread to her palms.

Kim placed two of his fingers on her right palm for a moment, then her left. Kari immediately felt a stronger pulsing sensation concentrated within the center of her hands, which now felt as if they were vibrating.

As she was told to slowly separate, then bring her palms back together, Kari felt a definite ball of energy forming between them. It was warm and quite tangible. Instinctively, Kari began moving her hands around the ball of energy.

"Good. Very good," Kim gently encouraged.

Kari smiled while basking in the heat which enveloped her hands. As she slowly moved her palms back together, she felt a resistance - the energy was keeping her hands apart.

Astonished by this, Kari's eyes popped open and she was greeted by Kim's knowing smile.

"Wow!" she exclaimed.

"You felt the energy?"

"Did I!" Kari answered. "Especially after you touched my hands."

"All I did was help to activate what's already inside you," Kim began. "Eventually, you will become aware of your own true essence."

Kim offered his hand and helped Kari to her feet.

"Stand comfortably," he said.

Kari watched as Kim raised his hands up into the air, then slowly, ever so gently, lowered them at his sides. Finally, he released his wrists, leaving his hands to dangle.

"What are you doing?" Kari asked.

"I'm releasing negative energy through my fingertips," he informed. "Now, you try it."

Kari gracefully lifted her arms high to the sky and

allowed them to softly waft downwards, as if she were creating a slow flying motion, like the gentle flapping of a bird's wings. After her arms reached down to her sides, without permitting them to touch her torso, Kari released her hands, allowing them to hang freely. She felt the subtle flow of energy emit from her fingertips.

"Can you feel it?" Kim asked.

"A little bit," Kari replied, wishing she felt more.

"You just need more concentration. This exercise takes some practice."

The sun slowly began to set, casting a rosy glow against the imposing canyon wall. A soft wind circulated through the trees, tickling the branches and stirring up a slight chill in the air.

"I think we should get going," Kim suggested.

As they hiked along the gurgling creek, towards the path leading back to the restaurant parking area, Kim elaborated, "There are three origins of energy."

"Does everything come in threes?" Kari interjected.

"You're very perceptive," Kim said.

"So what are the three origins?" Kari asked, as they retraced their steps over the metal cow grating.

"First is the physical energy, which you obtain from food. Second is the genetic energy, your body construction, which is inherited from your parents and ancestors. Third, is the pure energy, which comes from the proper breathing methods, meditation and prayer. The last origin is what we try to teach people."

During the long drive back, Kari ruminated on what Kim had talked about over lunch. She thought it was interesting that the restaurant seemed to be filled with a typical cross-section of society - individuals overeating, consuming alcohol and smoking. Because Kim's philosophies made so much sense to her, Kari felt conned by all the myths she had been told over the years, as well as a bit guilty. Indeed, her very business was responsible for promoting the prevalent falsehoods influencing people. First, advertisers hyped their products - selling the "cool" lifestyle that seemingly went hand in hand with drinking and smoking - mostly to the younger, wayward generation. Or they enticed an unsuspecting housewife with creamy chocolate dripping into porcelain bowls, or exquisitely decorated ice cream cake logs being sliced on silver trays. Afterwards, as if to add insult to injury, they began blaming the victims - telling them they had no self-control, while promoting billions of dollars worth of phoney weight-loss programs, harmful chemicals and experimental procedures; all claiming to help people with their problems. The vicious cycle had become a total waste of energy, time and dollars for all involved. The fallacies continued to pile up, as the people perpetually lost weight, then gained it back; quit smoking for seven days, then began again; the prevailing yo-yo effect. Kari herself couldn't believe how blinded she had been. All people truly needed was love - real love from the source, she thought. Otherwise, no matter how much cake they consumed, or cigarettes they smoked, they would forever be searching for it - yearning for it - desiring it. To what end?

Outside the hotel, still exhilarated from her experiences, Kari turned to face Kim. "How can I ever thank you for everything you've done?" she asked.

"I can ask you the same question," Kim replied.

"What do you mean?" she queried.

"When people respond to what I teach, it gives me great pleasure. My purpose is to help others realize who they truly are."

Kari didn't know how to respond. Never before had she encountered such a pure-hearted person.

"I would like to see you one more time before I leave," Kim said.

"When do you leave?"

"Tomorrow. I have to return to Phoenix, but I could meet you at the Chapel of the Holy Cross in the morning. Is eight o'clock all right?"

"Sure, I'd love to," Kari said.

"You are so very precious. Always remember that," Kim told her. "Have a wonderful evening and I'll see you in the morning," Kim added as Kari climbed out of the jeep.

Kari watched as Kim drove off. When the jeep was no longer visible, she stared at her right palm. For a brief instant, she felt a pulsating warmth. As she turned and strolled into the lobby of the hotel, a broad smile overcame her.

* * * *

Kari maneuvered through the parking area at the Chapel and immediately spotted Kim's black jeep. She slid into the vacant spot beside it and switched off the engine.

The view overlooking Sedona was spectacular and she remained sitting in the driver's seat for a few moments to take it in, while reflecting back on the previous night.

* * * *

Kari had returned in such a jubilant mood, but when she checked on Diane, her elevated spirits were slowly dismantled. Seething inside, battling the twin burdens of depression and pain, Diane lashed out with uncompromising venom. While she initially directed much of her diatribe at Kari, Diane soon fell into a wallowing pit of quicksand: self-pity dissolved into acute despair.

Before the night was over, Diane's subjective review of her life unleashed a tornado of tears and rage. To Kari's ever-lasting relief, Diane eventually succumbed to exhaustion and passed out. After entering the bathroom, Kari convinced herself that she wasn't responsible for Diane's angst. She remembered what people had told her about Sedona - everything, all emotions, were amplified within its red-rock parameters. Still, as she ran the soothing water into the porcelain basin for her bath, she wondered whether they would be able to salvage the rest of their vacation.

* * * *

Kari finally popped open her car door and quickly walked up the concrete, winding path that led to the Chapel. When she reached the top, Kari was soon caught up in the sweeping, panoramic view. As she stood over some low-lying benches, she caught sight of Bell Rock off in the distance. Then she turned slightly to her right and was able to view Cathedral Rock in all its grandeur as well. Rotating further, Kari was awestruck by the sheer, red rock cliffs opposite the entrance to the Chapel itself. What a perfect location to build a place of worship, she thought; no wonder it was Sedona's most popular tourist attraction.

Kari spotted Kim waiting just outside the immense double doors, dressed casually in a sharp green Windbreaker and white Levi's.

"Good morning," he said, effusively smiling, as his eyes appeared to be appraising her. Instantly Kari felt inhibited. She had never met anyone quite like Kim.

"You shouldn't feel responsible for your friend, Diane," he began.

"What are you talking about?"

"Sedona is the kind of place that causes people to become very uncomfortable. The energy heightens fear, causing much anger."

"Is there anything I can do?"

"Listen to her... but be aware that she's harboring a lot of negative energy. You should add salt to your bath at night. That helps to cleanse it away. Did you sleep well?"

"So so..." Kari answered. "But I always have trouble sleeping, even when I'm home."

Kim led Kari towards the stone benches.

"You're on a very sacred area. This location is at the heart of the vortex energy."

"Really?" Kari asked.

"Many high holy spirits congregate here. In deep

meditation you can communicate with them."

"What would I say?"

"That's up to you. Or you could just listen. If you're meant to get a message you will. Now, why don't we go into the Chapel and pray?"

"Pray?" Kari repeated, as her mind was immediately racked with memories from her childhood. Vividly she recalled her mother dropping her off at Sunday school. While the other kids would join their parents at the service afterwards, Kari waited outside until her mother returned to pick her up. More often than not, because she had been shopping and lost track of time, she was late.

"Why don't you and Daddy go to church?" Kari always asked.

"Because we don't need to go anymore," her mother responded hastily.

"So why do I have to go?" Kari persisted.

Her mother grew irritable. "Because you still have a lot to learn."

Mostly Kari was taught about Jesus' life. Many of the stories were frightening to her. When her bible teacher lectured about the crucifixion, Kari suffered from nightmares for weeks. She never understood why the son of God needed to endure such pain and humiliation. When she turned eleven, Kari ceased going to church. After that, the subject of religion was rarely brought up in her house.

Now, as Kari was about to enter the Chapel, she felt uneasy. Sensing this, Kim pulled her aside.

"You have to understand, I haven't had many good experiences in church," Kari blurted.

"This is a nondenominational place of worship for everyone to experience the spirit of God within themselves."

Kari nodded slightly, indicating that she was fine and that they should continue inside.

Rows of wooden benches flanked the center aisle. As Kari proceeded along its carpeted surface she observed the fantastic view stretching out before her through the ceiling-high wall of glass. On either side of these immense windows were narrow tables overflowing with an abundance of white votive candles in red glass.

"I want you to light a candle," Kim told her. "As you do, focus on the flame and start to relax your mind. When you take a seat, close your eyes and imagine receiving bright white light into your heart. Let that light expand to surround your entire body; allow it to purify your soul. Don't worry if thoughts keep popping up. Just gently try to dismiss them and concentrate on the white light."

Kari took a few more steps and gazed up at the high ceilings. She noticed that there were only two other people present. A tomb-like silence enveloped Kari, causing her to assume a solemn persona. Quietly, she retrieved a dollar bill from her purse and slipped it inside a donation box. Kari took a long, wooden stick and lit one of the candles, then dipped it into a container of sand, where it would remain until the procedure was repeated by someone else. Kari focused her eyes on the dancing, golden flame. After a few moments, she turned and headed towards one of the wooden benches where she sat down.

It was difficult for Kari to ignore where she was. For unfathomable reasons she invoked thoughts of Jesus looking down upon her. Stop it, she scolded herself. Kari emptied her mind, finally shifting her concentration to a ball of white light. She imagined it encircling her entire body and tried to feel its warmth penetrating her skin, entering into her heart. Taking deliberate, deep breaths, she visualized the light soothing her.

But something was troubling Kari. Deep-rooted emotions clung to her heart area, causing severe pain. Suddenly, her father's image flashed into her mind, and, despite Kari's deliberate efforts to banish him, he wouldn't go away. Kari felt that her father's presence came at a most inopportune time. She had wanted to proudly tell Kim what a wonderful experience she had. Instead, she was bewildered and troubled. Momentarily, she felt a constriction in her lungs. Finally, unable to bear the physical discomfort in her chest, as well as her confusion, Kari capitulated and opened her eyes.

She surveyed the room. Kim was nowhere in sight. Kari remained seated for a few interminable moments, before rising from the bench and walking back outside.

She spotted Kim standing near a water fountain embedded in the rock. As she approached him, she smiled, but deep down she knew he could detect her anxiety.

"You're having difficulty opening up your heart chakra." Kim stared right into Kari's eyes. "He's still there. I can see your father's face around yours, clinging to your aura."

Nonplussed, Kari turned away from him. She staved off the potent desire to run away. Why was he doing this?

How did he know so much about her? She felt uneasy. Her privacy had been invaded.

"You have a very pure spirit, but there are many issues you need to resolve before you will be able to find peace within your soul."

"So what are you saying?" Kari demanded. "That I'm screwed up? Isn't everybody?" Kari's dam had burst, releasing a flood of raw emotions that couldn't be controlled. Tears streamed down the mountains of her cheeks.

"Relax, Kari," Kim said gently.

"Relax? Since I've met you I haven't been able to relax. Why did you bring me here? It's like I was set up! I don't need you or anyone else to tell me how to live my life. Do you understand that? Please leave me alone," she said coldly, before storming past Kim to the concrete ramp. As she descended towards the parking area, Kim's pleas for her to stay grew faint.

* * * *

When Kari arrived back at the hotel, she was greeted by an apologetic Diane, who suggested they take a drive to the Grand Canyon. Only too anxious to get out of Sedona, Kari quickly agreed.

Looking out over the vastness of the Grand Canyon, both women were filled with a sense of awe. Having regained her health and good spirit, Diane was enjoyable company once again. The pair took lots of pictures and even purchased some expensive souvenirs. On the drive back, while passing through Flagstaff, they stopped to get some gas. While Diane inserted her credit card into the pump, Kari moseyed inside the adjacent convenience market where she spotted the man she had bumped into the day before. Smiling, Gil moved towards her.

"You're following me?" he jested.

"Doing a pretty good job of it, aren't I?" she playfully replied.

"I didn't catch your name the other day?"

"It's Kari. Kari Beacon."

"Gil Danton," he said, stretching his hand out to shake hers. "Don't I know you from somewhere? You look awfully familiar."

"I don't live around here if that's what you mean."

"Oh, you're from out of town?" Gil asked.

"Yeah. My first time in Arizona."

"Bet you just got back from the Grand Canyon, right?"

"How did you guess?"

"Are you staying in Flagstaff?"

"Actually, our hotel is in Sedona."

"Pretty amazing place."

"That's what they tell me."

"I just discovered some ancient writing in a cave there. The professor at NAU thinks the message was divinely inspired."

"No kidding?" Kari said, her curiosity piqued.

"A message from heaven, he calls it, except he's still trying to interpret what it means. For some reason I keep going back to the cave," Gil continued.

Kari's attention drifted to the window facing the gas pumps.

"I'm sorry, I don't know why I'm telling you this," Gil began.

"No, it sounds exciting. It's just that my friend is waiting for me in the car."

"How long are you in town? Maybe I could take you out there."

"Just a couple more days."

"Too bad. I just got a magazine assignment. The shoot is scheduled for tomorrow."

"You're a photographer? I work in advertising, back in LA. Maybe that's where we've met."

"Maybe. Here, why don't you take my card," Gil suggested, as he peeled one from inside his wallet and handed it to her. "If you're ever in town again, maybe we can get together."

"Sure, that would be great," she replied.

Kari smiled as she purchased two soft drinks before heading outside. She turned and opened the heavy glass door by leaning against it with her back as she glanced in Gil's direction one last time. Kari nodded awkwardly when she caught him staring back at her. As she approached Diane, Kari knew in her heart that she would see him again.

* * * *

For the remainder of their trip, Diane and Kari spent time sightseeing at ancient Native American ruins and shopping at the stores in the Tlaquepaque Arts and Crafts Village. They even spent an afternoon horseback riding at a local ranch. On their final day, they decided to experience a hot air balloon ride - hovering above nature's red rock creations.

Keeping busy during the day kept Kari's mind temporarily diverted, but each night she confronted an irrefutable reality: There was a reason Kim came into her life and she couldn't ignore the fact that all he had wanted to do was help her. But by attempting to inspire her spiritual awakening, Kim had inadvertently triggered Kari's fears. Her ever present ego, a formidable opponent, didn't want Kari to discover the purity that lay within her soul. No, her ego refused to accept guidance from others; it demanded allegiance to the status quo. Like a mantra, it kept repeating, "Why change what's working? Everything is fine." But Kari's dilemma was rooted in the simple fact that she didn't believe the mantra was true.

Chapter

When the trembling commenced, Kari was immersed in one of those anxiety-ridden dreams, in which she was late and unprepared for an important client meeting. As her bed began to sway, Kari restlessly grabbed for her pillow. The rolling motion must have triggered something within Kari's slumbering psyche, because she awoke just moments before tumbling to the floor. A loud crash in the kitchen instantly enlightened her: this was an earthquake. Struggling not to panic, Kari reached for the light switch, but there was no power. Dammit, Kari thought. With Brad still out of town, she was on her own. Her nerves raced as the tide of distress swept over her. Clutching her pillow as if it were a life preserver and she was out on the tremulous and unpredictable high seas, Kari remained in bed until the shaking ceased.

Uncomfortable with her dark surroundings, Kari forced herself to crawl in the direction of the hallway leading towards the kitchen, where she vaguely remembered seeing a flashlight in the cabinet below the sink. Kari proceeded carefully past her bed, then her dresser, wearing only a thigh-length, silk nightgown. As she extended her hands, reaching into the emptiness, Kari realized what it was like to be blind. Suddenly, her knee scraped against a shard of glass and Kari screamed in pain. As if responding to her cry, the lights came back on. Kari knelt to examine her knee and quickly removed a large sliver of glass. Laying beside her was a shattered picture frame which had fallen from the top shelf of her bedroom closet. It was a family portrait - her father, Charles, had one arm draped around Kari and the other around her mother. Staring at the photograph ignited the sparks of several memories: it was taken just before Kari had left for college, several months prior to her mother's untimely death. Overcome by conflicting emotions, Kari quickly headed for the bathroom to tend her bleeding knee.

Kari methodically rinsed the injured area with alcohol; the physical pain paled in comparison to the emotional void she suddenly felt. As Kari recalled the circumstances surrounding the tragedy, she grew solemn - even a bit guilty. Maybe if she had been home instead of away at college... Stop it, she scolded. The death had been a tragic accident - a mis-diagnosis made by overworked and exhausted emergency room doctors. Kari's mother should never have been released from the hospital. Within hours of being sent home, she died of kidney complications.

Kari would never forget the phone call. It was branded into her memory like a hideous label - marking her forever - a motherless daughter.

"Hi Dad," she remembered saying, "What's up?"

There was a protracted pause. All Kari could hear was her father's heavy breathing. Finally he spoke.

"I'm at the hospital."

"What's wrong?" There was alarm in her voice.

"Your mother died an hour ago."

"What?" Kari was not prepared for the emotional impact she felt. The blow caused her to sink to the carpeted floor while still clutching on to the receiver.

"There wasn't anything the doctors could do." her father continued. "It was too late."

"No! No! It's impossible! I just spoke with her the other day. Everything was fine. Dad? What happened?" Kari shouted in anguish.

The haunting memory of that scream jarred her back to the present. Kari felt a distinct ache in her chest, a loss that couldn't be soothed, even with time. The memories were as vivid now as when the events had actually occurred. As Kari slowly applied a bandage to her knee, she reflected back on the days immediately following the funeral. She had walked around in a mindless daze, wondering about purpose and meaning, sometimes coming to the forlorn conclusion that there was none. For a while, Kari longed to join her mother. But something, perhaps the enduring survival instinct that kept people clinging on to life, prevailed. Hope, although Kari did not know for what at the time, had triumphed.

After Kari returned to college, Charles enlisted the services of an aggressive young lawyer willing to work on a contingency basis. A month after filing the necessary paperwork, the hospital conceded; while not acknowledging any wrongdoing, they extended a handsome offer which was immediately accepted. The next thing Kari knew, her father, after negotiating an early retirement, had proposed to Dina Stemple, an attractive woman who had once been his secretary - the same woman her mother had always been suspicious of. Indeed, Charles had been conducting an affair with Dina for years; her mother's death conveniently provided the avenue for him to start a new life.

Encumbered by reluctant emotions which tore at her heart, Kari attended the wedding. Despite her friends' entreaties, Kari began to drink, futilely attempting to drown her indignant feelings. It was in front of the entire stunned congregation that an inebriated Kari told her father she didn't love him. The hush that ensued among the crowd was expected. What Kari hadn't anticipated was her father's complete disregard for her at that moment. He simply ignored her. Turning his back on his only child, Charles whisked his bride onto the dance floor.

Kari's relationship with her father had been forever tarnished. Since that time they rarely spoke. Their relationship became fraudulent. A wall was built between them - its bricks as flimsy as the occasional birthday or holiday cards that were sent. The artificial facade was created on top of an extremely shaky foundation of empty, meaningless salutations - between relative strangers.

Kari replaced the box of bandages in the medicine chest and headed back through her bedroom, down the hall, towards the kitchen. Various framed prints and china knickknacks had fallen from the walls. Only some had broken from the impact. Ignoring the damage, Kari shifted her attention to the digital clock read-out on the stove. It was almost five a.m. She realized it was pointless to return to bed, so instead, she flipped on the television where early reports had already estimated an earthquake in the 5.8 range. Yawning, Kari switched on the coffee machine. It was time to get her circulation going.

Kari wished that Brad was here to help her clean up the mess. Instead, he was visiting his older brother, Kevin, in San Diego. Kevin was an attorney; the only time Brad went to see him was when he desperately needed help. When Kari spoke to Brad the night before, he refused to divulge any details, but she sensed the concern in his voice. Brad was predictable that way. When things were going well, he was carefree and voluble. The moment conflict arose, he grew defensive and uncommunicative. Kari had begun to seriously question whether these were qualities she could tolerate in a long-term relationship.

After a quick shower, she caught updates on the news. The earthquake had officially registered at 5.6 on the Richter scale. Damage around the city was minimal; what had been stimulated were peoples' nerves. Kari couldn't wait to get back to work. She had been away long enough.

* * * *

When she entered her office, Kari was gratified that Brenda, her secretary, had already cleaned up the effects of the quake. As if craving the appreciation that Kari rarely gave her, Brenda began elaborating - telling Kari, in detail, about everything that had fallen from the desk and shelves. An ambitious young woman, Brenda had started coming in earlier every day. While Kari could find nothing wrong with her job performance, she felt Brenda lacked the people skills that clients demanded. Or perhaps, Kari just didn't want to face the reality that she would soon be losing Brenda - a promotion was imminent.

What Kari would miss most were the comprehensive charts and reports that Brenda prepared for her. Brenda's organizational skills were impeccable. As she sat down, Kari reviewed Brenda's summaries on everything that had transpired during her absence. Within twenty minutes Kari felt she was back up to speed.

Brenda peeked her head in the office. "They moved the staff meeting up to nine-thirty this morning," she said.

"Okay."

"Oh, one last thing..." Brenda began.

"What?" Kari asked, fearing the worst.

"People around the office know you went to Jack Streeter."

"What!" Kari shouted. "Who besides you could possibly know?"

"I didn't say a word, I swear!" Brenda stammered.

"I'm sorry. I didn't mean to accuse you."

The phone rang and Brenda sprinted back to her desk to answer it.

"It's Brad," Brenda called out.

"Hey stranger," Kari said into her phone. Allowing paranoia to run rampant, she fleetingly wondered if her calls were being tapped.

"I'll be home tonight. What do you say we go out to dinner?" he asked.

"I'd like that," Kari replied. "How are you doing?"

"Good. I'll tell you all about it later. I missed you," he added.

"I missed you too."

"Okay, see you," Brad said before he hung up.

As she sat back in her chair, Kari continued contemplating the various possibilities, until one leaped to the head of the pack. Could Jack Streeter have leaked the news? A pressure tactic? She realized, with keen awareness, that she couldn't trust anyone.

While briskly heading down the hall to the rest room, Kari suddenly thought about Kim, the man she had met in Sedona. Instantly, she regretted her impetuous behavior towards him. What had scared her was his prescient ability. He knew she had issues with her father that she stubbornly refused to acknowledge, let alone attempt to resolve. But how? Regardless, Kari couldn't refute Kim's genuine compassion for her, as well as his authentic powers. Perhaps her friend Diane had the right idea - while Kari often belittled her, maybe delving into spirituality was an option she too should explore. These thoughts and others were dashed when she ran into her boss right outside the conference room.

"Hi Linda," Kari quickly said.

"Welcome back."

"Thank you," Kari answered, all the while wondering if Linda knew about her meeting with Jack. She decided to confront the issue.

"Can we talk?" Kari asked. Linda nodded and motioned for Kari to follow her into the conference room.

"I know you may have heard some rumors about me looking for another job." Kari began, her voice laced with tension, "but I..."

"Why are you telling me this?" Linda interrupted.

"I guess I just wanted you to know that I haven't gone on any interviews yet and I don't know that I will."

"You're free to do whatever you want on your time."

"I know that," Kari answered awkwardly.

"Kari, let me just say one thing - in a few months you're up for a promotion that includes being made partner. Sure, there are a lot of good jobs out there for people at your level - Jack Streeter paints a wonderful picture. I should know, he used to paint them for me."

"What?" Kari was genuinely surprised.

"I used to date him," Linda conceded.

Kari came to the unsettling realization that Jack must have told her.

"Take a little advice from someone who has switched jobs - you have to start developing relationships all over again, and trust me, that's not as easy as it sounds. We brought you along slowly here and you've done great work. Now it's your turn to shine. Don't walk away from that. No matter what Jack tells you. I'll see you in the staff meeting."

Linda turned and exited, leaving Kari alone, staring at the large, oval table in the center of the room. Perplexed, Kari's pragmatic mind reviewed the conversation. True, Linda wasn't objective. Selfishly she wanted Kari to stay just to ensure the client relationships she had cultivated. She was like an investment to them. At the same time, Kari knew it would be a difficult, time consuming process to develop a rapport with new clients. At best, clients were moody and often impossible to please. Kari didn't relish having to appease a whole new set of personalities. But what about the promotion and possibility of being made partner? Yes, they would pay her more money, Kari knew, but partner? They dangled that carrot to many scrambling rabbits in the office. Kari decided that she would not rush into a job search right away. There were too many other things she needed to work out in her life, including her relationship with Brad.

* * * *

By the time Kari arrived at a trendy restaurant in Santa Monica, she was battling a throbbing headache - the pain pressed against her temples, demanding immediate attention. Popping a couple Advil, Kari joined Brad at a side table. He had already consumed a few drinks and motioned for the waiter to procure one for Kari.

"You look tired," Brad said.

"Long day. Nothing like having an earthquake for an alarm clock. Did you feel it in San Diego?"

"No," he answered.

"I wish you had been with me."

"Don't worry. I'm going to be in town for a while now."

"Good. So do you want to tell me why you went to see your brother?"

"It's a long story."

"We haven't ordered yet. Why don't you start?"

"I don't know if I want to burden you with this."

"Come on, Brad! You asked me to marry you two months ago! We sleep in the same bed every night, but suddenly you don't want to burden me with something!"

"Hey, why are you yelling at me?"

"Cause I'm losing my patience." Kari was silent a moment. "Maybe that's it," she said quietly.

"What?" he asked.

"Maybe a bed is all we share."

"Come on Kari, don't start this. I just got back."

"Yeah, but I don't know why you left."

Brad lifted his glass and finished the rest of his drink.

"No matter what it is, I'm here for you. Don't you know that by now?"

Brad wished he had the isolation and protection of a confessional booth. He couldn't look directly into her eyes; couldn't face her. Finally, Brad began to speak. He revealed that he had done some unethical things while starting his business. Those foolhardy mistakes had come back to haunt him.

"So you made some mistakes. We all do," Kari reassured.

"Not like these. And the worse thing is that I thought

I had a partner I could trust. He made me put all this stuff in my name."

"Hold it. Let's get something straight. Nobody can make you do anything. This was obviously something you agreed to."

"Oh great! Now you're taking his side."

"I'm not on anyone's side," Kari emphatically stated.

"This is not about sides. This is about you being a man and owning up to whatever you did."

"Am I going to get no sympathy here?"

"You want sympathy or you want to know what you should do?" Kari was growing agitated.

"Don't you realize, if I admit I did anything wrong I'll lose the company? That's exactly what my partner wants. He's blackmailing me."

"That's one way to look at it," Kari stated.

"Is there another way?"

"Yes, you could admit you did something wrong and face the consequences."

"I can't believe you're talking this way."

"Maybe you can walk away and start over," she suggested.

"Listen to you. Start over? Like it's that easy. You want to marry a failure? Is that it?"

"Since when is telling the truth being a failure?"

"You just don't get it, do you? But how could you unless you were in my shoes?"

"I don't think I would do the things that put you in this position," Kari quickly replied. The instant she said it, she regretted it.

"You bitch!" Brad stated as he rose to his feet. "And you wonder why I don't tell you anything."

"Look, I'm sorry. I didn't mean it that way."

"Oh yes you did. This is exactly how I knew you would be - self-righteous and completely intolerant. I hope the day never comes when you need a little support!" Brad fumed, before barreling out of the restaurant.

With the collective eyes of all the inquisitive patrons directed at her, Kari kept her head down and quickly paid the bill. Rushing to the parking lot, she spotted Brad's car speeding towards her. The gleaming headlights blinded Kari, as Brad screeched to an abrupt halt. He popped his head out the window revealing a seething countenance.

"Don't bother coming home tonight," he said.

"I live there too. Where do you expect me to go?"

"To hell!" he shouted, before speeding away.

Nervously rocking on her feet, Kari remained in place, acutely realizing there would be no point to going home. As long as Brad continued to grapple with his conscience, he would be impossible to live with. Like most people, his anger and frustration needed a target, and as long as they were living together, Brad would continue to conveniently direct his ill-tempered emotions towards her.

* * * *

Kari ended up moving in with Diane. Her friend seemed to take a perverse delight in Brad's travails.

"Bastard deserves everything that's coming to him."

"Diane, show a little compassion."

"Hell, Kari, he's like all the assholes who think they

can get away with anything they want. When they have a problem, they want you to feel sorry for them - refusing to acknowledge they did something wrong."

Kari pondered Diane's remarks. It was true: Brad didn't want to own up to his culpability. While she held out the hope that this was part of his maturation process, she wasn't optimistic about their future prospects. When he called the next day, Kari apologized for what she had said. A melancholy Brad suggested they postpone the wedding. Despite Kari's inner sadness, she quickly acceded.

On Diane's recommendation, Kari perused a few of the multitudinous books her friend had collected on spirituality. Diane's shelves were rimmed with volumes on religion, meditation and New Age philosophy. Kari found the reading compelling: especially some of the books depicting various spiritual journeys. They conjured up her recent experience in Sedona.

Kari attended a weekend psychic fair with Diane, where a clairvoyant blurted out that many of Kari's problems stemmed from a dysfunctional relationship with her father. Without any prompting, the psychic knew that Kari's mother was deceased. The woman's accuracy was uncanny.

"I see you going on a long trip somewhere," the psychic added. "In the very near future."

"Where?" Kari demanded.

"That, I'm not sure of. But, whatever you do, don't resist going on this trip. It's a journey that will permanently change your life."

"You probably say that to everyone," Kari scoffed.

The psychic's eyes narrowed and studied Kari's face.

"Some things are meant to be. Destiny can be postponed, but not changed. I see struggles ahead for you, but they're all necessary and you will endure."

Yeah, Kari thought. That's easy for her to say. Everyone has struggles.

"Do you see any relationships in my life?" Kari queried.

"You're involved with someone right now, aren't you?"

"Well..." she hesitated.

"It was serious. He asked you to marry him, but now he's having problems. That could go either way."

"What could?"

"Whether you get back together. It depends a lot on you - and what changes you end up going through."

By the end of the session, Kari was both amazed and doubtful. She had allowed a stranger to analyze her life - a totally self-conscious experience. In the process, it pulled Kari down a path to self-understanding. It was akin to a session of psychotherapy, only this was not a trained therapist. Rather, Kari felt this was a person who combined psychic power with keen insight and awareness. For days, Kari wondered about the trip she was supposed to take.

On the advice of one of Diane's friends, Kari went to a healer named Cassandra, who did her work under a giant copper pyramid. Cassandra massaged and applied heat to Kari's stomach area - soothing and, in her words, "working out the karmic wounds." She recited some chants and played angelic music in the background. By the end of the two hour session, Kari's pain was gone, and instead, she felt bliss. However, Cassandra didn't want Kari to leave with any illusions.

"You could come to me every week and feel better each time," Cassandra said. "But I wouldn't be expressing truth and love if I didn't tell people that they possess the same healing energy. It's inside all of us. Learn to listen to the rhythms of your own body. Through meditation and concentration, you can access this power within you, and radically change your life."

"How do I go about doing that?"

"There are many ways to reach the proverbial "spiritual pot" at the end of the rainbow. Everybody takes a different path to get there. When you're ready, you'll get directions. Then it's just a matter of how much you want it."

* * * *

To the dismay of some of her colleagues, Kari started to develop a conscience at work. When the company began bidding for a client wishing to advertise alcohol, Kari was one of the few to express disapprobation - once again facing the reality that her business willingly made profits by promoting the sale of harmful products to the public. But another side of Kari was subjectively rational - nobody forced people to buy the products. As for alcohol, even Kari wondered if her objection had birthed only because her own father had alcoholic tendencies.

Kari played a deliberate procrastination game with

Jack Streeter - putting him off for days at a time. When Kari alerted him to the fact that her boss knew what she was up to, Jack didn't miss a beat. He laughed and said, "You don't think she's looking too? Hell, she interviewed twice last week. She won't be there much longer."

Kari wasn't sure whether to believe him or not. "Why are you telling me this?" she asked suspiciously.

"You want to know why? Because when Linda leaves there's little chance of you getting that promotion."

Shocked and dismayed, Kari realized with piercing perception that Jack knew all the intricate details of her company. Was he the consummate puppet-master - cleverly weaving people in and out of their various stages - completely controlling their destinies? "You're afraid of change, Kari, but let me remind you of one thing - you're in a burnout business. You need to get out as much as you can, while you still have your health and clarity of mind. They need you now, but tomorrow, there's thousands of bright, ambitious sharks swimming your way."

"You should know, you're the one who charts their course."

After enjoying another egotistical laugh at Kari's expense, Jack finally said, "It's up to you, kid."

Kari was silent a moment. Swayed by Jack's ruthless rhetoric and realizing she wanted this man on her side, she finally replied, "All right. Start setting up some interviews."

"Now you're talking. I'll get back to you," Jack replied, before hanging up the phone.

The connection went dead while Kari was still holding

the receiver up to her ear. She paused, focusing on the tone, as if hypnotized by its monotonous sound. Kari pondered her life. A few weeks ago she had felt on top of the world. Now, her longest lasting relationship was all but dissolved - Brad wasn't even returning her calls. She didn't feel the same drive or intensity at work. Things that once meant so much, now meant so little. What was happening to her?

Kari continued to spend most of her free time with Diane. They frequented the Bodhi Tree bookstore where Diane purchased many of her spiritual books, while also trying to meet men. One night, while Diane discussed the future earth changes with a handsome, bearded man in his early forties, Kari poured herself a cup of complimentary tea and roamed through the store's wooden stacks. She passed a bulletin board on her way to the section on channelling. As she scanned the numerous flyers tacked to its cluttered facade, she spotted the word DAHN, printed in bold, black type on a small, white poster board. Underneath were details about Dahn Meditation classes being given in Los Angeles. Kari fished through her purse for a pen and quickly jotted down the times and location.

The next morning, while Diane had a breakfast date with the bearded man, Kari drove to an address in West LA to take a Dahn meditation class. It took place inside a converted warehouse - a spacious area with high ceilings. The walls were all white except for a series of framed posters depicting several meditation postures. The teacher was a long-haired man in his late twenties named Kenny.

Full of energy and zeal, Kenny directed the class through a series of limbering and stretching exercises. He continually reminded everyone to be cognizant of their breathing.

"Everything starts with the breathing," he said. "Try your best to breath deeply, down to your abdominal area."

Some of the exercises were difficult, requiring the kind of gymnastic flexibility that Kari didn't have. Still, despite feeling self-conscious every time Kenny glanced in her direction, Kari did her best to keep up, and quickly felt more energized.

After doing some back rolls on the carpeted floor, Kenny changed the CD in the player. The new disk contained sounds of nature: waves rolling across sand, wind whistling through a forest, birds singing in the trees. Every member of the class sat up in a half-lotus position. Kari followed suit. Kenny allowed them a few moments to unwind, before guiding them through a meditation. Kari experienced a peaceful, floating sensation; she became totally relaxed.

When the class concluded, Kari waited patiently until everybody else had gone, before approaching Kenny.

"What did you think?" he asked.

"It was wonderful. I've never done anything quite like this before," she responded.

"That's because there isn't anything quite like this."

"I'm beginning to realize that. Do you know someone named Kim? He's Korean. I met him in Sedona."

"Are you talking about Master Kim? Follow me."

Kenny led Kari into a back office where he scooped up

a picture frame from an oak desk and exhibited it to her. The glossy color photo depicted Kim and Kenny together on top of Bell Rock.

"Is this the Kim you're talking about?" Kenny asked.

"Yes, that's him. You're on Bell Rock in that picture. I met him there. He saved my life. Is that where you met him?"

"No, we actually met at the Grand Canyon. But he's the one who talked me into going to Sedona. I spent two days with him... one night we even slept on top of Bell Rock."

"Really?"

"Master Kim changed my life," Kenny stated with reverence as he replaced the frame on top of the desk. "I am one of his juniors. He trained me to teach Dahn Meditation. I'll admit, when he first told me about it, I was skeptical. I was a surfer. I got my highs riding the waves with the sun rising in the background, or smoking some weed. But Master Kim made me realize there was much more - to life and to who I really am. I'm still in the process of learning."

Something stirred within Kari. A feeling that she didn't quite understand. She suddenly missed Master Kim and longed to see him again.

"How can I get ahold of him?" Kari eagerly asked.

"Well, he comes to LA all the time..."

"No," Kari said emphatically. "I can't wait that long."

"Why don't you leave your name and number? Next time I speak with him, I'll..."

"When will that be?" Kari interrupted.

Kenny smiled. "Relax. Everything happens in due time. You can't push the universe."

Kari nodded, slightly embarrassed by how desperate she must have appeared. "You're right," she said, handing Kenny one of her business cards after writing down Diane's number on the back.

"Hopefully I'll see you in another class," Kenny encouraged.

"I'm looking forward to it," Kari replied, as he led her to the front door.

The moment Kari exited, Kenny returned to his office, picked up the phone and placed a call to Master Kim.

* * * *

The following Friday, Kari was in Linda's office. They had just returned from a meeting which culminated in the client threatening to pull his account. What exacerbated the situation was that this was an account they thought was impervious to change. Until now, the client seemed overwhelmingly satisfied: sales were up and the unique ads were considered to be on the cutting edge.

However, what wasn't taken into consideration was the personal life of Ralph Kever, the company's CEO. His wife had recently abandoned him, taking their two young sons with her. With his family life suddenly thrown into turmoil, Ralph seemed bent on sabotaging all his relationships, including business. Ralph had been vicious during their earlier encounter - insulting Linda with unconscionable regularity. Unable to sit by and watch, Kari sprang to Linda's defense. This caused Ralph to abruptly stand and terminate the meeting.

"So how do you propose we salvage this?" Linda asked.

"Recommend a few good therapists," Kari quipped.

"Talk about a no-win situation," Linda continued. "This happened to me once before with a client."

"What happened?"

"Bastard finally blew his brains out and things went back to normal."

"I don't think we can count on that. Ralph's not the self-destructive type."

The intercom buzzed and Linda pressed the speaker button.

"Yes?"

"Linda, is Kari there?"

"Right here," Kari answered.

"There's a Kim on the phone for you. He seemed to think you'd want to take it."

"I'll be right there."

"Okay."

Linda flicked off the speaker.

"Can we continue this later?" Kari asked.

"I'm looking forward to it," Linda replied.

Smiling, Kari exited and raced down the hallway to her office. She swiftly closed the door behind her and anxiously scooped up the phone.

"Hello?"

"Hi Kari. I thought about you a lot since our last meeting. When my junior phoned, I began sending you energy."

The mere sound of Master Kim's voice seemed to alleviate Kari's tension. Quickly, she apologized for her impulsive behavior.

"You were exposed to a lot very quickly. You needed time to digest it all. I understand. Tell me, how have you been?"

"Truthfully, not too good," Kari replied.

"I have a suggestion," Kim offered. "We're having an intensive weekend seminar in Phoenix. Why don't you join us? I would love to see you."

"That sounds great. When is it? I'll check my schedule."

"This weekend," he stated calmly.

"Tomorrow?"

"Is that a problem?"

"No, not really. I'm sure I could get a flight out tonight."

"Good," he said, before giving Kari the necessary details.

After she hung up, Kari asked Brenda to promptly arrange airline and hotel reservations for her trip. Immediately, doubts filtered into her mind. What was she doing? But the uncertainties were vanquished the moment she thought of Master Kim.

* * * *

Kari enjoyed every moment of the weekend seminar in Phoenix. She learned more about the fundamental principles of the Dahn philosophy and exercises. After one of the lectures, Master Kim spent extra time with her, demonstrating the proper way to breath. He wanted Kari to breath from her third, or solar plexus chakra, the power center - an area located three fingers width beneath her navel, in her lower abdomen. The Korean term is Dahn Jon. To help facilitate this, Master Kim suggested that Kari imagine an "invisible nose" at the same level as the Dahn Jon, but in her lower back. He instructed her to see her Dahn Jon as "invisible lungs."

"Pretend your upper chest doesn't exist," Master Kim said, as he guided Kari to breath exclusively via her invisible apparatus. When Kari inhaled, the Dahn Jon area expanded like a balloon, and contracted as she exhaled. "Don't force it. Relax and try to imagine breathing through your invisible nose and lungs, naturally."

It was a challenge not to consciously force the movement in her Dahn Jon, but Kari knew, as with everything else, this would take practice.

"Your Dahn Jon is the power center of your body," he explained. "Breathing deeply to your Dahn Jon is something we've all done as babies. These exercises are merely meant to help you re-learn how to breath correctly. Proper breathing, or in my country, Chosik, is one of the keys to enhancing your spiritual growth. Breathing is the bridge between our physical body and our emotions."

By the end of the weekend, Kari realized, with unforeseen clarity, that these Dahn exercises were not only a method to enhance physical health, but a way to begin feeling more centered and relaxed.

Naturally, Kari didn't want the weekend to end. Before she left, Master Kim gave her some meditation tapes and cordially invited her to rendezvous with him in

Sedona two weeks later.

"Why don't we meet at the Chapel that Saturday morning? By the way, feel free to invite your friend. What was her name?"

"Diane."

"Yes, Diane."

"She's starting to see someone again. That keeps her pretty busy."

"What about you?" he asked. "Are you seeing anyone?"

"Not exactly," Kari hedged.

"Do me a favor," Master Kim said. "When you see your boyfriend, try not to judge him. Do your best to understand what he's going through. He needs you right now."

Kari couldn't believe how much Master Kim knew of her present situation. It felt good to be understood so well. Perhaps that was what she was meant to provide for Brad: complete, unconditional love and understanding.

"I'll see you in two weeks," Master Kim added, before warmly embracing her. While Kari was relieved that he hadn't mentioned her father that weekend, she wondered why he had suddenly zeroed in on Brad. Did he know something he wasn't telling her?

When she returned, Diane told her that Brad had called five times. They met for dinner at one of their favorite bistros in Beverly Hills. After profusely apologizing for his behavior, Brad asked Kari to move back in. During the course of their meal, Kari tried to interest Brad in the Dahn exercises and meditation, extolling the seminar she had attended.

"Is this one of your new clients?" Brad cynically asked.

"No, I'm doing this because it feels right. I enjoy it and I think it will help me."

"You sound brainwashed," Brad started. Kari grew incensed, but she suppressed her rage, remembering what Master Kim had told her.

After moving back in, Kari tried to give Brad his space. When he continually refused to accompany her to the West LA Dahn center for the exercises, she didn't pressure him. He was still battling inner demons; consulting new attorneys in an attempt to salvage his pride. Adhering to what Master Kim had advised, Kari struggled to unconditionally support his efforts, listening thoughtfully when he needed her to. But something was missing. When they made love, Kari didn't feel the intimacy they once shared. And ironically, while Kari was going to sleep with more ease, Brad had developed an acute case of insomnia. One night, Kari found him on the sofa, tears streaming down his face. She rushed over and embraced him.

"Maybe it would be easier if I killed myself," he said.

"No, don't say that."

"You don't understand. My whole life was in that business. Everything I ever worked for."

"I know," Kari said, enveloping him with her arms.

"But Brad, I'm here for you, no matter what. I mean that."

Brad gazed into Kari's eyes. "Do you still love me?"

"Yes," Kari quickly said.

"You don't care that you're living with someone who did things he never should have done? Awful things?"

"I care about you. And I care about what you're doing now. Not what happened years ago. Do you understand that?"

Brad nodded, but he was still racked with guilt and torment. No matter how hard Kari tried, it seemed impossible to communicate with him. Frustrated, she poured more energy into her exercises.

At work, people noticed conspicuous changes in her. When she met with Ralph Kever, she boldly recommended the Dahn Center to him. Naturally he exploded with indignation, but Kari didn't care.

"How could you do that?" Linda chided her later.

"Because I thought it would help him."

"His personal life is none of your business."

"It is when it affects the work. Give me a little slack here."

"You want slack? Take one of those jobs Jack keeps calling you about. But while you're working here, you listen to me. Got it?"

Kari nodded.

She stopped taking Jack Streeter's calls, realizing that the changes she desired in her life didn't involve a promotion or making more money. Kari had begun her spiritual journey - that was her priority now. She couldn't wait to spend more time with Master Kim. Just being around him seemed to invigorate her. Intuitively she felt she needed his guidance and support. From a spiritual book she read while staying with Diane, Kari knew that mentors or sages manifested themselves at appropriate moments in a person's life. Kari felt blessed that Master Kim had appeared to her when he did. She felt she could learn so much from him. Little did she know that Master Kim had already handpicked another spiritual teacher for her.

Chon Hwa Won

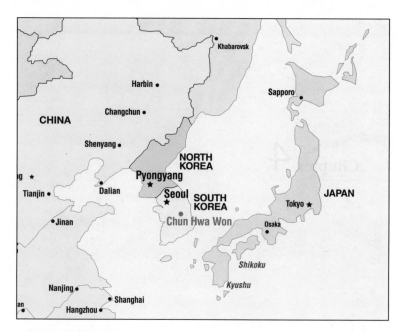

Chon Hwa Won

'Chon Hwa Won' is one of the Dahn Institutes established to train students with the special Dahnhak programs. It is situated in an area of Korea that is surrounded with graceful scenery and which has purified and harmonious energy. Deep mountains and a waterfall create the form of a pregnant woman playing the flute, and 'Chon Hwa Won' is located at her womb. In its front yard there is a stone monument which was built with the wish that all humankind shall find their True Self and achieve the completion of the soul.

Chapter 4

Unseen forces of fate conspired to keep Kari from reaching Sedona and meeting with Master Kim. While leisurely cruising north along highway 17, a tire blew out, causing Kari to lose complete control of her rented Taurus. Without warning, the car recklessly swerved into the oncoming lane. Desperately, Kari clutched the steering wheel, barely managing to avoid a nasty collision with a Greyhound bus. She found herself soaring off the side of the road. The car bounced into a gully, where it instantly stalled out. Unharmed, but in a state of shock, Kari quickly leaped out of the vehicle. She frantically signaled for help. Moments later, a Lexus glided to a stop a few feet ahead of her. After unsuccessfully attempting to soothe Kari's nerves, the driver, an older man named Bruce, used his cellular phone to contact the rental company.

"They'll have someone here in less than an hour," Bruce assured her.

"Thank you," Kari replied, still visibly shaken.

"Everything's going to be fine," Bruce continued. "I'd stay and wait with you but I'm on my way to my daughter's wedding."

"Oh, congratulations."

"We haven't exactly been close the past few years. She's never forgiven me for leaving her mother. I was surprised she invited me."

Kari's mind snapped back to reality. She thought about her own future wedding and the ramifications of inviting her father. After her behavior at his reception, she speculated on how he would reciprocate. At least there was one positive aspect to its postponement, Kari rationalized.

"Look, I wish I could stay but..." Bruce began, interrupting Kari's train of thought.

"Oh, don't worry about me," Kari quickly responded.

"Thanks for stopping. Most people don't anymore."

With a quick wave, Bruce hopped back into his car and sped away. The tow truck showed up an hour later. After getting her tire replaced, Kari was back on the road. She drove more tentatively, overreacting to every little bump along the stretch of asphalt. By the time she began to see glimpses of the Sedona red rocks, Kari had regained a semblance of confidence; rationally she convinced herself that the odds of another tire blow-out occurring were extremely rare.

Realizing how late she was, Kari headed right up to the Chapel of the Holy Cross. As she briskly strode towards the double doors, Kari spotted Gil sitting on a nearby bench. When he glanced up in her direction, his eyes beamed with recognition.

"It's about time you showed up," he joked.

"Did you know I was coming?" Kari asked, slightly perplexed.

"No. Just figured sooner or later I'd see you again. So what brings you back to Sedona?"

"I was supposed to meet someone here but my tire blew out on the way and I'm a little late."

"You okay?"

"I've had better days. How about you?"

"A lot of changes. I just moved here from Flagstaff," Gil said. "The moment I got here I started to get all these jobs. I'm flying down to Peru tonight to shoot some ruins."

"That's wonderful."

"Yeah. So I came up here to light a candle and bless my guardians who seem to be taking much better care of me," he grinned.

"We really have to get together," Kari blurted.

"We will. I still have your card," Gil said. "I should be swinging out to LA soon. When I do I'll call you."

"Great, I'd like that."

"Well, take care," Gil said before ambling down the ramp. Kari turned on her heels, swung open the doors and entered the Chapel. When she didn't see Master Kim anywhere, she strolled down the aisle and lit a candle for her mother. As Kari approached the front row bench to sit down, she spotted an envelope. Her name was neatly printed in pencil on the outside. Quickly, she opened it. The note read: Meet me on top of Bell. Can't wait to see you, Kim. After neatly folding the paper, Kari headed back out the door.

I guess this is my penalty for being tardy, Kari thought, slightly amused. Climbing to the top of Bell Rock can be an arduous task, even for people who do it regularly. It was Kari's second time, and while she wasn't quite as petrified, she proceeded with diligent caution. Every time she hesitated and wanted to stop, Kari imagined Master Kim on top waiting for her; holding that image coerced her into continuing. Careful to avoid the area that paralyzed her the last time, Kari climbed up an alternate route. Beads of perspiration began dotting her forehead as she ascended the last remaining feet. When she finally reached the top, Kari was out-of-breath, and she plopped down against a rock to recover. Suddenly, as if out of thin air, Kari felt two hands lightly massaging the back of her neck.

"I wasn't sure you would make it," Master Kim said.

"Neither was I."

"So far you've been able to overcome all the obstacles that stood in your way. But trust me, those obstacles will keep popping up."

"Terrific," Kari snapped.

After working on her tension spots, Master Kim joined Kari in a meditation. He was sincerely pleased by how focused she had become on her Dahn Jon breathing, and complimented her.

"You seem surprised," Kari said.

"Not really."

"Listen, I know I already apologized for storming off that day, but..."

"Just a necessary step," Master Kim interjected, smiling.

He and Kari spent the rest of the day hiking and exploring isolated parts of Sedona. After dining on French Cuisine at the L'Auberge Restaurant, Kari and Master Kim returned to her hotel. Outside her room, Kari felt awkward - it wasn't just a physical attraction. That would be easy to deal with, she thought. No, her feelings were more complex: deep-rooted and overpowering, but also very pure. She thoroughly enjoyed being with this man - on many levels. Kari could be herself around him; a degree of comfort existed that she never quite experienced before - not even with Brad.

"I want you to focus on your dreams tonight," Master Kim advised.

"What do you mean?"

"Before you go to sleep, speak to your guides. Ask them to give you any messages you're meant to receive."

"Is there something you're not telling me?"

"Have a good night's sleep," he said with a mysterious grin, before turning to leave.

It took several hours for Kari to fall asleep. Lately, she would meditate a few minutes, relaxing her body enough to ease into slumber. But tonight, her mind teemed with thoughts of what was happening in her life. She obsessed about what Master Kim had told her, recalling that many of the spiritual books she had read touted dreams as a pathway to enlightenment. But what would she dream about? She felt as if Master Kim knew but wanted it to be a surprise. How did he know so much about her?

Just before dawn, Kari had a vivid dream. She was sitting at home, when she heard a loud knocking on her front door. Reluctant to answer it, Kari grew apprehensive. But instead of going away, the noise continued, growing louder, sharply reverberating against the walls. Although fearful, Kari moved towards the sound. She peered through the tiny peephole, but saw nothing. As the pounding persisted, Kari lost her patience and flung open the door. Standing before her was a petite Korean woman with beautiful olive skin and short, black hair. The woman extended her arms towards Kari, offering a single miniature rose. After the rose was placed into Kari's hand, the woman disappeared. Kari suddenly awoke from her dream.

The next day Kari recounted the details to Master Kim.

He seemed quite pleased. "You've been introduced to your new teacher. Her name is Master Songwha and she's expecting you."

"Excuse me?" Kari began. "Have I missed something here? I thought you were my teacher."

"A good teacher knows when his student is ready to move on."

"Hold it. I was just getting comfortable with you."

"You need someone who could give you the intensive training you need. Someone who can spend more time with you. Master Songwha can provide that."

Kari was silent. Finally, a dejected, "If you say so," emitted from her lips.

"The last time Master Songwha was in Sedona, she meditated for ten days and nights on top of Bell Rock. She knew you were coming and saw an image of you struggling to climb up. That's why I was able to be there that day. Master Songwha had told me."

"What are you trying to say?" Kari asked.

"There are no mistakes. You were destined to meet me, so that I could guide you on your path to her."

"Does she live around here?"

"Not exactly," he hesitated.

"Where then?"

"South Korea."

"What!" Kari shrieked. "You've got to be kidding. Korea? What do you think, I'm just going to stop everything I'm doing and fly to Korea to meet a woman just because she showed up in my dream? That's crazy!"

"Is it? You're ready to begin your spiritual awakening."

"I thought I was, but..."

"You don't have to go," Master Kim stated. "But this is an unprecedented opportunity. Master Songwha is a renowned healer in my country. She is the 9th disciple of the Grand Master of Dahn. Usually she doesn't take on individual students."

"So why now?"

"There are reasons that can't be explained to you at this time. Keep in mind that you have the potential to reach ascension, as we all do."

"Ascension?" queried Kari.

"Ascension is what Dahn meditation is all about. It's when you become one with the divine spirit - source. When you lose your ego completely and understand the true purpose and meaning of life."

"Oh, is that all," Kari quipped, but she knew this was no time for levity.

She spent the remainder of the day with Master Kim, hiking around the base of Bell Rock. When she was ready to drive to the airport, she looked deep into his eyes and unveiled her inner emotions.

"I feel like I've lost control of my life," Kari said.

"Do you really think you ever had control?"

Kari pondered this a few minutes. Perhaps he was right.

"You can't lose something that you've never had," he added.

"But why do I feel so up in the air about everything? Like I'm in a perpetual state of limbo? It's not a feeling I'm comfortable with."

"Nothing remains the same. We're all in a state of flux. Your feelings are normal."

Kari gazed down at her feet, then back up at Master Kim.

"As crazy as it sounds, I'm actually starting to believe I'm going to Korea. I know I'm meant to do this. Not just because you're saying it, but something inside me tells me this experience will change my life... I just wish I could do it here. Are you sure that's not possible?"

"You need to get completely away - from your family, your culture, the pressure - away from everything. Often the hardest part of true spiritual enlightenment is the necessary isolation. You will meet Master Songwha at The Ascension Center which has been specifically established for this process. It's where you will embark upon the best and most difficult twenty-one days of your life."

"Twenty-one days?" Kari repeated. "That's three weeks! What am I supposed to do about my job? My life? Not to mention how much this is going to cost me! Can I try it out for a week? I think I can swing that much vacation time."

"Kari, you're free to do whatever you chose. No one is forcing you along this path. I know you can't possibly understand what I'm about to say now, but everything that you just mentioned - all your worries and what you thought were your priorities will completely and irrevocably change after this experience."

Kari knew, no, she felt, that somehow Master Kim was right. It was as if, she were living in an episode of "The Twilight Zone", in which everyone around her went along blissfully unaware of some major truth, yet she and she alone knew something was dreadfully wrong - but what? The building blocks of her entire life - everything she thought was important, everything she had been conditioned to value - was being torn down as if it were one massive, collective illusion. A sham. A fraud. Was this trip Kari's means to an answer? Perhaps the universe provided it as a bridge, enabling her to cross the ego-laden rivers of doubt and anxiety that have been ever present throughout her life, which, unbeknownst to her, was in fact, a process of growth - a spiritual journey all along.

"When am I supposed to go?"

Master Kim smiled. "Whenever you can conveniently arrange it into your life. Master Songwha is not going anywhere. Remember one thing, the sooner you get enlightened, the sooner other people will start receiving the message."

"Other people?"

"In time you will understand."

"Yeah, let's see if I can survive this first."

"Oh, you will," he assured her.

* * * *

As Kari fastened her safety belt aboard a Korean Airlines flight to Seoul, she reflected back on the past week: it was amazing to her how smoothly everything came together. Kari was able to make all the necessary arrangements without delay. When she requested a temporary leave of absence from work, Linda was stupefied, but eventually, after verifying that Kari had indeed purchased tickets to Korea, she relented and granted her the time.

Brad was a different story. Still burdened by business problems, he lambasted Kari, accusing her of deserting him in his time of need.

"Maybe by doing this, I'll be more of a help to you."

"You think you can just rationalize anything, don't you? Face the facts: I need you and you're leaving," Brad uttered.

"Why don't you face the facts? Are you the only

person in this relationship with needs? What about what's important to me?" Kari pleaded.

"You're going to fuckin' Korea! What's that about? Do these people have you so brainwashed that you'll do whatever they say?"

"No one is forcing me to do this," Kari insisted. "It's my decision. I want to go."

"Why?"

"I know it's hard to understand... you're right, it's crazy... but this is the first time in my life I'm relying on my instincts, not my intellect."

"That's for sure," he groused.

"It's something I have to do."

"Then consider our relationship over! As far as I'm concerned, if you get on that plane I never want to see you again. Understand?"

"Don't threaten me just because you're under pressure."

"Get out!" he wailed.

"I'll leave in the morning!"

"I never should have let you move back in here."

"I haven't even packed my stuff yet!"

"You want your stuff? I'll give you your stuff!" Enraged, Brad proceeded towards the closet door and flung it open wildly. He yanked all of Kari's clothes off their hangers and threw them to the floor.

"What are you doing? Are you crazy? You're acting like a spoiled child!" Kari shouted, while trying to prevent him from opening her dresser drawers.

"Get out of my way!"

"Stop it!" Kari screamed, unaware that Brad was

teetering between anger and the point of no return. Her defiance pushed him over the edge. That's when Brad lost complete control. He sharply backhanded Kari across the face. She instantly recoiled from the blow and fell to the carpet. What wrenched Kari most was not the stinging physical pain, but to stare up in fear at Brad. Fear was an emotion that he never before triggered within her - until this moment. Now, as Kari studied Brad's impassive face, she was wary and unsure of his violent potential.

"I'm going out for an hour. When I come back, have all your things out of here."

Kari didn't say a word. She merely watched as Brad grabbed his coat and headed out. The slam of the front door harshly punctuated his last words to her. Kari crawled across the carpet, reached up to the phone and dialed Diane who came rushing over to help.

"You should have called the police," Diane said.

"Do you think what I'm doing is crazy?" Kari asked, feeling very vulnerable.

"What's crazy is usually I'm the one asking you that. I can't believe this is you! We go to Sedona for one weekend and you come back a different person."

"Didn't you want me to start exploring my spirituality? Wasn't that the whole point?"

"Yes... I guess... but do you really need to go to Korea to do that?"

"This woman, this teacher, she came to me in my dreams. I know I'm meant to go to her. You see spirituality as some sort of a hobby. It's not something you do because you think it's fashionable - it's a way of life.

You can't be serious about it with one foot in and the other foot still wanting to spend the day at Bloomingdale's."

"You've changed," Diane stated. "You've really changed."

Kari felt a gentle tap on her shoulder and looked up to see a friendly flight attendant. "Would you like some more coffee, miss?" she asked.

Suddenly aware that she had been daydreaming, Kari shook her head and politely responded, "No thank you."

Kari settled back in her seat and studied the interior of the airplane's cabin. The plastic and metal encasing seemed as tenuous as society's belief systems. How protected was she from their flimsy falsehoods and misinterpretations of the great truth? Kari tried meditating, instead of dwelling on her irrational fear of flying. But each time she closed her eyes, stray thoughts about her life, rattled her calm.

Kari had called her father right before she left to let him know she would be gone for several weeks, but he didn't even feign interest in where she was going.

"Well, I just thought I'd let you know," she said.

"Call me when you get back," he replied.

"I will," and that was the end of their conversation. Her father had closed off his life to her, and as much as Kari tried to suppress her feelings, she was hurt.

* * * *

When Kari arrived at the Kimpo airport, it was early evening; she was both exhausted and hungry. After checking into a nearby hotel, she ordered up room service and drew a hot bath. She finished the remainder of sauteed vegetables and noodles, while soaking in the relaxing tub.

Still bleary-eyed, Kari collapsed on the bed, where she slept for ten hours. When she awoke, Kari peered outside her window and watched the sun slowly rising over the city.

After breakfast, Kari went to the front desk to inquire about the transportation schedules. Upon discovering she would have to transfer busses twice to reach her destination, Kari decided to splurge and rent a shuttle limo. A friendly Korean man who spoke broken English helped Kari negotiate a fair price.

The drive took a little over four hours. They stopped twice, once so Kari could use a rest room, and again to grab cold sandwiches at a roadside market. It was a beautiful spring day. The driver kept pointing out various locations; even though Kari couldn't understand what he was saying, she knew she was seeing some major visual sights indigenous to Korea.

The van drove up a slight incline, sweeping past several cherry trees in bloom and an abundance of pine trees, as they approached the Chunwha Ascension Center. It was a series of buildings nestled in the heart of a mountain, near a small, isolated Korean village called Young dong. A friendly, yet feisty dog barked out a greeting to Kari. She emerged from the van and kneeled to pet its beautiful coat.

The canine trailed Kari towards the main building. While inhaling the fragrant springtime air, Kari surveyed her surroundings. She was immediately taken with the location.

They were in the heart of nature: green trees encircled the compound, with mountains looming above; birds flew overhead; squirrels scampered about. Later, Kari would discover what Chunwha meant: becoming part of heaven.

Kari entered the main building and presented a card with Master Songwha's name written on it to a woman who smiled in recognition. She motioned for Kari to follow her down a hallway towards a far room. As she strolled through the corridor, Kari felt a powerful feeling of deja vu, as if she had been here before. Knowing it was impossible, Kari quickly dismissed that notion. The door of the room suddenly swung inward, revealing the woman who had appeared in her dream. The woman, Master Songwha, handed a single, miniature rose to Kari.

"Welcome," Master Songwha said gently.

Kari couldn't get over the fact that she was standing face to face with someone from a dream. She wondered: What was real anymore? Still feeling a bit unsettled, Kari nodded weakly in response.

"It will be an honor to train you," she said.

"Oh, please," Kari began awkwardly. "Master Kim spoke very highly of you. I know you don't normally do this and I appreciate..."

"You've had a long journey. Take tonight to rest. You will need it. The official training begins tomorrow morning. I will see you at four a.m."

Kari's mind raced. Four? In the morning? What had she gotten herself into?

In her soft-spoken way, Master Songwha had attempted to put Kari more at ease, but she could sense her inner conflict: anxiety was wrestling with Kari's soul, and Kari, as if wise to what was in her immediate future, was already starting to manifest an aura of insecurity.

Master Songwha bowed before Kari who didn't know how to respond. Feeling embarrassed and unsure, Kari managed a clumsy curtsy. Master Songwha smiled and gracefully left the room, leaving Kari alone to adapt to her new environment.

The accommodations were sparse: a thin futon mattress lay on the carpet; a lamp rested on a low table; some pill-box shaped cushions leaned against the far wall. Kari opened the door to the left of the pillows and entered a bathroom. It contained a stall shower, a toilet and a sink. Kari proceeded to open another door, revealing a closet. Hung neatly along its rod were white outfits that resembled karate uniforms. Kari lifted the two-pieces from their hangars and returned to the bathroom. She stripped off her clothes and entered the shower.

Kari shuddered as she recalled her anxiety attack just days before leaving for Korea. She had phoned Master Kim in a state of panic, insisting that she couldn't go. He acted like the drain in the basin below - remaining steadfast while allowing Kari to spew her fears, worries and angst, over him like a faucet. As soon as the pent-up pressure within her was relieved, Kari's trepidations slowed down to a trickle, then a few, occasional remaining drops.

In between the last inconsistent dribbles of Kari's

uneasiness, Master Kim had calmly relayed Master Song-wha's story to her.

* * * *

As a young child Songwha had been deathly ill; a fever consumed her body for days. When medication was unable to alleviate her physical condition, doctors feared the worst. Her parents summoned a minister to Songwha's hospital room. What none of them realized was that Songwha had already left her body; floating towards a bright, glowing light that bathed her in its loving warmth. As Songwha remained encapsulated within the light, an overwhelming feeling of purpose consumed her. Within a matter of seconds she was back in her body and her fever ultimately broke. This experience had a profound impact on Songwha. Never again would she doubt the presence of a divine source. Instinctively she knew the gift of life had been returned to her - but with certain stipulations.

As she grew older, Songwha began having mystical experiences. When she meditated, which she often did, she found herself leaving her body. Soon, Songwha discovered she had acute healing abilities: the kind that made her wary because of their profound impact on others. While some people were intimidated by her, others flocked to be healed by her touch. Yet, Songwha only grew more humble, as the powers that came through her expanded.

Songwha's recent visit to Sedona, in which she camped out on top of Bell Rock, solidified her sense of sacred responsibility. She was compelled to return to Korea,

where she could devote herself to the collective enlightenment of others.

* * * *

After showering and changing, Kari felt better. The
outfit was genuinely comfortable and felt pleasantly warm
against her skin. There was a knock at the door and Kari
moved to open it, revealing the woman she had given the
card to when she had first arrived. Kari later learned her
name was Lily.

"A light meal has been prepared for you in the dining
hall. If you wish, I will show you the way," Lily offered.

"Oh, that would be great. Thank you," Kari
responded.

Lily led Kari down another corridor towards a set of
double doors. She parted them, allowing Kari to enter.
"You may take a seat anywhere you wish," Lily said,
before allowing the doors to swing shut behind her,
leaving Kari alone in a large room of rectangular tables
and several chairs.

Kari was shocked by the emptiness of the dining hall.
There must be some mistake, she thought. As Kari was
about to turn and walk out, an older Korean man named
Kang Hoon entered and headed towards a seat. He noticed
Kari's curious stare and motioned for her to join him. To
her delight and surprise, he spoke English.

"I am Kang Hoon. Are you from America?" he asked.

"Yes. My name is Kari."

"You come a long way to a special place," he continued.

"I hope so," Kari answered.

"My son and daughter are here with me," Kang said. "But they are both fasting right now."

Kari glanced around at the sea of vacant seats. "Is that why there's no one else here?"

"Yes. Most everyone is in a fasting phase. I just completed a fast a few days ago."

"I've never fasted before. Is it difficult?"

"Only in the beginning. Once your spirit has been properly prepared it adjusts and receives energy from the other sources."

A demure Korean woman approached their table with a tray of food. She deftly placed two bowls of lentil soup and plates of salad in front of them.

"This seems more like a weight camp or spa than an Ascension Center," Kari said as she ate a fork full of spinach leaves.

Kang smiled. "Losing weight is trivial as compared to losing one's ego," he said. "That is the key which will unlock the door to your unlimitedness."

Kari realized there was a whole world of people who seemed to be more aware of things. It was bizarre and almost frightening to think about the ones she had left behind; Los Angeles seemed like another planet in comparison. Was everyone there sleepwalking? Going through the day-to-day trials of life in a permanent state of slumber? What was life, anyway? Perhaps, here on this isolated mountaintop in Korea, Kari would find out.

After dinner, Kari accompanied Kang for a walk along the grounds. They were joined by the dog, Chosun, who seemed to be the Center's loyal mascot. As they meandered through the lush gardens and strong Korean oak trees, Kang showed Kari the individual statues that stood erect in various squares near the main buildings.

Kang pointed towards one. "This is the Bon Seung Tower. It symbolizes the celebration of true self."

Kari studied the carved stone. "It's beautiful," she exclaimed.

The twilight sky changed many colors before darkness settled in for the night. Beneath the universe's palette of rosy pinks and lilac shades of purple, Kang led Kari to the base of another mountaintop.

"Look up," he instructed.

As Kari complied, Kang continued. "Do you see that rocky area way up there?"

"Yes," Kari nodded. "That's odd, it looks like a brain."

"Exactly," responded Kang. "You see, this whole area resembles a woman's body. From her head, with her brain, up there, down to her torso with her breasts - there and there," Kang pointed towards some hills. "The buildings of the Center are located directly where the woman's heart chakra is. If you go farther south you will come upon a waterfall - representing the flow from a woman's vagina."

"But how was this all formed? And so accurately?" Kari asked.

"Nature created this mountain."

"What an incredible image," Kari said while staring up at what truly resembled a human brain formed in the rocks above.

As the muted colors overhead slowly faded into

blackness, Kang escorted Kari back into the building.

"It was a pleasure meeting you," he said.

"I'm sure I'll see you around," Kari replied.

"I don't think so. Your training begins tomorrow. You're here for a divine purpose - all your concentration will be focused on that."

"Well, thanks again for allowing me to join you for dinner and showing me around. I would've been pretty lonely if you hadn't come along."

"Remember, you're never alone," Kang stated before shaking her hand and ambling down the hall.

Kari had trouble falling asleep. With no television or radio to distract her, she was forced to tune into her own thoughts. How did she ever allow herself to be talked into this? That question echoed relentlessly in her head. Finally, exhausted, yet still pragmatic, Kari rationalized that she would give the place a day or two - then, if she still felt like this, she would leave. While she was not optimistic, Kari remembered how she had always dreaded going to summer camp as a young girl. Kari fought it and fought it, until ultimately, she ended up having a wonderful time. Somewhere, deep within, Kari didn't think that what she was about to undergo was anything remotely comparable to the sportsmanship and teamwork she learned in her youth. As important as those earlier lessons were to her at the time, somehow, Kari knew this experience was profoundly more significant.

* * * *

Being wakened up at four a.m. had never been Kari's

idea of a wonderful time. She thought it was some sort of mistake, even a nightmare, when Master Songwha knocked on her door.

"Can we begin a little later today? I'm still exhausted from the flight," Kari spouted. She was irritable; sleep deprivation was a surefire way to trigger Kari's distemper.

"Come... it's time for your run," Master Songwha informed.

"Excuse me?" Kari responded. "You must have the wrong room. I need my sleep."

"Get dressed," Master Songwha said quietly, all the while staring into Kari's eyes with a look of consummate compassion. Kari lowered the blanket from her chin to her chest and gazed back at her. She understood that she didn't have to obey a thing this woman told her, yet instinctively, Kari knew that she should. Quickly, she got out of bed and headed for the bathroom.

It was still black outside the facility when Kari joined a small group of men and women, all barefoot, in the courtyard. Even the sun gets to sleep in, Kari thought to herself, slightly amused by her situation. A subtle breeze, redolent of the nearby gardens, wafted towards them. Kari inhaled the fragrant aroma as her eyes adjusted to the surrounding darkness. She noted a young Korean man standing before them. After announcing his name was Jai, he switched on a small flashlight, immediately illuminating his boyishly handsome face. He wore the same two-piece outfit as the rest - except his was black. After bowing to the group, he swiveled on his feet and began jogging towards the base of the mountain that towered directly above the center. Kari glanced around - everyone else had begun. With a shrug of her shoulders and an exaggerated sigh, Kari followed. As Jai and the others ascended the mountainside, Kari lagged behind, struggling to keep pace up the steep incline. Unable to see clearly through the dense blackness preceding the dawn, Kari continually jabbed her feet against sharp rocks along the path. When her toe impacted on a stray tree branch, Kari screamed in pain, but no one paid heed to her cries, except Chosun, who barked his sympathy and playfully licked her raw feet. Kari trudged onward. She felt slightly embarrassed, then annoyed, by her consistent trailing position. She had always been a leader, never a follower. Lagging behind was not acceptable to Kari's psyche and this caused her determination to swell. Despite her self-possessed resolve, her body began to falter - her abdomen cramped and her limbs trembled. Unable to endure the physical strain, Kari was forced to slow her pace. Once again, she fell behind the others. Her mind scolded her body, which finally, perhaps out of sheer obstinance, gave out. Completely out-of-breath, Kari doubled over.

When the group reached the summit of the hill, they took a brief rest, allowing Kari time to catch up. With a cramp piercing her right side like an arrow, she managed to move forward. A slow, but consistent walk had been established, as Kari plodded up the rest of the way. When she ultimately reached the top, Kari collapsed onto the ground, but to her dismay, the group had already begun their descent.

"Hey, wait for me!" Kari cried, forcing herself to stand up. "I'm coming!"

Finally, Kari was perpendicular once again and she struggled to keep pace. While it was considerably easier running downhill, she fretted about losing her balance and tripping over Chosun, who kept darting in front of her, playfully nipping at the air.

Suddenly, Kari felt different. The pain had lessoned considerably - her endorphins must have kicked in. Totally invigorated, she seemed to fly down the mountainside. That's more like it, Kari thought. But once she reached her destination and stopped, everything changed. Her cramp returned, throbbing mercilessly; sweat streamed off her brow, clouding her vision as she bent over to examine her feet. They were swollen and scratched, bleeding from the oddest places - even in between her toes. Yet, despite all the discomfort, Kari felt an overwhelming sense of accomplishment. She carefully rose and regained her composure, before slowly heading inside the building to take a shower.

After freshening up and tending to her foot wounds, Kari went to the dining room where she was joined by Master Songwha.

"You will be running three times a day. It's all part of a regimen designed to help build up your lower body," she explained.

"What if I don't survive?" Kari quipped.

"You will," Songwha stated emphatically as she placed a small plastic bag in front of her.

"What's that?"

"Breakfast," she said matter-of-factly.

Kari stared at the yellow powder inside the bag. "I'd join you, but I think I'd rather have some pancakes and eggs."

"No, you misunderstand. This is your breakfast."

Master Songwha proceeded to open up the bag and shake its contents into a shallow dish. Kari observed as she neatly poured water over the powder from a slender, silver carafe and expertly stirred the mixture into a fine paste.

"This is pine tree pollen. It comes from ground pine needles."

"You don't expect me to live on that, do you?"

Master Songwha gazed at Kari a long time before allowing a small smile to materialize across her face. "Just for your first week here," she said. "Then you'll begin the real fasting."

"Wait a second," Kari began, suddenly leaping to her feet. "This is all I'll be eating?"

"Taste it," Master Songwha ordered.

Kari twirled the utensil around the pale yellow paste. She lifted the bowl up to her nose, inhaled deeply, but couldn't quite detect an odor. Finally, Kari placed a small spoonful in her mouth. At first she wasn't sure about the taste - it was slightly bitter, yet at the same time, quite mild, almost chalky like Kaopectate, but with a hint of corn added in.

"This mixture is pure, from nature. It will begin to cleanse your body," Master Songwha said, while motioning for Kari to sit and finish the remainder of the bowl.

Master Songwha explained, "It will take your body a few days to adjust, but then you will feel much better. You are to eat the paste three times a day."

Realizing there was no other food to come, Kari began to savor each spoonful, as Master Songwha continued to speak. "This is all part of your purification process. First your body, then your mind, and finally your spirit. The dirty energy that's been weighing you down beneath layers of negativity, will begin to leave your body, allowing you to raise your vibration level."

"Dirty energy?"

"Yes, the energy that cloaks you in emotional filth - causing the pain in your stomach, as well as the depression and uneasiness in your mind."

"What about liquids? Will I be allowed to drink?"

"Yes, you can drink as much water as you like."

"At least I have something to look forward to," Kari said, before finishing the last spoonful of pollen mixture.

"It's time to start your breathing exercises. Follow me."

Master Songwha led Kari through the double doors and down another passageway towards a spacious, carpeted room. Soft, lyrical music played in the background, as a group of people commenced some elementary stretching exercises. Master Songwha indicated for Kari to join them, while she quietly observed.

The man who had led the morning hike, Jai, stood before the class. He inhaled deeply, gracefully spreading his arms, palms up, towards the ceiling, then exhaled by rotating his palms down and lowering them slowly in unison. Kari felt like her arms had become the wingspan of a bird gliding up and down during flight. The group took Jai's lead: bent over, hands on knees for four counts, then squatting for four. They collectively resumed an erect position and proceeded with what Kari felt was a form of dance. While maintaining their balance, they lifted up one leg, with knee extended, and swiveled it outwards, then back down in a circle. They repeated the same movement with the other leg. Eight times. After reversing the flow of movement, starting the leg away from their torso and swinging it around towards themselves for eight counts on each side, the group sat down.

After approximately ten minutes of straddle stretching and back rolls, the class was told to lie flat on the carpet.

Master Songwha quietly approached Kari and knelt beside her.

"Be conscious of your breathing," she advised, while her hands proceeded to massage Kari's stomach and Dahn Jon area. She kneaded and worked on her abdomen for several minutes. Kari did her best to relax her body and focus on her breathing.

Eventually Jai instructed the group to simultaneously raise their arms and legs off the ground. Master Songwha adjusted Kari's legs, bending them at the knee and aiming her toes towards the ceiling.

"Your legs shouldn't touch one another, they should be parallel."

Next, she fully extended Kari's arms, pointing her fingertips upwards.

"Your arms should be straight. This is called the baby pose. Try to keep this position for twenty minutes,"

Master Songwha said. "Keep concentrating on your Dahn Jon breathing."

At first, Kari thought this would be a breeze. But after about six minutes, her body began sending out distress signals. The position grew more uncomfortable the longer Kari maintained it. Her thighs began to tremble, her back ached, and her arms felt heavy. When Master Songwha announced that only ten minutes remained, Kari started to complain.

"I can't do this."

"Yes you can," Master Songwha encouraged. "You are not your body. You control your body. Don't allow it to give up. You're in charge. Pay attention to your breathing."

Kari tried hard to stay focused and ignore the pain. Her legs started to shake with more force, uncontrollably wobbling back and forth. It was a bizarre feeling, as if her legs weren't part of her, not attached, quivering on their own. Before long, Kari's entire body was vibrating; she felt she had lost complete control. She tightened her already closed eyelids and futilely struggled to disregard the agony. Every time her legs quaked and started to drop to the floor, Master Songwha was there to push them back up in the air.

"Dahn Jon... Dahn Jon... Dahn Jon..." Master Songwha began to chant.

Grimacing, Kari began counting to herself, hoping that would pass the time. Nothing was working - the discomfort turned to pain. When Master Songwha announced there was only a minute to go, Kari fought to hang on. Her thighs shuddered and throbbed intensely.

Finally, the time was up. Master Songwha told Kari to slowly let her legs and arms fall to the ground.

"Good job," Master Songwha said. "I wasn't sure you would be able to do it."

"Piece of cake," Kari replied, then wished she hadn't mentioned food. While her mind drifted to some of her favorite desserts, her body ached.

"Eventually you will be able to do that for two hours."

"What!" Kari exclaimed.

"It's all part of strengthening your lower body."

"Two hours!" Kari repeated. "Why don't you forget about the torture? Just kill me and get it over with."

Master Songwha laughed. "Think of yourself as a lump of coal. You have to endure much pressure and many trials before you can be transformed into a beautiful diamond. Your spirit is already that flawless diamond - but it's mired and hidden beneath years and lifetimes of accumulated falsehoods. This training, however difficult it may seem, will help you to uncover your true self. Why don't you take a short break? Then we can begin the real torture."

Kari did a double take. Despite her better judgement, she found herself glaring at her. The fury in Kari's eyes didn't escape Master Songwha's attention. "When you're finished with your time here you will understand. Until then, you don't have to like me."

"I like you. It's my body that's angry."

"That's what we want to do here - get rid of the anger stored within your body."

"So what's next on the agenda?" Kari asked, feigning

nonchalance.

* * * *

Kari spent the next two hours in a small, windowless room. Its walls were hospital white, completely bare. Kari was beginning to wonder if this was how mental patients were kept - totally isolated, left alone to deal with their innermost demons. Was this all one huge nightmare? Had Kari been committed? Was Master Songwha merely part of this elaborate illusion, all concocted within her own mind? Or was this river of paranoia meant to navigate and wear down the already fracturing boulders of Kari's sanity, before flowing out of her psyche? Perhaps it was all an integral part of the process that Master Songwha constantly referred to.

Kari had been instructed not to fall asleep. Indeed, every ten minutes, someone opened the door a crack and peered inside to check her status. Kari incessantly moved around, pacing, like a caged animal. She leaned restlessly against one wall, then quickly moved to another. At last, she surrendered to her confines and lowered herself onto a bamboo-thatched mat.

Naturally, some of Kari's thoughts revolved around her recent experiences which had led her to this point. While she had been initially prodded by her friend Diane, Kari had taken the reins and was now in full control of her spiritual journey. Or was she? Perhaps all she had accomplished since her first trip to Sedona was the realization that there must be something more to life - a divine order. Kari had awakened to the fact that her work had been a haven - a refuge for her to hide from the hideous truth. Her truth: that she was restless. Deep down, Kari had been on edge - living in a constant state of disquietude. As Henry David Thoreau so eloquently stated, "People live lives of quiet desperation." Kari could have been the poster child for that quote. She embodied its meaning - breathed life into its very words.

What was so inconceivable to Kari now was that she never knew this before. Despite an above-average intelligence level, and a successful career, Kari had never understood herself. She was the total stranger you casually wave to at a party - nothing more than a hologram projection. The reflection Kari examined in the mirror was that of someone else. Someone outside herself. Someone to groom for acceptance by others. A mere image - the true illusion.

During her mind's constant deliberations, Kari was on the verge of drifting off to sleep. As she was about to surrender herself to both physical and mental exhaustion, Kari heard a sharp pounding on the door. The noise ruptured the constant quiet, jarring her back to the reality of the room.

Kari thought about Brad and the other men she had been involved with. Had she ever had a satisfying relationship, she wondered? Or did she keep attaching herself to men in the constant search for love and approval? She relived all the details from her past romances and sadly concluded that none were truly fulfilling. She scolded herself over her lack of self-esteem.

Kari was relieved when the time was up. Besides the

stirrings of claustrophobia that had begun, she was growing more depressed with each passing minute. She was actually excited by the thought of running again.

Kari welcomed being near other people, out in the open. With Chosun scampering behind her, she kept up a much better pace, but still lagged behind the group.

* * * *

While Kari diligently mixed her tree pollen paste, she speculated on what was ahead for her. Although her body still ached, and her mind reeled with maudlin thoughts about her past, Kari had weathered most of her apprehensions - she had survived the first day. Maybe she would be able to conquer all her fears. But what was she afraid of? Perhaps she was afraid to face what was inside of her. Afraid of the unknown. Afraid of the truth.

After her meager dinner, Kari was exhausted. She longed to dive onto her futon and wrap herself inside a soft blanket, like a comforting cocoon. Sleep was Kari's one desire. To her dismay, she learned that bed rest was not permitted until midnight. Her protests fell upon deaf ears.

Master Songwha explained, "You need to force yourself to stay awake. This is all part of disciplining your body. Controlling it. You don't want to remain a lazy soul."

Heaven forbid, Kari thought to herself. Bleary-eyed and fatigued, Kari remained awake until midnight. She pretended that she was enduring one of her typical bouts of insomnia, and since she didn't have a television at her disposal, Kari recalled one of her favorite episodes of "The

Odd Couple," and replayed each joke in her head. It worked, but only for a little while. Soon her mind drifted back to unpleasant scenes from the ongoing, repetitive, episodes of her own life. Just as Kari began to sink into a permanent state of melancholy, Master Songwha entered her room.

She verbally guided Kari through an elaborate body meditation. While Kari lay upon her futon, eyes closed, Master Songwha instructed her to focus on her toes. Kari shifted her attention to each body part in turn. As her awareness moved up along her body on a conscious level, so did the flow of blood concentrate upon each area on an unconscious one, all the way up to her crown chakra atop her head. As Kari began to ease into sleep, Master Songwha gave her a message. Softly she spoke into her ear, "You are God," she whispered, "Divinity is within you. Soon, you will understand."

Kari was entrenched in such a deep state of slumber that she didn't remember her dreams. When she was precipitously awakened at four a.m., her whole body rebelled. It was painful to roll over; her legs felt tight and her feet were swollen. When she finally managed to make it outside, she had trouble keeping her attention focused. It annoyed her that everyone else seemed so chipper; even Chosun's friendly bark seemed forced.

Kari stumbled several times during the ascent up the hill. She felt empty: void of the energy necessary to perform something so strenuous. Still, despite wanting to surrender, she pushed herself on. On the way down, Kari completely lost her balance and took a horrible spill. Her head and left shoulder struck against a rock and Kari screamed in agony. As droplets of blood streamed down the left side of Kari's face, she stared up at the still dark sky and cursed as loud as she could.

"Goddammit! Why are you doing this to me?"

A harsh wind kicked up through the trees and ruffled Kari's hair. She decided to walk slowly the rest of the way. A resident nurse applied treatment to Kari's gash and assured her the wound was superficial. She was left with a patch of conspicuous white tape just below her left temple.

After returning to her room, Kari was greeted by Master Songwha. When she didn't display an iota of sympathy for Kari's injury, Kari erupted in a fury.

"What's next? Smashing my skull? Don't you people realize you could be sued! Has that ever crossed your mind?"

Master Songwha's countenance remained pleasant. "It's time for your morning meditation."

"It's time I got the hell out of here," Kari shouted.

"I'm hungry, I'm tired and I can't stop itching. What's that about?"

"Oh good," Master Songwha said quickly. "It means your energy is changing. Everything is on schedule."

"Except me!" Kari blared. "I'm getting out of here!" She stormed past a complacent Songwha and headed outside the building. The courtyard was vacant except for Kang, who Kari spotted sitting on a stone bench that wreathed an elaborate fountain. Though his eyes were shut, Kang seemed to sense her presence.

"Is that my American friend?" he asked, eyes remaining closed.

"Yes, but she's not in a good mood."

Kang nodded before opening his eyes to view her weary face.

"I guess I should tell you - I've decided to leave."

"Well, this isn't a prison. If you want to go you're free to. No one will stop you. It's completely up to you."

"So you don't care if I go?" Kari asked. There was a hint of desperation in her wavering voice.

Kang's eyes locked with hers. "Yes, I care. You're so close to realizing why you came here. If you stay you will experience the essence of who you are and you'll understand things that you never conceived of before. I know it's hard and I know it's frightening - that's why you keep resisting."

"You're not just a student here, are you?"

Kang smiled a mysterious smile. "Don't be surprised if along your journey you encounter many things that aren't what they appear to be."

"You didn't answer my question."

"I think I did," Kang rose from his seat and slowly strolled through the lush garden.

"Wait... what should I do?" Kari demanded, quickly joining him along the gravel path.

Kang abruptly stopped and gazed at another statue.

"This is Soon Jong tower - it means obedience to truth. Think about it. That's all I will say."

Kari watched as Kang disappeared through a series of cherry trees in bloom. As Kari focused on their gleaming white trunks and pastel blossoms, she pondered what Kang had said. Obedience to truth. What did it mean? To Kari, obedience referred to the discipline required of her over her physical body. Truth. Wasn't that what she was seeking - like the elusive Holy Grail? But why did she feel more like the biblical Job than a gallant knight? It's time to put myself to the test, she thought. If she could tolerate the hardships thrown her way, it would only serve to make her stronger.

* * * *

It took every ounce of Kari's will power to survive the second day. During her two hour isolation period, she kept succumbing to fatigue and nodding off. Only the incessant pounding on the door kept forcing Kari back to consciousness. She began to feel heavy hearted; for no discernable reason, tears kept welling up in her eyes. The itching was nettlesome; her constant scratching slowly started to break the skin.

Kari couldn't wait until midnight so she could close her eyes and escape the insanity. Master Songwha directed another body meditation, insisting that Kari attempt to soothe her painful areas. As she drifted off to sleep, Master Songwha's words floated in her ears. "You are stronger than you think," she insisted. "You will wake up feeling refreshed and will want to continue your spiritual odyssey. You love yourself and you can do anything you want."

* * * *

By the third day, although Kari started feeling physically stronger, a malaise seemed to constrict her spirit. She felt homesick, and despite Master Songwha's constant words of encouragement, still toyed with the idea of leaving.

"What's wrong with comfort? What's so hideous about a five course meal in a four star restaurant?" Kari asked.

"The physical dimension has many wonderful things to offer: the feeling of velvet against your skin; licking an ice cream cone; driving fast in a sports car on an open road... the material world provides for many a whim and fancy."

"So what's wrong with all that?"

"It's all an illusion. It only exists in your mind."

"But isn't that what counts?"

"That's for you to decide," Master Songwha said before turning and walking off in the direction of a beautiful sunset.

The magic hour sun reflected its surreal light off the surrounding mountains as Kari ambled down another path fringed with flowering dogwoods. She casually glanced upwards and noted how the branches and leaves of the trees intermingled, forming what appeared to be a crocheted blanket draping over her. What if Master Songwha was right? What if the leaves and branches were really the illusion, loosely woven together by the threads of fallacy? Kari admired the blush light that shone brightly through the numerous holes in the weave. Was that the light of truth?

Perhaps Kari's restlessness was really a longing for that feeling of life she vaguely remembered, as if it were a sketchy fragment from a dream. Was that why she drank when she was troubled or confused - striving for that altered state of consciousness that only alcohol could so easily and quickly provide? Maybe, just maybe, she was yearning for the quintessence of life, so expertly concealed by her apparent existence of death. Enshrouded in her robotic routines, Kari systematically disregarded every wake-up call that came her way.

She was too busy scheduling and working, maintaining and striving - to what end? What was she really afraid of? At this point in time it couldn't be lack of money or status. The constant rushing and harried lifestyle must have developed to stave off something, but what? What if all Kari's fears could be distilled down to one - the fear of death? Except, fearing death was really fearing life - for we are only truly alive, cognizant of our eternal unity with source, after we die. This... Kari thought, as she stroked the bark of a tree... is the dream. Reality is the hidden, invisible essence camouflaged within the bark.

Kari came to a realization: All the creature comforts, pleasures, and experiences that give humans solace, serve to thicken the haze of the collective dream - until the dream becomes more real than the truth. So real, in fact, that waking up is frightfully painful and only done with trepidation and caution.

It was in that instant, as Kari gazed up at the majestic crimson sky shining through nature's lacy blanket, that she decided to stay. No matter what the physical or emotional consequences, Kari would endure this test. She had never been a quitter, and despite her misgivings and fears, she wasn't going to start now.

* * * *

During the next few days, Kari's body, and more importantly, her mind, began adjusting to the Center's routine. She could feel her body getting more stout; while she was tightening her leg and stomach muscles, she also shed some unnecessary pounds, an added bonus. Kari developed a growing awareness and sensitivity to her physicality. Through the various meditation exercises, she became acutely conscious of every part of it, able to focus her concentration on a particular organ or limb, and in the process, feel the energy being transferred to that area.

During the fifth day, while in the midst of an extended, isolated meditation, Kari actually experienced what Master Songwha described as an "empty mind." She felt totally at peace, and for about three minutes, her mind was void of thought. Without warning, the waves of thought returned like a fast rising tide. Kari was unable to control the sweeping currents; soon her mind was conjuring up vivid images of her father. Several thoughts made her uncomfortable. But the more she attempted to block and banish them, the more her fragile dam sprang leaks and they consumed her.

As her father's visage filled her mind's eye, Kari felt both rage and contrition. She knew her father had been troubled his entire adult life, but still she had adored him.

Suddenly, with uncompromising clarity, Kari viscerally knew when her stomach pains had commenced - it was when he had told her he was marrying again. That day Kari felt abandoned, as if all her affection towards her father had been for naught. Feeling betrayed caused a dormant rage to flare up within her, resulting in the "dirty energy" tearing apart her stomach.

The unrelenting images sent distress signals to Kari's heart and she began to weep, neatly at first, with tears streaming evenly down her cheeks, eventually working up to full-fledged, uncontrollable sobs. In an attempt to regain her composure, Kari forced herself to think about other things. She tried to rationalize her behavior, concluding that making her father an insignificant part of her life was the right decision. It caused her too much pain to be close to him.

Kari shared some of her revelations with Master Song-wha, who was an eager listener. When she proudly told her that she had experienced the "empty mind" for the first time, Master Songwha's face beamed.

"Your soul is starting to awaken," she said. "Soon you will come to know who you really are."

* * * *

Kari finished off her first week in much better standing than when she had begun. Finally, she had started to take charge of her body. Now, Kari was running with the pack and not behind it. She was able to maintain the baby position for an entire hour without complaint. While pain still existed, Kari had trained her mind to ignore it.

Master Songwha continued to give Kari encouraging messages during her evening meditations, and she was waking up more invigorated each day. While she still couldn't recall her dreams, Kari often woke up with a smile draped happily across her face.

At the end of the seventh day, Master Songwha presented Kari with a small, cloth-bound, black book.

"What's this?" Kari asked.

"A journal."

"Why didn't you give me this when I first started?"

"The initial week is a time of abrupt transition. I didn't think it was necessary for you to put down all the negative thoughts and feelings you had when you first arrived here."

"What negative thoughts?" Kari joked.

"What you will experience during these next two weeks will far surpass anything you have felt up to this point. The work is just beginning."

"No kidding?"

"Keeping a permanent record of what you go through will only enhance the experience. Often when you write about something it helps to organize and clarify your feelings."

"Don't worry, somehow I think I'll remember everything." A cheshire grin formed across Kari's face.

"Oh, Master Songwha... thank you... for everything."

"It is my sincere pleasure."

"I'll start in the morning," Kari said, holding up the journal.

Immediately, Kari began to speculate on what Master Songwha meant by saying the work was just beginning.

Chapter **5**

Kari's Journal: Day Eight

Today was a physical and emotional maelstrom. Even in hindsight, I'm struggling to assess everything that transpired. While I know I'm not expected to fully comprehend what's happening, I'm accustomed to a clearer plan of action. Here, I feel I've relinquished all control. Only Master Songwha seems to know the limits and capabilities of both my mind and body; it's she who keeps reminding me how intertwined the two really are. Today started like every other day. I woke up at four a.m. and went running. Aside from the usual rabbits I've encountered along the path up the mountain, there were some wild pigs milling about. They were smokey grey and seemed rather friendly. After showering, Master Songwha reminded me that my fasting was to officially begin. To my dismay, I wasn't allowed any more pine needle paste. All that could enter my body now was water. Throughout the day, every thirty minutes or so, I drank a little water; or in Master Songwha's words, I "chewed" it.

She explained that the movement derived by "chewing" water would create the necessary saliva juices, as well as help to alleviate my impatience problems. The latter seemed not only incomprehensible, but impractical. She called my saliva a precious liquid and said it would blend with the water to be swallowed together. I did what she said and chewed, pretending that the liquid in my mouth was gum - I didn't want to give myself any false illusions of food.

What I couldn't ignore was the foul odor that emanated from my mouth - a putrid, horrific smell that demanded my attention. With each passing hour, the stench grew more severe. My pleas for a mint to dispel the odor went unheeded, despite my promises not to swallow it. The more I drank, the worse it got; even the water tasted sour.

I still had occasional cravings for my favorite meals, but fortunately my mind was slowly adjusting to the reality that no food was forthcoming. As for my body, I was surprised it still had sufficient energy to complete all the meditations and exercises that were required.

During one of the meditations, Master Songwha insisted I attempt to communicate with my father's spirit. When she casually told me that his spirit was with me at all times, I kept hearing Master Kim's words reverberating in my head. Why did everyone else see my father's spirit around me?

My stubbornness ruled the day. Despite Master Songwha's encouragement, I resisted. I told her that she couldn't expect me to see invisible spirits. "I don't have psychic abilities like you," I insisted. Fortunately, she stopped pressuring me, for the moment. Quietly she insinuated that I was afraid. Maybe she was right.

Master Songwha left me alone in the room to finish meditating. While I still didn't feel or sense my father's spirit within those bare walls, I did start to think about him. Quickly I succumbed to my usual forlorn feelings. These were supplemented by guilty emotions - what had happened to our once intimate relationship? Was his spirit hovering around me to demand emotional retribution?

I didn't dwell on my father for very long; fortunately there were enough activities planned to keep me preoccupied. In the early afternoon, I experienced the kind of enema I will not soon forget. It turned out to be an excruciating ordeal. A tube was inserted in my anus, filling my body with two liters of water mixed with lemon juice. Master Songwha insisted that I hold the liquid inside me for a minimum of ten minutes. Although I was lying down, it was grossly uncomfortable. Strange feelings lingered about my stomach and intestines. While parts of my body grew distended, I actually felt the water rising up through my chest, almost up to my neck. Master Songwha instructed me to shake and move around. I did, all the while feeling as saturated and bloated as a submerged sponge. After about eight interminable minutes,

I couldn't take it any longer and raced to the nearby bathroom. For the next seven minutes, my body did nothing but release itself - a discharge of liquidy gush clouded by an offensive odor. The smell was so rancid I desperately wanted to leave the room. How could so much come from a body that hasn't eaten anything of substance in over a week? Despite this curious dilemma, my stomach churned on - spewing and spurting. I felt awful; humiliated, like an animal. After the last bit of waste filtered out of my body, I was exhausted, but actually feeling a little better. This was the first complete bowel movement I had ever experienced and I felt fresher. I eased myself off the toilet, and on my own dare, before flushing, I turned back to examine the contents. They were dark and black - the color of tar - resembling the muck on the bottom of a swamp. I'll never forget what Master Songwha told me afterwards. "This is a physical manifestation of bad karma," she said.

Karma or not, I did feel immeasurably lighter - as if I could float in the air like a helium-filled balloon. For the remainder of the day I walked around smiling; savoring the feeling that my body had eliminated a tremendous amount of dirty energy. It was wonderful. Master Songwha was proud of me - she even complimented the way my skin looked, insisting that it glowed.

Afterwards, Master Songwha escorted me outside for a session of "skin breathing." After telling me to remove my clothing, she urged me to walk around the woods. "Air baths are important," she explained. "Concentrate on your whole body. You can get vitality from the trees."

Completely naked, I meandered through the towering pines for an hour, simply experiencing nature. It took a few minutes for me to overcome my inhibitions, but eventually I relaxed. I began to take mental note of the trees; I actually sensed they were watching me. For the first time, I felt welcomed by them; as if the blocks between myself and nature had been torn down and dispersed, like the collapsed Berlin Wall - a sense of peace stood in its place.

By the end of the hour, I experienced more energy - in actuality, it was a feeling of love emanating from the surrounding trees. Master Songwha informed me that my heart was opening and my ego had been slightly broken down.

I wanted to remain among the trees, but Master Songwha instructed me to slip on my cotton two-piece, and then led me to a clearing to begin a special form of chi training.

She guided me through an elaborate exercise in which it took literally thirty minutes to raise both my arms and extend them over my head. Master Songwha wanted me to feel like the bud of a flower, gracefully and slowly opening and revealing its velvety folds as it gradually transforms itself into a blossom. As I smoothly elevated my arms, millimeter by millimeter, I was circulating my body energy via my mind. As this invisible energy flow occurred within, a wonderful fragrance, akin to perfume, seemed to surround my body. Whether it was Master Songwha's intoxicating words, or my own feelings stirring up my imagination, I actually did detect a beautiful scent lingering about me like an aura. I felt comfortable with my body, truly accepting it for the first time. I had become the beautiful lotus, rising up from the dreck and muck of my insecurities, anxieties and prevailing negativity. With each upward movement, however measured or small, I shed more bad energy - until I vibrated as high as the spectacular bloom. I experienced the sixth sensation around my hands with more intensity - it was as if each finger had its own distinct halo of energy. Master Songwha directed me to lower my arms over a ten minute period, before telling me to repeat the exercise.

After fast-walking up the mountainside and down again, I joined everyone in a dance meditation. Soon, I was caught up in the rhythms of the music, and allowed my body to maneuver freely around the large room. My hands floated above my head in myriad directions. I distinctly felt the energy as it circulated throughout and around my entire being. Time must have stopped, because when they turned off the music I felt like we had just begun.

Now I'm taking a brief rest before Master Songwha joins me for a final meditation. I never had a teacher quite like her. With each passing day, she seems more devoted to me; I feel a tremendous obligation and I don't want to disappoint her.

Kari's Journal: Day Nine

I met an unexpected new friend today. Someone I embraced, communicated with and felt a magical connection to. We melded our energies together, and my body felt euphoric in a way it never has before. I feel grateful to my new comrade, who by the way is not a person, but one of nature's wonders: a pine tree.

After a short indoor meditation session, where once again I struggled, and ultimately resisted any communication with my father's spirit, (Master Songwha assured me that I would soon be "ready," but I had my doubts) she escorted me to an isolated area in the woods.

She advised me to select a single pine tree to work with. In one way or another, all the trees seemed appealing. But finally, one seemed to beckon me with its tantalizing branches and robust stature. It was standing off by itself; and although it seemed slightly aloof, it was quite down-to-earth. Instinctively, I made my way over to this particular tree. The sturdy trunk was tall and lean; the way its branches extended and dipped slightly before sloping upwards, was quite formal and stately looking, as if it were poised to be adorned (not needlessly killed) for a festive occasion. Its needles were a rich green: radiant and healthy. Master Songwha complimented my choice. "You selected a young, male pine," she said, before teaching me more than I ever thought I would know about tree etiquette.

While I initially felt self-conscious, I obeyed her every command. Standing approximately three feet away from the tree, she told me to observe it - from the top of the highest branch to the base of its trunk - gently caressing it with my eyes, three times. After that, I bowed before the tree and greeted it silently to myself. I said, "Hello.

How are you? I am honored to be in your presence. May I engage you in this exercise?" Although this sounds bizarre, I felt very reverent towards the tree and continued my dialogue with it by saying, "I love you," three times. Eventually, Master Songwha urged me to move closer - I was now within one foot of the tree. I raised my arms to chest level and encircled the tree without allowing myself to touch its trunk.

The next step required intense concentration. Fortunately this was a discipline I was getting much better at. After closing my eyes, Master Songwha suggested I focus my attention on my heart chakra. At her prompting, I began to imagine energy circulating from my chest, to my left shoulder, down my left arm, out through my left hand, and flowing into the tree. "Your negative energy is being released. Imagine dark emotions discharging from your left fingertips, the way plumes of blackened smoke are emitted from a chimney," she said, prodding me to continue. Then I was instructed to visualize positive energy coursing through my right hand, up my right arm, to my right shoulder and finally pulsating within my chest. "Imagine the fresh vitality of the tree as white light, streaming into your body." I focused my complete awareness on this energy flow, twice, doing it very slowly. At Master Songwha's urging, I continued this circulation pattern ten times, until eventually, without prompting, my hands were lightly touching the tree. Spontaneously I embraced it, draping my arms fully around its circumference. "Press your heart softly against his trunk and listen," she said. As I inched still closer to my wooden partner, I placed the ball of my right cheek against him as well. I took three deep breaths and listened, for what I did not know, but I've learned not to question anymore. Within a few seconds I heard a heartbeat. At first I thought it was my own, but clearly it was emanating from the tree. I heard the heartbeat of a tree!

By this time I was fully relaxed. I felt like I'd made a connection with this handsome pine. But then, to my amazement, I sensed a distinct pulsing sensation coming from within his trunk. Oh my God, I thought, now I'm feeling his heartbeat! Now I knew the tree was fully aware of my presence. With my eyes remaining shut, I pressed my body as hard as I could against its bark. I heard a faint voice, "Kari," it whispered. "Be brave. I am your friend. You have great potential."

Shocked, my eyes popped opened and I gazed curiously at Master Songwha. "Listen to the tree," she said knowingly. "This is very natural. There's no need for you to be surprised." I closed my eyes again, allowing the warmth of the tree to envelop me. While I didn't hear any more words, I felt as if invisible arms were hugging me closer to the tree. Mine and the tree's heartbeat had become one. A nexus had been formed: pure and profound. My body was surrounded by white light energy and somehow I felt I was disappearing. I was enraptured - in a complete state of harmony and fulfillment. I became the tree: experienced fully the many facets of its existence. My toes seemed to plow into the ground, becoming roots. My torso straightened as if by sheer reflex. I felt very tall. My hair flowed as gracefully as leaves, with each gentle caress of the wind. My arms swayed like sturdy branches. Master Songwha described the experience as akin to "making love," but at the time, I only focused on the sensations I was receiving. It was as if I were momentarily enclosed within a photosynthetic womb; infused with a continuous surge of pure energy that was both inspiring and invigorating.

Master Songwha's voice broke my reverie and jarred me back to reality. I slowly opened my eyes and smiled at her. I knew that she was cognizant of everything I had just experienced. "Step back three paces and thank the tree for your encounter. It's time to say goodbye," she said. I was reluctant to let go, but knew I couldn't stay. As I moved backwards, I stared back at the tree and smiled - not only in happiness, but in gratitude. "Thank you very much. I truly appreciate this meeting. I love you and will never forget this moment." After I said goodbye I felt sad. This tree had transmitted such unprecedented bliss and unconditional love towards me, I didn't want to leave.

"It doesn't seem fair," I said to Master Songwha at the time. "All I did was leave all my negative energy inside the tree, while I got to feel only wonderful, uplifting sensations."

"Your negative energy will not stay in the tree. Trees are able to circulate and raise the vibration of the energy in ways that human beings haven't yet learned. The tree had a wonderful time with you. He sensed and received your love and is truly happy," she remarked.

I'm still reeling with the memory of my encounter with that pine. Master Songwha was right - it had been like making love, but without the ubiquitous inhibiting emotions that inevitably arise when two people connect. In contrast, this was exchanging energy on the purest of levels. I would recommend the experience to anyone. All they have to do is step out into nature and make new friends among the trees.

Kari's Journal: Day Ten

The expression, "The grass is always greener on the other side," took on a radically different meaning for me today. Indeed, I felt I went to that proverbial "other side" - not only was the grass greener, exuding an emerald radiance, but it took on a persona all its own.

In the early afternoon, with the heat of the sun blazing down, Master Songwha took me to an open field of vibrant, lush green grass - nature's carpet. After shedding my shoes, she watched quietly as I roved about. I closed my eyes and focused on the sensations - the grass felt soft and warm against the soles of my bare feet. Having just completed a lengthy meditation, my mind was totally relaxed; in a state of lightheadedness, almost to the point of being giddy.

I suddenly heard what I construed to be a soft murmuring sound inside my head. As I was about to progress with my stroll, stepping down onto the grass with my right foot, the indistinct murmur suddenly became intensely clear. A voice spoke: "I am alive. Please, don't step on me." Stunned, my foot remained frozen in mid-air, causing me to resemble an out-of-place pink flamingo perched awkwardly on someone's front lawn.

What was happening to me? Had all these days of not eating and barely sleeping finally taken their toll on my sanity? Or was I finally awakening to sounds that have always existed, but that I had conveniently chosen to ignore in the past?

I turned to Master Songwha, who was quietly communicating with an orange and black butterfly that had landed, ever so gently, on her fingertip. Its impressive wingspan resembled polished marble, glinting topaz and obsidian, as it caught the natural light, while smoothly flapping its glorious expanse in the sun. As if she knew the very second my concerns originated, Master Songwha released the butterfly into the air with a playful upwards toss and turned to face me.

"I can't continue," I told her.

"Yes you can."

"No," I protested, still teetering on one leg. "The grass knows I'm here. It feels me walking on it. Every time I step down it feels pain."

"Why do you think that is?" she asked.

I paused a moment, trying desperately to maintain my balance while pondering her question. Then, a revelation struck me like a power surge, causing my mind to scramble, sort out, and recondition my previous way of thinking.

"Because the grass is me!" I uttered in astonishment.

"It's just like me! It has thoughts and feelings! I wouldn't want to be stepped upon either!"

"Yes! That's right," Master Songwha exclaimed, smiling broadly. "You got it. You're finally understanding some of the fundamental principles."

"Great, but what do I do now? Never walk again?" My foot was still dangling in the springtime air.

"You must speak with the grass. Remember your experience with the tree? Tell the grass you are not here to do it any harm. You have no malicious intent. You come before it with understanding and love."

I gazed down at the expanse of grass. It was different than relating to a single tree, for here, there were millions of individual blades awaiting my next move. Although a bit daunted, I thought, okay, I can do this. I observed the green sweep, imagining a collective set of eyes staring back. "Hello," I said softly. "I don't want to hurt you. Is it all right if I walk around for awhile?" I waited for an answer, but none was forthcoming. This is ridiculous, I thought. Did I really expect the grass to keep talking?

Again I turned to Master Songwha for guidance. She motioned for me to place my right foot down and continue walking. When I did, I received a profound, irrefutable answer to my inquiry. As I ambled a bit farther, I felt as if the sides of my feet were being lightly tickled; the grass subtly brushed against my toes in a distinct back and forth motion. I was receiving a massage from the grass, and it felt wonderful!

What occurred next was so incredible, it seemed nearly sacrilegious to believe that it could happen to me. While stopping in mid-stride, marveling and enjoying the flirtatious antics of the grass, I watched in amazement as several hundred blades actually lay down before me, as methodically and gracefully as an Olympic team of synchronized swimmers - creating an organized, perfectly arranged and measured pathway. As I proceeded, I felt like one of Moses' disciples when they crossed the Red Sea - completely in awe. I followed the path so lovingly created for me, without talking, for a full hour. The grass had provided an elaborate labyrinth for me to walk upon - its detailed design invoked a wonderful meditative state, akin to the intricately-tiled mazes which adorned the back courtyards of landmark churches.

As I reflected back upon this experience, I realized with absolute certainty, that like me, the grass was fully alive, possessing a consciousness and intelligence all its own. Another bizarre occurrence worth noting, was that after this incident my pangs of hunger were greatly reduced. Master Songwha explained, "You received energy from love. By opening up, the grass was able to transmit energy directly to your body. If you reconcile with your father's spirit, your hunger will go away completely."

"Anything you say," I replied. And I meant it. I had not only seen miracles, but had experienced them. I knew I could trust her. In the past few days, all of her expert and loving guidance has led me further along on my journey towards enlightenment.

"You are ready to receive the love from your father's spirit," Master Songwha said later that night.

At the word father, my body immediately grew tense.

"So when do you want to do this?" I asked, not sure I wanted to know the answer.

"Tomorrow. Don't think about it too much. Trust me, it will be a wonderful experience."

A lot easier said than done. Intuitively I knew I was destined to do this - get closer with my father - but I still harbored an inordinate amount of resentment and anger towards him. Let's face it: the truth, is I'm terrified.

Kari's Journal: Day Eleven

With Master Songwha's guidance, I finally confronted my father's spirit. The experience, which was wrenching but ultimately rewarding, coerced me to fully understand his essence. Not only will I never perceive him in quite the same manner, but I now feel connected to him in a way I never would have thought possible.

After tossing and turning all night, the day proceeded like all others - until I threw up. Since beginning the actual fast I've had several near misses - the kind when some of the noxious, bitter liquid rises up from your stomach and irritates the back of your throat with its harsh, repugnant taste; only to be swallowed again, causing insidious burning sensations as it flows down your esophagus like molten lava.

My body tuned into my apprehension concerning today's reconciliation exercise with my father by expelling a yellowish substance, streaked with red, resembling the texture of a snail's entrails. Although I felt physically better afterwards, somehow I longed to remain hunched over the toilet instead of embarking upon this particular communication.

Random and chaotic thoughts were fermenting inside my head. Like a fine wine, I felt they should remain within me, waiting to be released at the appropriate time. I tried to convince myself that now wasn't it. But my stubborn and irrational volition quickly unravelled as I grew fretful: "Let's just get this over with," I finally concluded.

When Master Songwha arrived she showed no sign of being cognizant of my emotional plight. She proceeded to direct a couple of breathing exercises, before guiding me through an hour of meditation so that I would be appropriately relaxed. Once she sensed I was cloaked within a blanket of tranquility, she escorted me to a spacious room that I didn't know existed. It had high ceilings and open windows. In the middle of the room were two wooden chairs facing each other. Master Songwha motioned for me to sit on one of them and close my eyes. I complied and soon sensed her sitting opposite me.

"Try to control your breathing," she said. "Now imagine a spot three feet in front of you. Call to your father's spirit. Beckon him to come to you. You will see him as a bright, white light, not as a face. Concentrate. When you see the light, just nod."

I focused my concentration on my father and visualized a bright light before me. Finally, I nodded.

"Your father's spirit is with us. Inside the light. Do you sense him?"

Despite my skepticism, I truly began to feel the presence of my father; his image flashed through my mind. While I focused on the light, my heart began to beat more rapidly, as if I were experiencing the feelings of anticipation and expectation that come when you are in love. I knew at that moment, with unerring conviction, that my father was in the room with me. As I continued to consciously breathe, struggling to remain at peace, my mind focused on the animated rhythms of my heartbeat. Were they trying to convey a message?

While my heart persisted with its melodious palpitations inside my chest, I felt the spirit of my father, yet something else began to happen. Images began to formulate within the bright light. I saw a white glow, barely discernable, like a spark, darting rapidly through a dark tunnel.

"Your father's soul is entering into your Grandmother's womb."

I couldn't believe what Master Songwha had just said. Yet, while I tried to grasp the concept, odd forms of substance started shifting and coagulating. The hazy images began to slide together like a jigsaw puzzle, revealing the distinct shape of a human fetus. It possessed a large head with protruding eyeballs that seemed to be staring directly at me.

"Your father's soul is creating his body," Master Songwha told me.

I was actually witnessing the formation of my father's fetus - his soul was merging into a physical body! Mysterious feelings of wonderment swept over me as if I were sprinkled with enchanted fairy dust. How was this possible? I continued to stare at the image of creation, both amazed and stupefied. As I watched my father grow within my grandmother's womb, I lost track of who I was. Had I become Alice? Was this place within my mind's eye,

"Wonderland?" Indeed, I felt I had fallen into the "looking glass."

What in reality took close to ten months to accomplish, I observed within a span of seconds. I shouldn't have been so surprised, for as I'm learning, all time is truly simultaneous, with no beginning and no end - just an all-encompassing, eternal now moment. I felt my father's struggle as he slowly inched through the narrow canal with each contraction. Amidst shudders and spasms, my father's body was pushed through my grandmother's, tearing through muscle and flesh, as he was born into the physical world. His head magically appeared to the doctor looming above, then his shoulders, and quickly, the rest followed. In one fluid motion, my father was lifted into the chilled air and he began to wail. I felt his confusion. He was taken from the warmth and comfort of his mother and abruptly thrust into a cold, brightly-lit room. Tears streamed lightly down my cheeks as I watched the miracle of my father's birth - an unbelievable experience to behold. I felt honored to have been permitted to witness it.

"Look into your father's eyes," Master Songwha instructed. "Now, take hold of his hand."

In my mind's eye I gripped his tiny, soft and crinkly hand. It vibrated within my palm. Immense unconditional love embraced my entire being. I wanted to protect this baby, to nurture him. Instead, feeling like an infant myself, I continued to weep, succumbing to a bizarre array of emotions that I had never previously encountered.

"Continue to watch," Master Songwha said.

Before my eyes, the baby began to grow. I observed

my father's first crawl, his initial smile, and heard him
utter his first words. Every moment was precious. As he
took his first step, I watched his eyes. They were glowing
with an inner vitality - a happiness that I had never seen
in them before, when he was the adult and I was the
child. What had changed in him? Why did the joy he so
effortlessly possessed as a youngster disappear when he
became an adult?

Master Songwha must have sensed my mind
wandering and said, "Focus on your father's childhood.
See him going to school for the very first time."

I shifted my thoughts back to my father's youth and
saw him riding his first tricycle. I watched as my grand-
parents taught him how to steer and push down on the
pedals with his little feet. I observed my grandmother
dressing him in a nice shirt and dress pants and grew
weepy once again as I felt his fears when she dropped him
off for his first day of kindergarten. He was very inquisitive, constantly asking questions of his teachers.

While studying my father's interactions with his fellow
classmates and friends throughout grade school and junior
high, I became keenly aware of the similarities of our experiences. Although a generation apart from each other, I
felt quite the same. Was the age gap between us merely a
myth designed to allow us the freedom to be different,
when in fact we were alike all along? What purpose does
that apparent space hold? Twenty some odd years is a blip,
a second - nothing more than a discrepancy of time. In
reality, while viewing my father's life, I was truly witnessing my own. Tears of understanding, of grasping the

sometimes ungraspable, rolled down the mountains of my cheeks like winding rivers.

As the profusion of images materialized before me, I felt like my father and I had become one - we were the same person. I was able to experience his feelings as profoundly as if they were my own. When he struggled through puberty, I shared both his guilt and shame over his first sexual thoughts, but I also felt the exquisite pleasure when he fell in love for the first time. It was amazing! I couldn't believe, and never pictured, that my father had endured the same experiences that I did during adolescence.

Soon I became the ultimate voyeur - both watching and feeling my father lose his virginity. At first I was mortified. How could I continue to view this very personal aspect of him? It wasn't natural. Yet, something kept my mind's eye glued to its imaginary television set which unfolded each episode of my father's life like a well-made documentary - exuding the full spectrum of emotions - so real, so full of truth. How could I deny the depths of understanding that I was becoming privy to?

But this was different. I suddenly felt a stirring within my own body as I observed and experienced my father's pure, unbridled passion. As I'm coming to know, there really is no sex, per say. We are all both male and female - yin and yang. Each time we incarnate to this physical dimension we choose the gender of our expression. Source is beyond male and female and since our essence is source, so are we. Yet, because I'm only conscious of myself in this lifetime as Kari, a woman, it's both astounding as well as intriguing to make love as a man.

Since it was my father's first attempt, the experience was both nerve-racking and brief; I felt his initial pride sink into a sea of dissatisfaction. While it lasted, I was able to dive through one of those infamous, tempting windows of opportunity - the ones, however narrow and short-lived, that allow you to break free of your surrounding illusion and create a whole new set of circumstances. As I caressed, stroked and kissed the body of a woman, I felt as if I achieved the ultimate freedom - traversing across unconventional landscapes and interdimensional time zones - harkening back to when I had chosen to express as a man.

My father possessed a range of human emotions that ran the gamut from innocent bliss to harrowing despair. Throughout this exercise I noticed that he was truly an honest person - a pure, loving soul. But something was missing. There was a sense of perpetual anticipation - a constant search for someone to fill the void that was growing within his heart. Little did my father realize at the time, that the emptiness he was experiencing was a longing for more - much more than a loving relationship with a woman could provide. His search for the ultimate woman with whom to share his life was in essence a quest to remember who in fact he really was.

Unfortunately, I doubt he'll ever come to that understanding of truth in this lifetime.

As the movie played on, I witnessed the touching moment in which my father first saw my mother. They were at a party given by mutual friends, when his eyes locked with hers from across the room. A definite connection was made - he felt as if he knew her from somewhere. When I saw my mother through my father's eyes, I was taken with her casual beauty: the way she held her head in such a poised manner; the way she caressed the rim of her punch glass, lightly encircling it with her fingertips. The attraction was immediate for my father, who moved closer.

While viewing their courtship I was caught up in the whirlwind of their romance - seized onto the grand white horse of the majestic carousel - spinning out-of-control along with their loving emotions. Finally, I was privy to the brass ring. Actually, it was gold, but there was a horse present. My father drove my mother up to a rustic ranch in the mountains. As the horses lumbered beneath them, my father withdrew a small velvet box from his jacket pocket. My mother's radiant face blushed as crimson as the setting sun when he asked her to be his wife. A passionate kiss was shared, while the horses flanked each other passively, unaware of what was transpiring atop their backs. There was something enchanting to this kiss. A carefree abandonment that was enhanced by the balmy warmth in the air. It wasn't long after their honeymoon that I was born.

Witnessing my own birth through my father's eyes was a complex experience. I could sense his fears and apprehension, yet at the same time, I shared the feelings of joy and pride which overtook his being.

At this point during the exercise, my own body seemed to necessitate a pause in the action. Tears flowed rapidly down, spreading a warmth over my entire face; simultaneously, my nose began emitting a thick, milky mucous. Later, Master Songwha would explain to me that it was more "dirty" energy spilling out.

Remaining inside my father's head, I relived my own childhood. What I sensed more than anything was how strong his love was for the baby he held in his arms; the toddler he bounced on his lap. As his passion for my mother waned, his attention was consummately directed at me. He poured all his energy into ensuring that I had the best of everything. When I disappointed him, he felt a personal sense of loss. What seemed to discourage him more than anything was when I commenced dating. My father had no desire to share his affections. He saw other boys as a threat to his own imagined dominion. He never wanted me to grow up; the more independent I grew, the more disheartened he became. Was I the only person he was ever able to unconditionally love?

My father's spirit was in chaos; as his obsessive feelings towards me intensified, I increasingly pulled away. An emptiness swept through him. He felt as vacant as my childhood room, now a hollow shell; although it contained sentimental paraphernalia, it was void of life, void of laughter, void of me. Now I understood why he committed adultery. My mother became the brunt of vicious attacks - onslaughts that he wanted to direct at me but instead unleashed onto her. Why Dad? Why couldn't you let me go?

I became quite melancholy. My parents used to be so much in love, it was hard for me to comprehend how their lives together unravelled. Had I been watching their whimsical courtship through rose-colored glasses - so befittingly supplied by the beautiful sunsets that cloaked them during their capricious times, ultimately capped off by their romantic proposal? Or were those magic-hour skies merely a veil, concealing a much deeper, harder to comprehend reality?

Master Songwha's voice interrupted my pleas. "Your father's spirit is now in front of you," she said.

Thrust back to focus, I tried to clear my mind.

"His spirit will start to take on his physical body. Watch for your father's face."

A few moments elapsed before my father appeared in front of me. Oh God, I thought, what do I say to him? Suddenly, I burst into tears. After living through my father's entire life, I felt only complete empathy for him. It seemed so unfair. All those years he devoted to me had resulted in utter turmoil, as he suffered the anguish of knowing he had lost his place in my life. What had I done? Nothing, I realized. I merely grew up.

Unbeknownst to him, his longing for completeness could never be fully satisfied through me. He must go deeper within himself to rekindle that ever elusive, ultimate connection we all yearn for.

"Reach out and hold your father's hands," Master Songwha instructed. I did and she said, "Feel the tempera- ture of his hands. Have you ever felt his hands before? Now look into his eyes."

While I gazed into my father's eyes, I felt only one emotion: his love for me. I had to battle the onslaught of tears fighting their way down my cheeks. Finally, unable to resist, I gave in to their attack.

"Listen to your father. He has something to say to you."

"Kari," he began. "Do you know how much I love you?"

I nodded emphatically, "Yes."

"Just enjoy being with him," Master Songwha said.

A pulsating sound had commenced. With each passing moment the rhythm grew louder and more insistent.

"Can you hear that?" I questioned. "What is that sound?"

"Your father's heartbeat," she replied.

"Really?" The beat was deafening - his heart had suddenly become the center of the universe. My universe. Its sound enveloped me, bathing my entire body - moving around and through my flesh. The methodic noise resembled the ticking of a bomb - unnerving, yet, possessing an intense energy. I felt distinct changes occurring within my lower body, in particular my abdomen. It grew warmer, while my head remained decidedly cool. I flashed back to my encounter with Master Kim on top of Bell Rock. He had explained that a cool, fresh head and a warm torso were physical proof of a genuinely healthy body. However, my experience with him only lasted a day - it was quite temporary. Now, Master Songwha insisted, "Your body is finally being restored to its natural state. You will be able to maintain this always."

After a few minutes, the heartbeat sounds diminished in intensity. Master Songwha directed, "Now, fully embrace your father. Allow your spirit to merge with his."

For the first time in my life I understood my father completely. Master Songwha told me that because of this newfound comprehension, my spirit had been awakened. After a few eternal moments within my father's embrace, Master Songwha said, "It's time for him to leave." As I started to pull away, he spoke again.

"I love you," he said. "You must never lose your courage, Kari. Remember, I am always with you. My spirit will never leave you. I will protect you." His words still resound inside my mind. I sensed his absolute sincerity. A feeling of pure love swirled within my heart as he spoke. I wanted desperately to remain in his presence, but Master Songwha urged, "It's time."

I told him it was an honor to be his daughter. After expressing my love and eternal gratitude once more, I pulled back and resumed my original position on the chair. Master Songwha directed me to bow my head down. She explained, "If you watch him disappear, there's the possibility that his spirit will stick to you - he may not want to leave, and he must, in peace."

I kept my head lowered until Master Songwha assured me it was okay to lift it back up. The instant I did, I saw an unforgettable sight: Double rainbows, bright and sparkling, unfolded in front of me as gracefully as a woman spreads the accordion folds of a decorative fan. The shimmering expanses of color loomed over my head as Master Songwha explained, "This double rainbow symbolizes that the vibration of your father's spirit has been elevated as a result of this encounter."

After the session I was emotionally drained but physically rewarded: My stomach no longer felt any discomfort. I had been fed with the food of spirit - chi energy.

It had been a unique and profound experience. While viewing my father's life, I was forced to emotionally conn- ect with him in ways I never imagined possible. Now, I fully understood the source of his pain, anger and frustration; sadly, I realized why our relationship had never been a healthy one. In a sense it had taken the form of spiritual incest with me, my father was trying desperately to replace what was lacking in his own life with my mother. Although nothing physical had ever transpired between us, over the years he treated me more as his spouse than as a daughter.

My guilt had dissipated as a result of this exercise because I now knew that growing up and leaving my father's house was quite normal according to the laws of nature. If only he was able to come to that understanding and realize that it wasn't me he was seeking, but himself.

Unfortunately his dilemma could never be solved with the limited knowledge he possessed, or that was instilled in him from his own parents - his longings could only be satiated by his own awakening and spiritual insight.

I feel the need to express these newfound feelings to my father in person, and vow to visit him after I leave Korea.

If only everyone could experience what I did today! Imagine the kind of world it might be.

Kari's Journal: Day Twelve

Master Songwha paid me a compliment today.

"Your face is getting rounder," she said.

"It is?" I replied, perplexed by this notion. "Are you saying my face is actually changing its shape?"

"Yes. Enlightened people lose the harsh angles and lines on their faces as they evolve spiritually. As you continue this process, your spirit will get rounder and this will be reflected by the circular shape of your face."

After my morning shower, Master Songwha used a similar meditation ritual to conjure up the spirit of my mother. Because I was at a higher level now, I only needed a half hour of meditation to achieve the same deeply relaxed state.

The exercise turned out to be bittersweet. As I reviewed my mother's life, I couldn't keep myself from fast-forwarding to her sudden, tragic death. Master Songwha must have sensed this because she guided me slowly and lovingly back to my mother's ironic and harsh beginning.

Just seconds before it was too late, an inexperienced and fatigued hospital resident noticed that the umbilical cord was choking my mother's neck. The cord had to be severed and clamped before they allowed my grandmother to push once again. My mother's face looked morbid; it had taken on the tone of a severe bruise, a ghastly bluish-black. The horrific circumstances bore likeness to a scene out of a sci-fi thriller, as my mother's tiny gray head strained and moved about while the rest of her remained lodged within the birth canal. The ineptitudes of the medical profession flanked my mother's life like bookends. Why did she have to endure hospital traumas at both her birth and death? What did her spirit feel she needed to learn from this? I suppose I'll never know.

Except for a developing passion for dance, my mother's childhood was uneventful. She began early: taking ballet, tap and modern jazz lessons when she was only four years old. It was wonderful to see her joyful countenance during recitals. Myriad swathes of bright colors, sequins and fringe flashed before my eyes, while I viewed her flamboyant costumes over the years, as if I were doing a chronological fashion retrospective.

When my mother turned eighteen, instead of going the academic route like the majority of her high school friends, she chose the exciting, yet unstable, vocation of dance. Like many dancers, she was labeled a gypsy - always on tour with some dance company - travelling aboard buses and trains, in an attempt to find that ever elusive audience. I suppose she had been seeking approval.

I didn't blame her after witnessing the countless sea of rejections during numerous cattle call auditions. It was at that time in her life that she stopped by a friend's party and met my father.

I wasn't quite sure what prompted her to give up her dream. Her motivations at the time were muddled and unclear to me. But maybe I just didn't want to see.

As I gazed upon my mother in an empty rehearsal room, staring at her own reflection in the wall-to-wall mirrors that surrounded her like endless windows to inner understanding, I began to realize why she had insisted that I attend dance classes. Was she living out her dream through me? Did she give up her aspirations because of impending motherhood?

Although my mother truly loved my father when they met, their intimacy distinctly waned after I was born. Was it the countless sacrifices she made for my father, as well as for me? Perhaps, it was the hypnotic expression and rhythmic movements of dance that she longed for. Or was her quest for something deeper? Did her unhappiness stem from the same roots as my father's had? Were they searching for the seeds of truth from which they both sprang, that were part of them all along? All my mother's anxieties regarding the choices in her life - giving up her career, getting married, having a child - were a massive smoke screen, as attention-grabbing and blinding as the set designs of her performances. In order for my mother to dissipate the haze of uneasiness and doubt, she would have to elevate herself to another stage - one of higher understanding.

While she had always been a loving and conscientious parent, my mother's growing unhappiness often sapped her energy and enthusiasm. I recognize now, that while all parents instinctively love their children, misconceptions inevitably occur. The main source of the problem is communication. I saw that once my parents stopped expressing their feelings to each other - whether they were ones of discontent, frustration, even the occasional bouts of happiness - slowly, their mutual trust and respect abated as well. After cutting the common ties of understanding amongst themselves, they had nowhere to vent their overflow of emotions - except, of course, to me. It was never an outward form of expression. In fact, it was the read-between-the-lines type - quite subtle.

My mother craved my father's affection, while he outwardly doted on me. Although she camouflaged her jealousy, almost to the point of being dormant, I sensed how lonely she had become during her last years.

It seemed as if death was necessary to allay her pain. I felt as if my mother's spirit needed to be released; set free into the wild like a noble bird of prey - able to soar through the clouds - able to dance once again.

I cried more during today's communication than I did at her funeral. I felt a profound connection to my mother, similar to what I had experienced yesterday with my father: a bond of understanding and love that could never again be strained or broken. I was grateful for the opportunity to express my deepest love and gratitude to her.

After the session, I remained seated for a few minutes. Finally, my tear-stained face turned to Master Songwha.

I stumbled over my own words. "Did you have any impressions about... I mean... what did you feel about my mother?"

Her answer was blunt but full of truth: "Your mother had trouble loving herself. When you can't love yourself you can't love anyone else."

Thoughts of my mother mingled with Master Songwha's words inside the basin of my mind for the rest of the day. It dawned on me that my own spiritual journey must continue, however difficult and painful, if only to prevent myself from repeating the mistakes both my parents had made.

Kari's Journal: Day Thirteen

I woke up this morning feeling quite hesitant, as hostile memories of my last encounter with Brad exploded to the forefront of my mind. When I agreed to undergo the reconciliation exercise with him I must have been crazy. Most people would construe invoking the spirit of an ex-lover as being obsessed. But then again, nothing I had done so far would conform to the ideals of most people.

Today I needed a mere fifteen minutes of meditation and relaxation before Master Songwha was able to initiate the process. Watching Brad's birth and early childhood was quite moving and caused my feelings for him to swell. My mind drifted to our relationship and kept pondering why he couldn't open up and truly love me.

What had caused him to be so closed off? What had been the trigger? Sadly, I found out. During our time together I had always thought of Brad as a young boy needing love. Now, I understood why. My own body grew tense as I watched his life unfold.

It was startling to witness: an innocent child's spirit being completely torn apart - by mere words. I came to realize there was nothing trivial about the power words contained. They were as lethal as a vial of poison. But most frightening is that, once said, they're gone without a trace - leaving no proof that they were ever even uttered. Except to the recipient, who experiences their invisible and insidious toxicity as if it were radon gas.

The effects of words are long-lasting. Poisons have antidotes, but words remain spackled within the tears and holes of someone's aura, as entrenched as sand thrown onto wet cement. Words can never be erased from the receiver's psyche - they're dwelled upon and worried about, until finally, the person, no matter how hard they try to resist the onslaught of negativity, caves in and actually starts to believe what was said. Then, it's over. The damage has been done.

Unfortunately, Brad's parents had married very early in life. They didn't understand themselves and each other's needs, much less the requirements of raising a child. As their own frustrations mounted, they continually belittled, criticized and attacked him. A flurry of biting remarks played within my head: "Why can't you act your age?"; "Sit up straight!"; "What makes you think you can do that?"; "You'll ruin it!"; "You're incapable!"; "You're inept!"; "You'll never amount to anything!"; "You're the cancer of this family!"; "You're a failure!"

Each word whittled away at Brad's spirit, like a sculptor chips away at the perfect block of marble. Brad's ill-fated artists were his confused and unhappy parents - instead of revealing the masterpiece hidden within the stone, they were burying it deeper.

I longed to turn the volume down on their misguided obscenities - knowing all along that Brad could not. The more I heard, the more clearly I saw why Brad had done what he did with his business. As he struggled to make something out of himself the honest, hard-working way, his parents' toxic words echoed throughout his head, prompting him to take short-cuts, however illicit or illegal they may have been - all in a futile effort to prove his parents wrong.

It was awful. I saw a genuinely loving boy being transformed into a closed-off, cold-hearted, ruthless man. What had caused me to enter into a relationship with someone like that? Did I feel that undeserving of love as well?

Brad and I were lost souls coming together in the frantic search for love. We didn't know at the time that neither one of us was capable of giving it, let alone receiving it. As I watched our courtship unfold, I realized that I had been just as responsible for our problems. There were countless times when Brad needed me and I wasn't there for him. We were both too calculating, unwilling to reveal our innermost feelings to each other until we thought it was safe. But when is it ever safe? Both of us had erected our own self-imposed barriers and inhibitions which precluded our natural love from surfacing.

Communicating with Brad's spirit enabled me to see the painful truth. He loved me as much as his battered emotions would allow. Like everyone, Brad had the unlimited potential to love - sadly, it had been diminished against his will.

Reflecting back on today's encounter, I see that all mankind has the same potential to love, fully and unconditionally. Love is not something that needs to be learned. It resides within our genes, our cellular memory banks, and our spirits. We, as a society, have to prevent it from being quashed to the point of extinction, and replaced with the ever present, runaway emotion of fear.

Alas, the plight of mankind teeters like a seesaw atop the fulcrum of comprehending this truth. Someone has to put a stop to this never-ending cycle - silence the harsh words, end the violence. We have to break the chain of misunderstanding with regard to our human condition in order for us to survive our misdeeds.

Kari's Journal: Day Fourteen

This morning I awoke feeling something quite bizarre: happiness. Over the past few days I had emotionally cleansed myself, purging many burdens and guilts that I'd carried around as long as I can remember. I tore apart the cumbersome web of conflict, intricately strung with the filaments of human dynamics, and, in the process, eliminated the discords and contradictions that had kept me mired in a swamp of fear and negativity. Finally, light illuminated the darkness of my misunderstanding, and I was able to see and grasp the source of contention, friction and dissonance that comprised my interpersonal relationships. The illusion of separation and confusion had reaped my inner turmoil. Indeed, I had discovered that by truly experiencing someone else's life, only then can you fully comprehend why they behave the way they do. In lieu of taking their actions and words personally and reacting defensively, you can be compassionate, loving and forgiving.

It was by becoming one with others that I finally

understood their motivations and was then able to accept them for who they truly are - just like me: a frightened seeker of joy and love, grasping for the true understanding of self.

Although my body is in the best shape it's ever been - experiencing more strength and vitality with each passing day - I now feel lighter. The torrent of conflicting thoughts that used to weigh me down had finally dissipated. Master Songwha said I'm experiencing "peaceful energy" for the first time. I learned that this sense of harmony can only be realized when we start to detach ourselves from our personal and separatist emotions and begin to understand that we are part of everyone and everything - one with all.

Kari's Journal: Day Fifteen

Today I discovered a secret energy channel in my body. After Master Songwha informed me about the two main energy channels (horizontal and vertical) that all humans possess, she helped me to experience the one that circulates around the waist.

After assuming the lotus position, I was told to relax and fully concentrate on my breathing. Not long into the training session, I began to feel a rush of something quite tangible swirling clockwise around my circumference. The flow of the energy belt soothingly caressed my waist like a gush of warm water, spiraling down like a whirlpool.

Master Songwha directed me to feel specific body parts. As the movement of energy grew more palpable, my kidneys began to throb. Without warning, my large intestines started to stir. It seemed as if my internal organs had taken on lives of their own; pulsating and moving beyond my control. Even my ribs took flight, heading downward and disappearing out my Dahn Jon area, like skeletal birds taking liberty from their flesh confines.

Master Songwha sensed I was becoming overwhelmed by these sensations and slowly eased me out of the meditation. Upon opening my eyes, I immediately stood up and ran my hands over my chest and abdomen. I guess I wanted to make sure my body was still intact. It was!

Before leaving, Master Songwha informed me that tomorrow I will experience the vertical channel. Her eyes seemed to twinkle with zeal as she said it. All I could conclude was that it was going to be another unique encounter. Each new experience elicited more enlightenment. Where would it end? I realize I should have no expectations. All I need to do is go with the flow, energy or otherwise, to see where it leads me.

Kari's Journal: Day Sixteen

What a day! I keep discovering dimensions to my body I never knew existed. Most people are being kept in ignorance, but why? Is there a conspiracy going on? Shouldn't everyone be encouraged and taught about the incredible energy that courses through their flesh, quicker than the blood that circulates within their veins?

With Master Songwha's guidance and assistance, my vertical channel was opened up today. While it was an exhausting, time-consuming and unnerving experience, it also proved to be exhilarating and excruciatingly pleasurable.

I was told to focus on an area midway between my ribs and navel, directly beneath my heart. This was to be the starting point for the exercise. Master Songwha placed her two fingertips onto that spot, while I concentrated and felt the energy.

She told me to direct the energy down towards my navel, where its warmth treated and soothed my large and small intestines. As the energy moved towards my bladder it grew hotter. According to Master Songwha, the healing energy was completely restoring each individual organ to its optimum, robust condition.

The energy flowed south, massaging the area around my sex organs. Master Songwha cautioned me that although the region between my sex organs and anus was a critical one, I shouldn't allow the energy to linger there too long. Instantly, I found out why.

My thoughts abruptly ceased. I was no longer grounded in the real world; all sense of time and space had been vanquished. Most astonishing of all, my head felt as if it had shifted location, travelling downwards, nestling in my lower abdomen. I imagined myself as Kali, the Hindu Goddess who carried around a head in her hands. Was losing my head, my mind, the brain - ultimate of all body parts - a necessary step towards self realization? Did the elimination of the most mysterious and prestigious organ, one that secured my very identity, become the prerequisite for truth? Yet, how could I label something as truth unless

I could identify its falsehood? And who was I to make that determination?

Perhaps the only way to recognize my real self was to first become something other than me. Was my feeling of decapitation actually the shedding of my persona? Kali was as destructive as she was kind, as cruel as she was tender; who was I to decide which? It's all interpretation - an earthquake or flood may appear tragic in one sense, yet healing to mother earth in another. I needed to go beyond my own critiques and deductions. Wasn't losing that incessant tendency to label and judge everyone and everything around me, in essence the destruction of my ego? I recalled what Kang Hoon had said and realized that my "beheading" was more than the elimination of my individuality - it was the realization of what was left in its place.

Master Songwha explained to me later, "When your consciousness resides in your Dahn Jon, you will have only the purest feelings of joy and peace. Only then can you truly love."

The sensations that followed were beyond comprehension. First, I felt profoundly grounded, like my body had magically connected with the center of the earth. My entire physicality was stronger and more powerful; while it grew heavier, my mind became lighter - all things seemed possible. We must have reached our goal. This must be completion! Overwhelming feelings of love enveloped me - was this heaven? But as if she could read my mind, Master Songwha informed me that we were only just beginning.

As the energy funnelled towards my rectum, my anal hole instinctively squeezed and contracted. When this happened, my entire body was swept up into the throes of unmitigated ecstasy. While in some ways it was tantamount to having an orgasm, nothing I had sexually experienced prior to this came even remotely close. The intensity of the pleasure was too staggering to comprehend - far more powerful than any climax I'd ever had. Every cell in my body shared in the unending rapture. I kept thinking: "This is impossible! How is this happening?"

I became the actual manifestation of the birth of pleasure itself. My entire body vibrated as the incredible sensations expanded upon themselves in undulating waves. I longed to remain forever in that blissful state. But Master Songwha's soft voice slowly induced me back to reality (I still wonder about the illusion our mind perceives as reality), to recommence the energy circulation.

As I focused on moving the energy upwards, past my tail bone, I was confronted with severe difficulty. I desperately needed Master Songwha's assistance. Once again, she placed her fingertips to the area, prompting the energy to continue its journey. Only my body was protesting: It trembled, and I heard loud, discordant sounds that grew deafening, almost explosive in nature - my pelvic bones were literally reshaping themselves. I had trouble hearing Master Songwha's voice through the din.

"Don't be frightened. You need patience," she said. I used all my powers of concentration to forge the energy upwards. It took fifteen minutes for it to traverse past my tail bone area. I learned that if I didn't focus and keep the energy from dissipating, it could have been very dangerous.

As the energy travelled to my kidneys, the discomfort increased. My kidneys twisted and squeezed tightly, as if they were sponges being wrung out over a sink. "Allow the dirty energy to be expelled," Master Songwha urged.

My back bone grew warmer with the flow of energy. Each vertebra realigned itself - I could feel my bones straightening and my spine becoming erect.

Before I knew it, hot water, originating from my kidneys, streamed midway up my back. While this occurred, my heart raised approximately five centimeters within my torso. This process was very difficult. I worked at it for nearly ten minutes, until Master Songwha finally pointed her fingers towards my back and sent her energy to help. In an instant, my entire body flung violently backwards, causing my chest to assume its optimum condition and my shoulders to go down. It was an excruciatingly painful ordeal. My body felt as if it was spiraling out-of-control as I attempted to pass through this area. My muscles compressed and squeezed; I experienced lightning flashes of pain beneath my skin. When the cataclysmic changes subsided, my chest organs and bones resumed their proper position and once again, my heart was in a state of peace.

The energy climbed up the bones of my neck, causing my lungs to expand, almost to the point of explosion. A growling sound commenced - more "dirty energy," this time originating from my bronchial tubes, air sacs and tonsils. My body felt like it was on fire. As I imagined flames engulfing me, and tried to quash stray thoughts of spontaneous combustion, my jaw gaped slightly and the gurgling and rumbling noises increased.

Master Songwha said, "Relax. Your body is in the process of purifying its organs. There is no cause for alarm." After allowing me ten minutes to rest, Master Songwha resumed the circulation. The energy had substantially cooled off before she directed it further upwards. As the flow wound over my head, passing the area between my skull and neck, each vertebra in my neck was restored.

"That area of the brain is what controls our physical movement," Master Songwha said. "When the meridian channel there is destroyed, paralysis results." My mind drifted to the potential healing possibilities. If only we could learn to work with this incredible energy that we all possess and that originates from the moment of our creation.

I experienced the feeling of soft snowflakes caressing my brain, slowly melting, as the cool energy flowed up and down within my head. This was accompanied by a gentle floating sensation; my body seemed to waft upwards through the air like a feather. Was this ascension, I wondered? It was as if my ego was gone; I had become one with the cosmos.

Just when I thought the pain had stopped, I was abruptly whipped back to my body, where more discomfort ensued. My eyes endured intense pressure, like they were being dug out of their sockets; squeezing and shifting, as if they were becoming centered and realigned from within. My nose suddenly felt like it was cracking; yellow and red mucous streamed from my nostrils, oozing over my mouth like a garish waterfall of negative energy.

My entire head underwent a substantial transformation, beginning with my temples. They seemed to open and I experienced the sensation of a cool wind blowing through them. My ears became connected via this intense energy. In actuality, my face and head were reshaping - becoming rounder. At one point, I was able to move my brain. It was a euphoric feeling to physically exercise this most incredible, yet elusive organ.

Throughout this energy meditation I experienced unprecedented sensations; my entire skeletal body altered and realigned itself beneath my skin.

Finally, the energy returned to the point where it had begun its unbelievable journey. Once again I was encapsulated by the ultimate feelings of peace and tranquility. It had taken a full hour for me to circulate my energy via the vertical channel.

Master Songwha informed me that the feelings I was experiencing were only temporary - maybe they would last three to five months. But, if I maintained the training, they would remain with me forever.

Afterwards, when I gazed upon my reflection in the mirror, my face did look rounder. What was happening to me? Was I shape-shifting into another species of human being - one that possessed the infamous knowledge that all mankind sought?

As I began to digest the magnitude of what had transpired, I realized that this exercise far exceeded anything I could have imagined. And yet, I instinctively knew there was still more. How many more doors of perception were there left to open?

* * * *

Note: I should note that my fasting ended today. At noon I was allowed a half of cup of pine tree pollen mixed with water. It still tasted bland and on Songwha's instruction, I allowed each teaspoon to mix with my saliva for about 2 minutes before swallowing. Songwha informed me that this mixture is all I would be ingesting for the rest of my stay here. Now I know why there are no pictures of food in their brochures.

The pervasive pains that haunted me since I arrived at the center had mysteriously and pleasantly disappeared after this particular exercise.

Kari's Journal: Day Seventeen

Although the pervasive hunger pains that haunted me since I arrived at the center had mysteriously and pleasantly disappeared, my fast ended yesterday. At around noon, I was permitted a half cup of pine tree pollen mixed with water. Using a teaspoon, I allowed nearly two minutes for the yellow paste to combine with my saliva before swallowing.

Eating seemed cumbersome at first. It was like my system had regressed back to that of an infant. I had to relearn the pleasure and technique of food consumption.

Today I was able to have two meals: one at noon and the other at six p.m. Master Songwha informed me that this was to be my schedule for the remainder of my stay.

Under Master Songwha's direction, I repeated the vertical circulation twice. The energy flowed with less difficulty and the process seemed more natural: not as much pain but plenty of pleasure. As the energy surged and streamed, I imagined the invisible channel as a ribbon of bright light curving over and around my entire body, glowing like neon glass tubing.

Afterwards I pondered the ramifications: Whither this hidden power of the human body? Why was it so rarely talked about? With uncompromising clarity, I realized that human beings are capable of not only healing themselves, but tapping into an energy source that has unlimited potential.

Kari's Journal: Day Eighteen

Today Master Songwha suggested that I perform the vertical circulation exercise without any guidance from her. Although she was present to observe, she would only intervene if absolutely necessary. To my amazement, I was able to move the energy with relative ease. Now, each circulation was only taking approximately five minutes. As the energy flowed I became more in tune with my body and began feeling truly comfortable within the shell of my flesh for the first time. I blessed each organ and as I came to know my body more intimately, I felt utterly grateful for its existence. Indeed, without it I could not elevate the level of my soul.

But after repeating the circulation several times, the feelings of pure bliss became overshadowed by more languid thoughts. What was the purpose of this? It suddenly dawned on me that this wasn't completion. So what if I could perform circulation exercises on command. Was that all there was? Perhaps I had become a trained monkey, able to dazzle onlookers beneath a circus tent. For unfathomable reasons, the void inside me grew more vast.

I reflected on my time here at the Center and knew I had accomplished a great deal. I had called forth the spirits of both my parents and Brad, and reconciled all my conflicts with them. I even restored the love for my physical body. Yet, who was doing this training?

Abruptly I stopped the circulations and remained seated in a lotus position. Except now, I resembled The Thinker, with my chin perched on my hand, forever pondering purpose and existence.

A flurry of questions barraged my mind with the impact of a hurricane. Where did I come from? Where am I going? Although I realized the potential of human consciousness, what did it all mean? An insight ignited a modicum of understanding inside my brain: love of my parents, Brad, even the pure and profound love I felt for all of humanity, is not completion. But then, what was?

While I ruminated further, I came to the conclusion that no feeling is permanent. Then I queried, what is permanent? As the day went on, even Master Songwha kept her distance from me. For some reason I had veered off the path towards enlightenment, or had I? I no longer knew. With each hour that elapsed, I forgot about all human relationships, my past, my job - I even lost track of where I was. Everything that used to consume and concern me had ceased to exist. My focus had been narrowed down to one solitary question: Who am I? I became obsessed by it. Who am I? followed me around like an annoying fly, buzzing in my ears as I meditated outside for hours. I waited for an insight to sweep the nagging insect away and answer my persistent question. But no enlightenment came. So I continue to ask:

Who am I? Who am I? Who am I?

Who am I? Who am I?

Who am I?

Kari's Journal: Day Nineteen and Day Twenty

Yesterday I was so despondent, I couldn't even muster up the necessary energy to write in my journal. Instead, I spent my time aimlessly wandering around, selecting new and unique locations to meditate. For the first time, without the direction of Master Songwha, I was able to achieve very profound and natural states of relaxation from deep within my own soul.

I took long, solitary walks. But no matter where I went or what I did, no lucid answers were forthcoming. I felt as if I were going around in circles, spinning haphazardly and uncontrollably, as unbalanced as a wayward top. When would I crash to the floor?

Master Songwha watched over me, and although occasionally she would nod or wave in understanding, she never provided an explanation for my chronic dilemma. Why couldn't I get past this mental maze? I felt she must have read my mind, which had been screaming: "I need to get out of here," because she suggested that we take a trip to the hot springs.

My mind required an experience potent enough to jolt me off the repetitive and monotonous train of thoughts I was endlessly riding - a train that was about to career off its tracks.

Maybe getting away will trigger some insight. I hope so, because tomorrow is my last day.

Kari's Journal: Day Twenty-One

This morning we drove about thirty miles south to the world renowned hot springs called Chojeung. Open to the public, people flock to this locale for its mineral rich waters that are said to possess healing and transforming powers.

Many thoughts had surfaced over the past couple of days. I came to recognize that every experience I'd ever endured throughout my entire life, remained locked inside me in the form of energy. Every praise, every scolding, whether consciously forgotten or not, was still there, ingrained upon my soul like a permanent tattoo.

While fasting had eliminated many negative thoughts, some bad memories still lingered. I came to learn that they interrupted my meditations, preventing me from realizing who I truly was. But being aware of this was not enough to cleanse them out. I needed total concentration and deeper meditation on questions such as: "Who is the controller, the real Lord of my body?" I feel that my body is me, but Master Songwha says I must eliminate this way of thinking. But how? Perhaps coming to the hot springs would provide the answers.

At first I thought I would be able to indulge myself by relaxing and soaking in the warm soothing water. Naturally Master Songwha had something different in mind - an exercise that initially proved less relaxing, but ultimately was far more rewarding.

After removing my clothes and taking a brief shower, Master Songwha pointed to two large tubs of water: one hot, one cold.

I didn't have much time to admire the beautiful inlay designs of the surrounding tile work, before she motioned for me to hop into the chilled basin. I stepped in and eased my body into a sitting position. Instantly the cold jump-started my brain; simultaneously my body shivered and trembled. Using a stopwatch, Master Songwha timed ninety seconds before directing me to climb out and enter the hot bath. As I submerged into the scalding water, it suddenly felt like my body was slightly removed from me. The steamy feeling of heat quickly abated while I floated in the water.

I ended up switching back and forth between the tubs

ten times. The bubbly mineral water invigorated my skin until I couldn't think of anything but the sensations. I had stopped being able to distinguish between hot or cold; I became numb from head to toe. My body didn't feel like my own anymore; it was a paralyzing experience.

I used to think that I was my body, but I'm quickly realizing that this body is not the true essence of me. I could no longer feel the heat while submerged within the hot basin. There was something inside me that was not affected by external circumstances, such as temperature. Something within myself, that's linked to my consciousness, that can freely separate from all outside conditions. The experience became a revelation.

Spontaneously, my skin began to squeeze and expand, engaging in a type of skin breathing designed to release dirty energy. It was amazing!

After dressing, Master Songwha handed me two liters of bubbly spring water and told me to drink. The carbonated liquid was refreshing. I later learned that it would move my internal organs and purify my intestines.

On the way home I reflected back on the exercise. Clearly it was designed to prove that my body was not me. It was only by being temporarily separated from it that I once again came to the overwhelming, seemingly obvious conclusion: My physical body is not who I really am. Yet, this didn't seem to answer the infamous question that continued to plague me, even as we pulled up to the center. Who am I?

At around six this evening I took a stroll outdoors to watch the sun set. Upon reentering the building, I heard a chorus of melodious sounds emanating from the main lounge. Loving feelings swept through my consciousness. Hope emerged where doubt had previously existed. Somehow I sensed I had gained insight to my dilemma, yet it was still unclear. But, for the first time I knew there was an answer. I was naturally drawn towards the chanters, as if I were a child being beckoned by the Pied Piper's flute. Resolutely I gravitated in the direction of the room and peered inside. A dozen young people were sitting in a circle, their faces radiated pure energy as they intoned certain sounds.

Transfixed, I remained standing in the doorway. The energy was palpable, almost tangible; the vibrations being chanted resounded and echoed throughout. I felt hypnotized by the enticing rhythm. Soon my entire body was affected; every cell was awakening. As the harmony grew in intensity, I was mysteriously drawn, until I too joined the circle.

By now, the group had stood up and was moving their bodies to the beat of their own voices. I found myself thrust into the dance. Round and round I went - arms swaying, rapturously twirling within the spiral of energy. Recklessly out of control, my limbs moved on their own. A drum appeared as if from nowhere; loud, piercing thumps matched the beating of my heart.

I had lost all track of time when I happened to catch a glimpse of Master Songwha watching me from the doorway. A moment later she disappeared and I raced out after her.

I demanded to know what the chanting was all about

and she calmly explained that the sounds originated from an ancient "Manuscript."

"What Manuscript?" I asked.

Master Songwha escorted me outside where we sat together on a wooden bench. The inky sky above us was pocked with numerous glittering stars.

"From your understanding, it's not really a Manuscript, but a grouping of Sacred Symbols. Eighty-one to be exact. They hold the key to understanding the mysteries of the universe."

"Really?" I said, intrigued.

That's when Master Songwha proceeded to relate a story about an old Korean Sage and how he came to enlightenment through these eighty-one symbols. As best I can recall, this is what she said:

"9,000 years ago mankind lived like animals. But one man, Chun Ki Doin, felt he didn't want to live that way anymore, so he started to mull over the mysteries of life and asked himself, who am I? He instinctively realized that human beings possessed the strongest energy in the world. Alas, he began to wonder why he was living on Earth. So entrenched in his thoughts, Chun Ki Doin stopped eating and sleeping. His meditations grew longer and deeper. Soon he focused all his energy on trying to come up with the answer. After seven days, he had eliminated all of his dirty energy. The low-level spirits that had surrounded and clung to him were banished and replaced with pure guardian spirits from heaven, completely connected with God. These spirits helped to awaken him and revive his understanding of truth.

Upon awakening, he was so inspired that he wrote down the keys to understanding and harmony as eighty-one symbols in the form of doe print on a mountain cave wall. But no one found it.

An oral tradition evolved from the doe print wherein people handed down the principles incorporated within those sacred symbols. 4,000 years elapsed before someone interpreted and translated the doe print symbols into Chinese characters. They etched it into the side of Bak Too Mountain, bordering China and North Korea, where they remain to this day.

Over the years, the essence of the symbols' original meaning became sullied by misunderstandings. As the Korean people stopped living by the principles of the symbols, their lives became more corrupted. Today, most contemporary Koreans see the manuscript as simply a legend."

When Master Songwha had finished her story, I bombarded her with questions about the ancient symbols.

"Once you grasp the complete essence of the Manuscript, you will be fulfilled," she said.

"How do I do that?"

"You need to seek out the Grand Master. He knows you are coming."

My frustrations mounted. I demanded to know why Master Songwha couldn't explain the meaning of the Manuscript to me. She glanced down at the floor, then focused back on my face. Surprisingly, she admitted that her own understanding of it was limited.

"What are you talking about?" I exclaimed. "How can

you not understand it?"

"So far I am only able to grasp it consciously, on an intellectual level. But you have the potential to fully comprehend its meaning."

"Where exactly is this Grand Master I'm supposed to meet?"

"Go to Sedona. You will find him when you're ready."

"Sedona! That's where I started." My mind reeled.

Before Master Songwha said goodnight, she read me a poem of self-realization:

Everyone has it
Close your eyes and you will see
Truth is what you aspire to be
Open your eyes and you will know
Allow all emotions and thoughts to flow
Everyone has it
It's time to awaken from your deep sleep
You have infinite potential flowing deep
Don't hesitate when you start to weep
You have an appointment with your soul to keep
After travelling long and far
You will soon realize who you are
What a wonderful thing!
What a wonderful thing!

After Master Songwha recited the poem, my physical body felt as if it had disappeared; only my breathing remained. While I continued to inhale and exhale, something strange occurred. Suddenly, I couldn't recognize the existence of my own ego. Lost in the rhythm of breath, I, myself, was missing. Confusion and fright took over. Where had I gone? But as I realized that breathing was all that existed, all that linked our spirits to our bodies, joyful wonder emerged.

Something within me resonated deeply and I began to weep. But, as the tears streamed down my face, I thought about what Socrates had once said: "Know yourself." Despite my misgivings and all the drawbacks associated with my spiritual journey, I realized that this was my way.

Master Songwha told me that my intense emotional reaction was a direct result of the spontaneous opening of my twelve meridian points. Once again, I was hovering within a state of pure being; blissful peace. She reiterated that only when I fully understood the meaning of the Manuscript would I feel complete.

Master Songwha commended me for my accomplishments and insights over the previous twenty-one days. She said my face had become brighter. I'm starting to realize how much I will miss her guidance and support. I have grown attached to her, and while I know I still have a long way to go, I don't know if I'll ever find a mentor that I'll feel as comfortable with. I told her how eternally grateful I was for everything she had done for me.

"May I hug you?" I asked awkwardly, knowing it wasn't part of her tradition.

"Yes," she nodded.

As we embraced I was enveloped within a nurturing cocoon of love, where I longed to remain. These past twenty-one days had truly been a metamorphosis. Just as the caterpillar is miraculously changed into a glorious butterfly, I too had been transformed. When Master Songwha pulled away, I knew I was being released back into the wildness of society, free to fly about and find my own way to truth.

Chapter 6

Kari peered through her window overlooking Korea's beautiful landscape, before the plane headed out over the vast ocean. It was hard to believe that she was leaving. Her experiences up in that tiny mountain village had truly become a part of her. Kari grew wistful as the last patch of Korea disappeared: The Land Of The Morning Calm.

During her flight back to Los Angeles, Kari spent the majority of her time meditating, achieving deeply relaxed states of consciousness. Reflecting back on the past three weeks, Kari swelled with enthusiasm. She knew she would never be the same again, nor would she want to. Nothing in her past rivaled what she had just accomplished. Not only did she survive the vigorous physical training, but she surprised even herself by reaching levels of awareness that most people only fantasize about. Having realized that life in the physical dimension was ultimately restricting, Kari couldn't wait to continue to press the limits of her spiritual potential.

A major difference in Kari's attitude was that she had finally shed the burdensome cloak of insecurity which she had worn wherever she went. Now Kari felt more confident and completely safe. She believed that what Master Songwha had told her was true: "The 'holy thing' is within you. It will protect you and steer the path of your future."

As Kari continued to review recent events in her life, she couldn't deny that the tentacles of destiny had chosen her. They had clasped onto her energy limbs and guided her, via myriad synchronistic circumstances, to her present situation. But what did fate have in store for Kari now? A rendezvous with the Grand Master that Master Songwha spoke so reverently about? Who was this man? What if she didn't get along with him? It was painful for Kari to imagine any teacher other than Master Songwha. Yet, hadn't she once felt the same way about Master Kim?

Futilely she attempted to picture what this Grand Master looked like, conjuring up countless images in her head. But none felt authentic. Kari knew she would have to wait until she met him in person.

Moments before the plane began its descent, Kari had made her decision: She would only stay in Los Angeles a few days before heading to Sedona. She was eager to know what, if anything, this mysterious Grand Master could teach her.

In the taxi, Kari felt her energy dissipating. She hadn't slept much on the plane, but then again, her body had adjusted itself to requiring less sleep. No, what she was reacting to was a lifestyle that she had completely removed herself from. The noisy, congested traffic of Los Angeles was oppressive. Between the impatient driver and the polluted skies overhead, Kari struggled to remain unruffled. She realized that she needed total concentration and an abundance of energy to counteract the harsh and negative effects of this onerous environment.

Kari instructed the driver to search for a modest motel in her former neighborhood. Before she had left for Korea, except for some clothes at Diane's place, Kari had stored all her belongings. Now all she had was a suitcase, which she had no interest in opening. For some reason, her luggage had become alien to her. Kari had grown accustomed to needing very little, especially when it came to material things. If it had been appropriate, Kari would have been quite content to wear her white cotton two-piece to the airport. It wasn't, and as the taxi came to an abrupt halt in front of the hotel, Kari's skin itched beneath the fabric of her designer blouse.

It was early evening when Kari checked into her room. The first call she made was to Diane, who was excited and immediately wanted to get together. Kari agreed to meet her friend for dinner the following evening. Tonight she longed for a good night's sleep as her mind and body continued adjusting and acclimating to the energy of Los Angeles.

* * * *

He came to her in a dream. Kari was exhilarated,

flying high in the sky, floating above red rock mountain-tops. Off in the distance, she spotted a diminutive figure atop a level plateau. As Kari drifted closer, she recognized an older Native American man calmly sitting in the lotus position. Intuitively Kari felt she knew him. Though his eyes were closed, he gestured calmly with his right hand for Kari to join him. She remained hovering above the ridge, until her body, almost against her will, began to waft downwards. Moments later, Kari found herself standing on the ledge. The man spoke her name softly, in a voice Kari vaguely remembered hearing before. Then the man stood up; his face transformed itself right in front of her. Kari was looking into the eyes of Kang Hoon, whose smile melted through the layers of Kari's consciousness, causing her to awaken and wonder what it all meant.

* * * *

Linda wasn't the least bit surprised when Kari tendered her resignation. In fact, during Kari's absence, Brenda had been promoted and was already assuming most of Kari's former responsibilities.

"If you change your mind," Linda offered, "there's always a place here for you. But trust me, the longer you stay away the harder it will be to come back."

"Well, I'm not thinking about coming back right now," Kari said.

"You look different," Linda stated while assessing Kari up and down with her eyes. "Did you lose weight or something?"

"Oh, about fifteen pounds I didn't need."

"It's not just that. Your face... it's... got a different shape to it."

"Rounder?" Kari prompted.

Linda nodded. "Well, anyway, you seem really happy. Otherwise I'd try and talk you out of this."

"You've got to try this training sometime Linda," Kari began.

"No, what I have to do is snare a few new clients. In fact I've got a meeting in five minutes with the Motorola people. Wish me luck."

Kari smiled. She felt she was gazing through a window into her own past. Once upon a time, she too had been so consumed with work that she couldn't stop to consider anyone or anything else. But the fairy tale had ended. Sleeping beauty had been awakened.

"Good luck," Kari said with little emotion.

"You too," Linda said quickly. "Keep in touch. Oh, by the way, if you ever find the real meaning of life, be sure to give me a call."

Kari smiled to herself. If Linda only knew.

Before leaving, Kari stopped by to see Brenda, who was entrenched in her old office. But as Kari peeked in the doorway, which ironically still bore her name, she saw that Brenda was preoccupied: screaming obscenities at a copywriter. Kari backed away, roving past clusters of cubicles, quickly heading towards the elevators.

Kari was looking forward to her next stop. Ever since she confronted her father's spirit at the center, Kari had wanted to communicate her newfound feelings to him in person.

Odd emotions swept over Kari as she approached the entrance to the house she grew up in. So many things had changed since she skipped through the sprinklers on summer days and put on shows with the neighbor's children in the backyard, using four wooden patio benches wedged together as a makeshift stage. It was strange walking up the same slate path she used to roller skate across.

What seemed truly foreign to her was the fact that she no longer possessed the key to the front door. Instead, she rang the bell, like any apparent stranger would.

A surprised Dina swung open the door. Upon recognizing Kari, Dina's expression soured.

"What do you want?" she said coldly.

"Is my father here?" Kari managed to ask beneath Dina's icy and scrutinizing stare.

"He's busy right now," Dina began, but the pretense soon got the best of her. Kari focused on sending loving thoughts towards her, maintaining a friendly smile, until Dina finally caved.

"Do you want to come in?" she asked, but wasn't exactly sure why.

"Yes, thank you," Kari replied. "Actually, I wanted to speak with you, too."

Dina became anxious, stopping in her tracks before swinging back around to face her. "What did we do now?"

"Nothing. Nothing. It's about what I did," Kari waited until she knew she had Dina's full attention before continuing. "I know this might not mean anything to you now but I want to sincerely apologize for the way I've acted towards you in the past."

Confusion overshadowed belligerence and finally Dina conceded, "You had your reasons."

"No. I had my judgements. And I never should have imposed them on you. I'm truly sorry."

Kari sensed Dina's seething hatred dissipate beneath her genuine gaze.

"It's okay," Dina said, uncomfortably staring at her feet, then the wall, finally, back up at Kari. Hostility seemed easier to handle than understanding. Why was that? Why did people feel more comfortable displaying abhorrent behavior, than exuding love? Kari wondered.

"Please forgive me," Kari said.

Dina nodded, closed the front door and motioned for Kari to follow her down the hall, into the living room.

Kari's eyes widened. The decor had been completely transformed from the warm, rustic tones her mother had chosen, to a stark white, blue and green. Perhaps her father felt compelled to exorcise her mother's presence by instituting this massive change. Gone was the pine wood furniture and the wicker accents. Gone were the antique shadow boxes containing quaint miniatures and sea shells collected from past family vacations. They had been replaced by a domineering, white lacquered wall unit, white leather couches and white carpet diagonally striped with blue and green. Overall, the room left Kari cold. But despite her nostalgic feelings towards what once was, Kari realized that the style and color scheme of a room was in fact meaningless window dressing to an already over-played illusion.

"Are you in some kind of trouble?" Dina asked. "Is it money?" she continued, falling back into the dark sea of suspicion. Kari acknowledged to herself that it had taken less than three minutes for Dina to revert back to skepticism and doubt regarding her. Obviously Dina was more at ease with negative feelings and less able to accept expressions of kindness.

"No," Kari said. "Really, I would just like to speak with my father."

"He's in the den. But please, don't upset him."

Tears came to Kari's eyes as she studied Dina's face. "Haven't you been listening to me? I just want to tell him that I love him. That how I acted towards him in the past was wrong. Terribly wrong. I know I hurt him and I'm here to seek his forgiveness."

"I forgive you," a voice resounded from the other side of the room. Kari swiveled around and saw her father standing there. His countenance beamed with joy as he faced his daughter. Clearly he had heard every word she said. Yet, Kari felt it was more than that. She now knew that she had indeed contacted his spirit.

"Daddy," Kari began, as she ambled towards him.

"You look great," he said.

"So do you. I missed you."

Without another word, Kari nestled into his chest, allowing his arms to encircle her shoulders. She remained within his warmth; their spirits communicated without words on many unseen levels.

Kari ended up spending the entire day there. After canceling plans with Diane, she dined with Dina and her father. While consuming small portions of salad from her plate (Kari's body was still very sensitive to the intake of food) she told them all about her journey to Korea, detailing many of her unique and extraordinary experiences. In lieu of his customary indifference to her life, Charles was genuinely interested, asking many questions. After dinner he implored his daughter to keep in touch. Kari insisted she would and embraced her father one more time. Silently she thanked Master Songwha - this reconciliation had far exceeded Kari's expectations.

* * * *

Kari made reservations to fly to Sedona the next morning. She agreed to allow Diane to drive her to the airport. On the way she tried to explain her immediate need to return to the place Diane had originally forced her to visit.

"I don't believe this," Diane stated. "You're just running away from your life."

"What are you talking about? This is my life," Kari responded.

"What? This so-called journey? What about your job? What about Brad? When does it end?"

"That's what I'm trying to find out."

"I think you might be losing it kid. Going to Korea was crazy enough. But this is insane! What do you know about this Grand Master, anyway? What if he's some psycho waiting to brutally murder you?"

Kari tried to analyze Diane's constant fear. Why had she been so conditioned to opt for paranoia instead of love? But then, Kari solemnly acknowledged, wasn't everybody indoctrinated into that mode of discernment - perceiving differences where none existed? She tried to make light of the situation. "That sure would put a quick end to my journey, wouldn't it?"

"You think this is funny?"

"Why don't you join me, Diane? You're the one who tried to get me to be spiritual in the first place. So now who's the hypocrite? Listen, if you really want to find out the truth about who you are, you have to start taking all this seriously and go within. Spirituality is not a part-time thing."

"No, with you it's more like an obsession!" Dina shouted.

"Call it what you want. It's what I have to do right now."

Frustrated, Diane changed the subject. "You know a lot has happened since you left."

"Like what?"

"Brad has started to turn his life around. He confessed to everything. Don't worry, the worst he could get is probation. Apparently, with his testimony, his partner might be indicted."

"Really? When did this happen?"

Kari wasn't surprised to find out that Brad's radical transformation occurred on the very day she communicated with his spirit.

"He was looking forward to seeing you," Diane added.

"Please, tell him I'll see him the next time I'm in town."

"Whenever that will be," Diane swiped.

"Funny, I thought you'd be happy for me."

"I guess I am," Diane finally conceded. "It's just that I miss you. Three weeks was an eternity without having you around to bitch to and go shopping with. And now you're leaving for Sedona and you don't know when you'll be back. Who am I going to spend ungodly amounts of money with at Neiman-Marcus?"

"Ungodly is right. Anyway, three weeks is nothing in the scheme of things."

"Tell it to the empty seat next to me at the Saturday matinees. All three of them."

"One day you'll go down a similar path... and then our friendship will reach far beyond charge cards and Chinese chicken salad lunches on Sunset Blvd."

"You think so?"

"No, I hope so."

Diane dropped Kari off at LAX and wished her luck. While she knew she wasn't ready for such an experience, she wondered if Kari was. And if so, how? Despite lingering feelings of jealousy, Diane was curious to know what would happen to Kari next.

* * * *

Kari turned off highway 179, leisurely parking her rented car in front of the Bell Rock Inn. She felt invigorated; the energy in Sedona was a striking, welcome contrast to what she had left behind in Los Angeles.

After checking in, Kari relaxed for a few minutes in her room, casually gazing out the window at Bell Rock, looming in the distance. Suddenly she thought of the man that she kept running into: Gil. Since she didn't really know anyone else in town, she decided to phone him. Gil was thrilled to hear from her.

"Hey, I was just thinking about you."

"I bet you say that to everyone," Kari said.

"Actually I do, but sometimes I mean it. So why don't we get together? I was heading out to get a bite to eat. Care to join me?"

Kari admitted she had no plans and Gil insisted on picking her up at the hotel. When Kari emerged from the lobby entrance, Gil leaped from his jeep. But before opening the door for her, he couldn't help staring at this woman who looked distinctly different - much healthier, more radiant and in Gil's eyes, more attractive.

"All right, what's going on?" Gil asked.

"What are you talking about?"

"You're either in love or you've decided to move to Sedona permanently. Is that it?"

"Why do you say that?"

"You're practically glowing. Or is this all in my imagination?"

"Not exactly," Kari grinned mysteriously.

"Come on..." Gil said as he gestured for Kari to enter the passenger side of his jeep. "You can tell me when we get there. I'm starved."

Kari began unraveling the tale of her recent adventures on the way to The Sage, a vegetarian restaurant in West Sedona. Gil remained silent, completely absorbed in her words. The story continued to unfold while they were seated; even the maitre'd craned his neck to catch an earful, as Kari described in detail everything significant that had transpired in Korea, including the little she had learned about the Manuscript. Something seemed to ignite in Gil's eyes, a hint of recognition, but he kept his realization to himself, at least for the moment.

"It all sounds so unbelievable, almost surreal," he said when Kari stopped speaking to take a sip from her water glass.

"I know. If it didn't actually happen to me I wouldn't believe it myself."

"So what brings you back to Sedona?"

"Well," Kari hesitated, trying to feel Gil out with her eyes.

"What... don't tell me it gets more far out than this."

"Well, okay. Here goes... I returned to Sedona because I'm destined to link up with the Grand Master."

"That sounds exciting. So what's wrong?"

"I have no idea what his name is, what he looks like or where he lives. The only thing I have to go on is that he's Native American."

"That could pose a bit of a problem. And you're sure you're supposed to meet him here?"

"Positive. I was told he was expecting me."

Gil thought quietly for a moment. "You know who might know?" Gil suddenly blurted. "Kit Polcyn."

"Who's that?"

"You've got to meet this guy. I'm renting a room from him right now. If anyone would know where this Grand Master hangs out, he would."

"Great," Kari exclaimed.

"This guy has done wonders to keep me inspired. Did I ever tell you about that cave I discovered?"

"I vaguely recall you mentioning it once."

"Well, when you talked about that Manuscript, I thought of the symbols I saw in the cave. Didn't you say there were eighty-one of them?"

"Yes, I did."

"Well, do you think it's a coincidence that this cave also has eighty-one symbols?"

"I learned there's no such thing as coincidence."

"Why don't you come with me to the cave? How about tomorrow?" Gil urged.

"Okay. Other than trying to find this Grand Master, I'm free."

"Great. So what do you say we head out to Kit's ranch after we finish eating and see if he has any ideas on where this guy is?"

Kari nodded. "Thanks, I appreciate all your help."

The pair drove about ten minutes, most of which was along a bumpy red dirt road, to reach the ranch. When they arrived, they found Kit sitting beneath a copper pyramid situated beside the house. Kari followed Gil as he sauntered towards the peaceful-looking man, who appeared to be in his early forties.

"Kit, I'd like you to meet a friend of mine," Gil began.

Kit rose and stepped out from underneath the copper enclosure, turning to face Kari. His eyes lingered over her entire body, as if he were appraising her.

"This woman is vibrating at a much higher level than you, Gil."

"What are you talking about?" Gil asked.

Kit smiled warmly and extended his hand to greet Kari. She clasped it, while he continued to stare.

"Is everything okay?" Kari finally asked.

"Oh yes. It's a pleasure to meet someone who's approaching a level of enlightenment that few of us will ever achieve."

"You can tell that just by looking at me?"

"Of course, I can feel your energy. It's a sheer delight to be around you. I've been in Sedona for many years. Everyone claims to be closer to God here, but trust me, few of them truly are. But you - this is the real thing, Gil. You could learn a lot from this woman."

Gil grinned sheepishly. "Well, let's hope she starts teaching me."

Kari spent the remainder of the day with them. Kit was a wonderful host, serving iced tea and cranberry-orange muffins out on a wooden deck. Several animals scampered freely about the property. Kari spotted rabbits, dogs, cats, even a goat.

While admiring the splendid mountain view, Kari remembered to ask Kit about the Grand Master. He set down his glass and nodded knowingly. Kari leaned in closer as he prepared to speak.

"The last time I saw him he was out in Fay Canyon."

"Have you ever spoken with him?" Kari asked.

"No. Legend has it he takes on a new student only about every ten years."

"Really?"

"Consider yourself lucky if he agrees to teach you. He might be able to take you all the way. But it won't be easy. It's an arduous path."

"Tell me about it. It hasn't been easy up to this point."

Kari proceeded to tell Kit about the genesis of her spiritual journey. When she was done, Kit studied Kari's face. He seemed to send messages of support with his eyes. She met his gaze and smiled. Later, as they were leaving, Kit offered Kari an open invitation to stop by whenever she wanted.

When Gil drove Kari back to the hotel, he confirmed what time he'd be back in the morning. But Kari had other plans in mind. In no uncertain terms she told him that she didn't want to postpone her fate any longer. Tomorrow she was going to try and find the Grand Master.

* * * *

The next morning, after a light breakfast, Kari asked someone in the lobby for directions to Fay Canyon. She felt relaxed and confident as she headed out. Thoughts of what Kit had told her resonated within her head. Was she destined to achieve total enlightenment? Then she wondered: Why wasn't this the goal of all people? Was it simply the fact that society itself was designed to keep people living in fear? Is fear of enlightenment tantamount to a fear of the unknown? But why? Perhaps the powers that be, i.e. the Church and government, insist on keeping things just the way they are, conjuring up falsehoods and misconceptions, so they can maintain their misguided sense of power and dominion over people who, in truth, are their equals in divinity.

After parking next to a pink tour jeep, Kari proceeded to hike down a dirt path in the direction of Fay Canyon. She wasn't sure exactly where she was going but she was determined to make contact with the Grand Master.

An hour passed. Kari perspired from the sweltering heat. As the sun beat down, she found relief under a ponderosa pine and dabbed at her moist flesh with the dangling arm of a sweatshirt knotted around her waist. Kari sipped from a bottle of water and closed her eyes, trying to relax while tuning in to the sounds of nature surrounding her.

The comfortable stillness in the air was broken by the sound of wings flapping. Moments later, Kari felt movement on her right shoulder, as if something had landed there. She opened her eyes and was startled to find herself face-to-face with a Stellar's Blue Jay. It was a beautiful periwinkle blue and silver with an impressive dark crest. Its forehead was striped black and white which somehow reminded Kari of a Native American. The bird craned its beak towards Kari, staring endlessly into her curious eyes. Kari tried not to move, afraid she might scare the bird off , but the feathered creature exhibited no fear. Finally, it lifted off her shoulder and floated in the air directly above her. Soaring in a circle, the bird emitted a low pitched, raucous call, before turning in the direction of the spires behind them.

Kari felt compelled to stand up and follow the bird's path. She trudged up a steep incline, strewn with rocks and blooming prickly pear cactus. The majestic bird remained in her sight until it dipped under an expansive archway. Sweating and slightly out-of-breath, Kari continued to climb. As she glanced upwards, she caught a glimpse of its wings gleaming sapphire in the sunlight, as they gracefully fluttered and disappeared off to one side within the spacious opening.

Kari reached the top and marveled at nature's sculpted archway. She edged closer and discovered that the arch was like a false cave front; there were a few feet of space between it and the back wall. This created a naturally-formed skylight of sorts. Shafts of noon sun poured in between the stone, illuminating the entire area, but the jewel-colored bird had vanished.

All of a sudden a wave of uneasiness roiled through Kari's mind. She felt as if someone was watching her. Kari advanced a few more steps until she was beneath the archway. She gazed up at a cluster formation of rocks to her left and spotted an older Native American man sitting in the lotus position on top of an elevated spire, as if perched on a throne. Kari froze. She knew in an instant: This was the Grand Master.

Suddenly, Kari felt as if she had been transported through time and space into an ancient Temple. Feelings of peace, love and gratitude enveloped her within that sacred space, framed by massive, smooth red rock.

Kari managed to observe him despite her overwhelming intimidation. He wore a white tee shirt over khaki shorts and tan sandals. A multi-colored bandana encircled his neck like a rainbow. Kari noted the roundness of his face and serene expression as he stared directly at her with his intense brown eyes.

Slowly and with a hint of apprehension to her movement, Kari inched closer to the base of his regal stone seat. While he remained silent, his eyes continued their unwavering scrutiny.

Kari wasn't sure whether to say something or linger within the quiet stillness. Without warning, he deftly uncrossed his legs, stepped down upon what appeared to resemble a stone stairway wedged within the rock between his grand chair and the canyon wall, and leaped as gracefully as a panther, landing two feet before a stunned Kari.

"I've been awaiting your arrival."

Kari opened her mouth to speak, but nothing came out. Somehow she seemed to have lost her voice. He smiled and gently extended his hand. As if caught up in a slow-motion day dream, Kari lifted her hand to meet his. Upon contact, Kari noted the warmth that emanated from his palm - not your typical weather-related heat, but a powerful surge of energy.

"I am Owl From Heaven."

Kari nodded, still fumbling with her speech.

"Please, sit down," he said, pointing to the ground.

Kari quickly knelt and took a seat. Owl From Heaven sat directly across from her.

"Place your hands in a praying position in front of you. Now close your eyes and imagine the energy between your palms as you slowly move them apart."

Although Kari complied with his wishes, she didn't understand why he was having her do something so basic.

"Do you feel the energy?" he asked.

Kari's eyes opened and thanks to her ego-driven determination, she found her voice. "Of course I feel it," she scoffed. "How could I not feel it? I've only done this particular exercise hundreds of times! Maybe you weren't fully informed, but I'm a little more advanced than this."

The Grand Master grew solemn.

"You are not ready," he said gravely.

"What are you talking about?" Kari shouted. "Do you know how hard I worked to get to this point? I've done things I never thought I could do. I know I'm ready for more."

"You still think this is all about you and what you can do. I am not here to indulge your personal accomplishments. Perhaps what you're ready for is more of what you can do, not what I can teach."

Abruptly Owl From Heaven stood up and walked outside the arch. Kari turned and followed him with her eyes as he strolled along a narrow path which hugged the canyon wall and disappeared beyond some bushes.

"Hey, where are you going? I think there's been some kind of misunderstanding."

Kari stood up and looked around. There was no sign of him. Instead, perched atop a tree was another Stellar's Jay, its beautiful plumage shining brightly beneath the noon sun. Kari approached it curiously. Was it the same one she had seen earlier? As she gazed into its eyes, it turned away and burst into flight. Kari stared after it until she could no longer see. Her vision became blurred by her own angst-ridden tears.

Frustrated, Kari turned and marched back down the hill. During her descent, she wondered why Master Songwha had ever sent her on this pointless trip. She decided to continue her spiritual journey herself, concluding that under no circumstances did she need the help of an ill-mannered teacher to achieve enlightenment.

Kari grew restless on her way back to the hotel, so she stopped off at a pay phone and called Gil to see if he still wanted to go to the caves. He eagerly said yes and on their way there, she told him what had transpired with the Grand Master.

"Maybe you aren't ready," Gil said.

"Oh, I see. So you're on his side now?" Kari blurted.

"I didn't say that. I'm just speculating. I wouldn't take it personally."

"Well, if he doesn't want to teach me I sure as hell don't want to be around him."

"So then you can hang out with me," Gil offered with a smile.

After parking the car, they hiked on foot the rest of the way, about thirty minutes into the heart of the canyon. Finally, Gil pointed upwards; Kari found herself standing beneath a narrow cave-like opening in the stone. They climbed up towards an elevated ledge and sat before it, resting and taking sips from their bottled water.

"Let's go," Gil said, retrieving a flashlight from inside the zippered pocket of his backpack.

Kari and Gil crawled inside the cave entrance. It was dark and Gil immediately clicked on the flashlight, illuminating the small, but cozy cavern. Kari couldn't believe her eyes. Etched perfectly within the rock were a series of symbols. She counted them almost in disbelief - there were eighty-one: The exact number Master Songwha said the ancient Korean Manuscript contained.

"So this is what they look like," Kari stated. Almost instinctively, she tuned her mind to the distinct energy vibration of the cave. Gil watched in silence as she sat down to meditate. Moments after Kari closed her eyes, all she was conscious of was her breathing. The feelings that swept over her were similar to those she had experienced just after Master Songwha read her the poem on self-realization: consummate peace, love and joy.

Kari remained in that euphoric state for over an hour. Feeling awkward, Gil tried meditating himself, but he couldn't quiet his mind and ended up just observing Kari. Intuitively he knew she had slipped into a profound level of consciousness.

When Kari finally opened her eyes her face beamed. The recent frustration she had experienced with the Grand Master was now a distant memory.

"Thank you for bringing me here," she told Gil.

"My pleasure," he began. "Actually it seemed like it was more your pleasure. You're glowing again."

Kari emitted an enthusiastic smile. "This place... it conjures up feelings I had in Korea. Incredible feelings. I want to continue to explore these sensations. You know what, maybe it's a myth that you have to have a teacher. We all have unlimited capabilities inside us. Who better to bring them out than ourselves?"

During the hike back, recalling what Master Kim had

told her about Bell Rock being one of the best places in the world to meditate, Kari decided she would stay in Sedona a little while longer.

* * * *

The next morning, Kari climbed Bell Rock. This time she felt no fear, just the sheer will to reach the circular platform that sat atop a rocky spire and resembled an eagle's eye from above. Full of vigor and confidence, Kari was determined to prove that she could vertically circulate her Kundalini by herself.

Memories of her accomplishments in Korea gave birth to feelings of immodest power: Ignoring the telltale signs that her ego, fueled by arrogance, was running rampant, Kari erroneously believed she was in control of her body.

While she had no problem initially activating the energy to commence the exercise, everything went awry immediately afterwards. Kari's body couldn't sustain the circulation, and worse yet, against her will, it began to reverse itself, triggering extreme discomfort and pain. Her head felt as dense and heavy as the stone she was sitting upon. Kari's eyes turned red; her cheeks bulged out. Her ribs felt as if they were breaking; as they rattled within her chest, she thought that at any moment they would pierce her skin. When it became too painful for Kari to remain seated, she stood up. Her head was hot and her torso cold. Hands trembling, chest expanding, Kari discovered that she could no longer control her breathing. To compound her hardships, the atmosphere surrounding her grew dark. Feeling the distinct presence of low-level spirits encircling her, Kari became frightened. Were these the "greedy" spirits Master Songwha had warned her about?

Left with no other options, Kari stopped the training exercise. From what she had been taught at the center, she was able to gradually resume authority over her breathing. Heavily laden with her ego, Kari began her decent. It was a struggle the entire way; her balance was askew and she continued to have problems controlling her breath.

Back at her hotel, Kari pondered whether or not she had done something wrong. Had she taken for granted her new skills? Was she the "greedy" one? No, she firmly concluded. Today had simply been an anomaly. But, when she had the same exact trouble the following day, even Kari fell victim to self doubt, conceding that maybe she did need a teacher after all.

Surrendering to her persistent nature, Kari attempted yet another energy circulation on top of Bell Rock. This time the negative effects were more severe. Not only did her body succumb to a high fever, but it triggered intense hallucinations. Once again Kari felt low-level spirits hovering about. They taunted her with their voices, spewing their toxic egocentric beliefs over her aura like a can of black spray paint. "You don't need the help of a master," they insisted. "You are so strong. Don't you know that? You can become God without anyone's guidance but your own." Accompanying the chorus of repetitive and seductive voices, music swelled within Kari's head. Fantastic imagery unfolded before her mind's eye: endless fields of yellow flowers, all illuminated with a surreal, bright glow. What was this place, Kari wondered? Was it heaven? It resembled the limitless pastures of poppies that rendered Dorothy asleep with their soporific smell in The Wizard of Oz. No! This was not heaven! "I don't want to be asleep any longer!" Kari shouted. "I want to wake up!" Frantically she fought the illusion which had looked and sounded so inviting. Kari summoned her inner strength and believed with all her heart that the holy thing within her soul was still working to protect her. "This is not real," she said to her inner mirage. Kari clenched her fist and proceeded to beat the tempting illusion.

As the images began to fade, Kari's head was about to explode in frustration and despair. She grew dizzy and felt that Bell Rock itself was no longer stable, imagining it to be spiraling uncontrollably counter clockwise - the circulation direction of death and destruction. Kari thought she herself was spinning, turning upside down and sideways, feeling at any moment that she might be tossed off the rock.

She was teetering at the edge of a ghastly abyss when the Grand Master magically appeared. He placed his two fingertips on the large collar bone at the back of Kari's neck and pressed down. Kari felt an instant catharsis. He had repaired the flow of energy by reversing its direction within her channel. After a few moments, the Grand Master had restored her balance.

Sensing Kari's depleted state, he quickly placed his two fingers on her lower back and injected pure energy into her Dahn Jon. While experiencing an intense surge of energy, Kari noticed that her lower body had bulged in size; she felt bloated. Despite the temporary discomfort, the inoculation of energy settled Kari into a pleasant state of peace. She noticed a stream of colorful lights radiating around her body. This must be my aura, Kari thought. She shifted her gaze back up to the Grand Master and observed glowing, white light encapsulating his head like a halo. If the Grand Master could read Kari's thoughts, he would have known how grateful she was. But he was in no mood for congeniality.

"You are a greedy person, Kari," he began. "You're only interested in techniques - not truth. But without the truth you will achieve nothing. I don't think you will be able to receive truth with your attitude."

"How can you say that?" Kari protested.

"When I observe you, I don't see a longing for truth. Where is your desire, your yearning for truth? This path, the path of enlightenment, is the way of truth, not techniques; without truth, techniques are meaningless."

"So what are you trying to tell me?"

"You are not ready yet. You think you have accomplished so much. You are so proud of yourself, but you are nothing! Your training is nothing! Your life is nothing!"

Kari was too stunned to muster up any objection.

"You thought you had put a lot of effort into this path - much training and hardships - but you are still nothing. Your life is nothing!"

"Who are you to say my life is nothing? You hardly know anything about me! Are you crazy or do you enjoy insulting me?" Kari exploded in a fury.

"Life is nothing," he stated impassively.

"What is that supposed to mean?" Kari demanded.

"If you fail to comprehend this one sentence you will never understand the truth."

Kari stared directly into the Grand Master's eyes, barely able to contain the rage swelling inside her. But when she tried to articulate her anger, she found herself assaulted by a wave of energy that countermanded her immediate instincts. Oppressed by his force field of energy, Kari lost her voice and was rendered incapable of verbally expressing herself. Her thoughts churned in a seething manner, yet she had no defense for his overwhelming presence. His penetrating eyes intimidated her before his words presented another challenge. "Oh, you don't take my word? You don't agree with me?" he asked.

Unnerved, Kari felt as though she'd been discovered; her thoughts and emotions laid out before him like an open book. She decided to remain silent.

"You are still prisoner of your ego. You think you are so special, but remember, you are nothing. Life is nothing."

After declaring those seemingly harsh words, the Grand Master deliberately turned on his heels and strode away, beyond another jagged rock. Kari didn't have to check; she knew he was gone. But she didn't care anymore. What kind of teacher spends all his time insulting a potential student? Enraged, Kari considered stopping her spiritual odyssey altogether, but quickly concluded that that wasn't a sensible resolution. She had worked too hard to get to this point. The unceasing chatter in her head presented many suggestions. Kari knew she could be satisfied with just circulating her Kundalini. Yes, she thought, that would be enough. There was nothing to dissuade her from continuing the training and exercises herself. That's it, Kari concluded: She would be her own Master.

* * * *

That evening, Kari and Gil dined together at a local Mexican restaurant. The atmosphere was festive and spacious. A multitude of colorful, animal-shaped pinatas hung from the rafters; strikingly-glazed pottery was displayed for purchase across hand-painted wooden shelves. A young woman, cloaked in a red-and-white uniform, led the pair to a corner table and placed over-sized menus in front of them.

Kari detailed her latest experience with the Grand Master to Gil. "So what do you think I should do?" she asked.

"You could always move in with me," he quipped. "Seriously, I can't tell you what to do. This is something you're going to have to decide for yourself."

"I know... it's just that I'm so confused by it all."

"It'll come to you, you'll see."

Kari smiled and resumed studying her menu. It didn't surprise her that Gil spent most of the night flirting. What did startle her was how much she appreciated his playful banter. It had been a long time since she had enjoyed a man's company. Something strange was occurring between them - a comfortable, yet exciting chemistry was forming. Lustful thoughts began to crisscross Kari's mind. As they indulged themselves on guacamole, chips and vegetarian tacos, she noticed his strong hands and the way his tanned muscular arms moved as he reached for the salsa. Not wanting to monitor herself any longer, Kari allowed her eyes to drift upwards, past his shoulders, to his face. Her gaze lingered there a few moments, taking in his ruggedly handsome features - his perfectly-formed lips, his inviting eyes - until finally she switched her attention back to the spicy rice that covered her plate. What was going on? Kari wondered. A need had sprouted within her. A void that longed to be filled. Sex had become a distant memory for Kari, ever since she had left for Korea. But why now? Kari wished the voices in her head would stop pestering her. She yearned to be free of their judgements - free to act out on her innate, animal passions.

After dinner, Gil drove Kari back to the hotel. He shut the engine off, leaving them consumed by an awkward silence. Although it was obvious neither wanted the evening to end, both hedged on how best to continue it.

"Why don't you come back to the ranch," Gil suggested. "We could play some cards. Kit could join us."

"I don't think we need Kit," Kari said, leaning in closer to him.

"No, I guess not," Gil replied.

"Would you like to come up to the room?" she offered.

"Good idea. Maybe we could get some cards from the front desk."

"I'm not really in the mood for cards, are you?" she asked.

"No, not really."

Seizing the initiative, Kari passionately kissed Gil on the lips. His response was immediate. He embraced her, caressing her hair and cheeks before pulling away. For a moment their eyes locked, searching for answers. Finally, Gil said, "Let's go upstairs."

Once the door to the room closed behind them, Kari and Gil made their way to the bed in a heated frenzy: pulling, yanking and tossing various items of clothing to the carpeted floor; kicking off shoes and undoing zippers. Slender shafts of moonlight filtered through the angled blinds, illuminating their still partially-clothed flesh with a subtle glow.

Gil was bursting with anticipation. He had felt an attraction to Kari from the very first time they met, one that had grown with each subsequent interaction. Indeed, she was beautiful, but her allure went deeper than the way her hair flowed about her shoulders in undulating waves, framing her intense eyes and slender nose - which he couldn't resist lavishing with kisses.

When their bodies became entwined, Kari relished the intimacy. It had been so long since she felt warm flesh against hers. Kari basked in the primal intermingling of passion, sweat and skin. There was something raw and exciting about physical interaction with another human being - an intangible lure that was completely captivating. Kari suddenly experienced a sensation she had never before achieved in the bedroom: She felt as if she was in control, able to orchestrate the duration of their encounter. Energy shot up through her legs like meteors. It was akin to a surge of intense heat, that rushed within her and swelled around her second chakra - pulsating and vibrating to an uncompromising ecstasy.

So entranced by Kari's pleasure, Gil couldn't contain himself. Sensing his swelling passion, Kari began infusing his body with her own energy. This exchange took immediate effect, and to Gil's astonishment, he no longer had to focus on staying off his own orgasm. Instead, while experiencing powerful sensations within each one of his own cells, Gil tuned in to Kari's feelings and began kissing every part of her body. The more excited Kari became, the more energy she emitted; the energy, like a dip in a mineral bath, invigorated Gil.

This incredible cycle of pleasure continued for several hours; they were raised to unbelievable and heightened levels of enjoyment with each moment that elapsed. When Kari sensed Gil's physical exhaustion, she encouraged him to surrender to the rapture. Sweating and panting, his release was touched off by a loud sigh of exultation. After collapsing on the bed next to her, Gil found himself too enraptured to speak. Savoring the pleasure, he closed his eyes and drifted off to sleep.

While she had enjoyed every moment of their passionate interlude, Kari was troubled afterwards. Her energy had been completely depleted; she felt an itching sensation over her entire body. It was an overall disturbing feeling that mere scratching could not alleviate. As Kari studied Gil's peaceful, slumbering face, one solitary sentence rose within her mind: "Life is nothing." What was going on? Kari had always thought that connection with another human being was the ultimate goal, that once ideal physical intimacy was achieved, happiness would follow. But Kari was not satisfied; like an addict needing another fix, Kari craved energy: the energy obtained from making love.

Without disturbing Gil, Kari managed to slip from beneath his nurturing arm and climb out of bed. She lumbered towards the bathroom, flipped on the small light over the sink and studied her reflection in the mirror. On the surface everything appeared normal, but the cloak of Kari's flesh concealed much suffering and discomfort. When she focused on her own eyes, "Life is nothing," resounded again in her head. She shook herself wildly, trying to extricate the sentence, but to her dismay, it fought back by repeating itself over and over until she thought she would go mad. In hopes of escaping the words, Kari moved back into the bedroom and observed Gil once again. Without question, she had just experienced the best sex of her life. How could that mean nothing?

Kari stepped out on the balcony and stared up at the sprinkle of stars inlaid in the sky like jewels against black velvet. Ignoring the slight chill in the air, Kari assumed the half lotus position in an attempt to meditate and successfully move her Kundalini. What she didn't count on was an enervated state that completely inhibited her flow. Compounding her problem was the annoying itching sensations that continued unabated.

Finally, acknowledging her less than robust physical condition, Kari reflected back on the sex with Gil and the palpable exchange of energy thereof. What suddenly dawned on her was something Master Songwha had once said:

"When you direct energy to someone else, you incur their karma; while invigorating the person receiving the energy, this transfer can severely deplete the sender's energy source." Thus, while Kari had triggered the most intense sex of Gil's life, she was now enduring the consequences.

It made Kari more appreciative of the countless times Master Songwha, Master Kim and Owl From Heaven had made the energy exchange - each time they had voluntarily polluted themselves in a determined effort to clear up Kari's karma. Her teachers had suffered from this, as it is difficult to purify dirty and negative energy. This was the first time Kari had an intimate encounter with someone vibrating at a lower level than herself. Now, having been on the other side, Kari understood the process. This awareness activated an onslaught of tears, which Kari allowed to paint her face and neck. She realized that her ability to manipulate Gil's energy had indeed elevated her to another level of consciousness. These thoughts, however, were telltale signs that Kari's ego was still alive and well.

* * * *

After a light breakfast with Gil, Kari had an exigent desire to be alone and meditate. With all kinds of questions swirling through her mind, she needed the combination of isolation and tranquility to ease her fermenting anxiety. Gil suggested Long Canyon and jotted down directions for her on a napkin.

"Call me when you get back, okay? Believe it or not, I don't have any plans tonight," he grinned.

"I promise," Kari replied as she headed out the door.

After arriving at Long Canyon, Kari hiked for about a half hour before discovering a sequestered area guarded by stout cactus plants. There were no other hikers in sight and the atmosphere had a distinct coziness to it; the energy was pristine.

After doing a few fundamental stretching exercises, Kari sat down to meditate. As she concentrated on her breathing, her mind quickly emptied itself. She felt relaxed until an uninvited mantra trampled through her mind.

"You are nothing," it stated indifferently. "Life is nothing." Kari instantly thought of the Grand Master. Only he had the capability of sending her these messages. Dammit! she thought, this was worse than E-mail!

Stubbornly, Kari attempted to ward off the message. With resolute determination, she tried to close her mind and resume her meditation, but failed miserably. Abruptly she stood and began traipsing through the desert brush. It took a tremendous amount of energy to maintain her equanimity. Wandering aimlessly, she searched for a place where she could relax and meditate, but those three infamous words: "Life is nothing," seemed to follow her around like a lovesick puppy. Kari couldn't escape the desperate animal. It trailed at her heels at every turn, occasionally nipping into her flesh with its biting words.

Kari didn't understand why that sentence had haunted her so. She wanted to object, scream her protests out loud to the universe, more importantly, to the Grand Master. But the disturbing curse endured. "Life is nothing," seemed to rise up from every rock, plant, tree and bird she laid her eyes upon - it ricocheted off the canyon walls, reverberating inside her skull like a vexing echo.

Not wanting to spend the night alone, Kari continued what was quickly becoming a ritual: having dinner with Gil. Still in a euphoric mood, Gil spent most of the evening boasting about how everything in his life was going so swimmingly. Kari learned that Gil not only had a surfeit of photographic assignments to choose from, but several prominent galleries in Phoenix had recently approached him about exhibiting his work.

"Life has never been better," he raved. Little did he expect the response Kari gave.

Almost absentmindedly, Kari blurted, "Your life is nothing." But while even Kari was stunned and a bit embarrassed by the harshness of her emission, she quickly detected the kernel of truth contained within her inadvertent remark.

"What?" Gil shouted.

"Everything you've been talking about," Kari began.

"None of it has any relevance. They mean nothing. Your life is nothing."

"How dare you! Who do you think you are to say that my life means nothing?"

When Kari didn't reply, Gil became more riled.

"Answer me dammit!" he insisted.

Kari remained silent a moment. Through Gil, she finally understood herself. His outraged reaction mirrored her own when confronted by those same words from the Grand Master. In one rash instance, Gil's kind and gentlemanly exterior had been shaken away, revealing the fear that otherwise lay dormant within his being. As Kari watched him unravel before her, she identified with his plight. But she still couldn't fathom the meaning of those words and why they stimulated such fear.

"Look, don't take what I said personally. This is not just about you. It's everyone's life. None of it means anything."

"Are you angry at me about something?" Gil asked.

"Because I thought we were really getting along and now you suddenly start demeaning me!"

"I'm sorry. Besides, what does it matter what I think? If you feel good about yourself, you shouldn't care what I say."

Gil's face remained riddled with turmoil. They barely touched the rest of their meal when Gil hastily summoned the waitress for the check. Gil drove Kari back to the hotel in silence. This time he didn't join her inside. Instead, he peeled out of the parking lot, feeling unsettled and not sure if he ever wanted to see Kari again.

* * * *

Kari was too restless to remain in her hotel room. After spending ten minutes anxiously pacing the carpeted floor, she briskly headed back outside to her rented car. The sky was at its grayest, just prior to turning completely dark. As her car steered along highway 89A, the silhouettes of red rock mountains loomed menacingly on both sides, resembling colossal-sized dinosaurs. Kari flipped on her high beams to increase visibility, but the eeriness surrounding her prevailed. She found herself heading towards Long Canyon. After parking, Kari trekked out into the silent darkness, guided only by instinct and the subtle illumination of stars. Still yearning for enlightenment, she felt that deep meditation might provide the answers she had been seeking. After roving about for ten minutes, Kari randomly chose an elevated spot atop a stone plateau.

This time, instead of dreading the onset of the Grand Master's message, Kari reversed her tactics: She would welcome hearing it. So when the words: "Life is nothing," repeated themselves over and over inside her head, Kari didn't resist. The mantra continued, until the sentence faded away and her mind grew quiet.

Kari meditated through the night, all the while receiving nourishing energy from the stars and moon above. She felt their overwhelming presence and allowed the comforting energy to embrace her. Soon, a layer of tangerine light began ascending from the horizon. As the sun lifted itself over the canyon walls, washing Kari with its brilliant radiance, she began a gradual transformation. While her body grew intensely warmer, Kari noticed the distinct sensation of cold energy streaming downwards and ultimately exiting through her toes.

Losing that icy energy triggered a massive change in Kari's attitude. When her body had clung to the cold energy, Kari's way of thinking was dictated by lower spirits who relish a frigid habitat. Only by reverently meditating all night was Kari able to expel the chilled energy and supplant it with warmth. This changed Kari's way of thinking, and when she finally opened her eyes, she realized that she desired the Grand Master's advice.

From that moment on, Kari would willingly bow down to this holy man and obey his every word.

* * * *

Kari drove to Fay Canyon, determined to find Owl From Heaven. Hopefully, he would give her another chance. But after roaming around for several hours, Kari grew frustrated. The Grand Master was nowhere in sight. Fretting over whether or not she had blown her one opportunity, Kari quickly became disillusioned. Maybe the Grand Master was just a crotchety, stubborn old man who had never intended to give her a fair chance.

Kari's ruminations ceased when a voice, his voice, rattled her mind like a shrill bell from an alarm clock.

"Kari," he said in an authoritative manner, clearly designed to command her full attention. "Do you have a sincere mind for seeking the truth?"

"Yes," she whispered.

"In order for you to achieve your final goal of truth, you need genuine sincerity - a pure mind, pure heart and total obedience. Do you understand?"

"Yes," Kari responded. "I will do whatever you want. Please take me on as your disciple."

When there was no immediate answer, Kari's hopes were dashed. But then, she felt a distinct change in the energy field surrounding her. Whirling around, she stood face to face with Owl From Heaven. He appeared as if from nowhere, Kari thought. Or, did she have it backwards? Perhaps, he appeared from everywhere, because he was a part of every thing.

Clad in a white robe, he resembled a sage from centuries past; his right hand clasped the naturally-curved top of a wooden staff. Without uttering another word, he simply motioned for Kari to follow him.

They climbed a steep incline, leading to a Native American ruin. Owl From Heaven stood before a semi-circular wall, which formed an ancient room atop the plateau. It had been constructed many years ago by the Native Americans that had lived there, out of several hundred pieces of red rock, that resembled bricks. Many of them were chipped and parts of the wall looked fragile, like they could collapse at any moment.

Holding his walking stick skyward, Owl From Heaven closed his eyes and uttered a silent prayer. With sudden, rapid motions, he lashed out at the wall with his wooden staff, smashing the bricks until they tumbled to the ground in scattered piles. He wreaked his havoc, making certain not one brick remained standing atop another. Satisfied with his act of destruction, the Grand Master turned to face a stunned Kari. "Rebuild this wall," he said.

"What?" Kari asked tentatively.

"Rebuild this wall," he repeated. "Make it better than it ever was. Pretend you're living in this cave and you need this wall for protection."

"Okay," Kari quickly replied. If this is what he wants me to do, fine. Obviously this is a test. Once I complete this task to his satisfaction, he'll begin to teach me the truth, Kari concluded.

As soon as Kari commenced with the arduous task of

rebuilding, the Grand Master disappeared. To keep herself distracted from the drudgery of the work, Kari sang the lyrics of old songs out loud. As the hours passed, the temperature increased to sweltering levels; Kari sweated profusely. The job was much harder than she had anticipated - not only were there hundreds of rocks, but each one had to be carefully placed to maintain an even balance. But hell-bent on pleasing the Grand Master, Kari worked diligently. It took all day, approximately ten hours, for Kari to complete her assignment.

When she was finished, Kari felt a sense of accomplishment, confident that she had exceeded all the Grand Master's expectations. Every brick fit snugly in its place. This wall, she concluded, would withstand all the forces of nature, and, like its predecessor, would remain standing for years to come.

Collapsing from sheer exhaustion, Kari slept within the confines of the brick wall. She awoke the next morning and spotted the shadow of Owl From Heaven hovering nearby, quietly appraising her creation. Springing up, Kari eagerly approached him.

"Well, what do you think?" she asked confidently. "Great, isn't it? If you want to know the truth, I've even impressed myself. I didn't know I had it in me."

"What you have in you," Owl From Heaven stated, "is a lot of pride."

"And why shouldn't I? Look at the job I did!"

"You laid these bricks with pride and greedy feelings. You built it because you expected something from me in return. That is greed, not truth."

"What difference does it make where it came from if it's a masterpiece?" Kari exploded.

"You call this a masterpiece? Well I call it a house of pride and it doesn't deserve to stand!"

The Grand Master raised his staff into the air.

"Hey!" Kari shouted, but it was too late. Owl From Heaven sliced against the wall with his stick as if he were hitting a golf ball off to a distant green. Within seconds, hours of painstaking labor were reduced to a heap of rubble.

"Build it again," the Grand Master commanded. Before a flabbergasted Kari could reply, he had vanished.

"I don't believe this!" she ranted. "Who do you think you are?" Kari screamed into the emptiness.

It took Kari an hour to calm down. When she did she realized that maybe he had a point: She had taken too much pride in her work, and as a result, held lofty expectations. But couldn't he have expressed that without making her rebuild the entire wall? she mused.

Reluctantly, Kari turned her attention to the task of rebuilding. Ironically, what inspired her this time was her irritation. What a colossal waste of time, she thought. But if this is what he wants, Kari decided she would comply with his wishes, however irrational they appeared. It was all part of the same test, she concluded.

As she replaced each stone, her frustration mounted. By the time the wall was completed, it was nightfall. Weary and annoyed from spending two full days laying bricks, Kari plunged into sleep.

The next morning she awakened to renewed hopes,

but one look at the Grand Master's face cast out her misplaced optimism. When he started dismantling her brick creation, she realized that again, her efforts had been in vain.

"What did I do wrong this time?" she shouted.

"This time you built out of irritation and impatience. You felt it was a waste of time. Those emotions were transmuted into the wall,"

"So I was a little irritated. Big deal," Kari protested.

"It's time to build it again. Here," he said, placing a few pieces of fruit and some nuts on top of a stray rock.

"I brought you some breakfast," He strode away without uttering another word.

Kari had indeed been frustrated the previous day, but now she started to question the very reality of this man and her situation. Perhaps this entire scenario was ingeniously fabricated just to humiliate her. Was someone trying to play an awful trick at her expense? Flagrant doubts about the Grand Master surfaced in her thoughts throughout the day until she began to question his very existence.

"What have I done?" she asked herself. Flashes from her previous lifestyle invaded her psyche. Kari had given up her whole way of life, but for what? Nothing made sense to her anymore. She felt as if she was caught in between worlds - the world of material comfort and ignorance, versus the world of truth and knowledge about her real essence. Yet, somehow Kari feared the authenticity of that truth. She had backed herself into a corner. What were her options? She couldn't go back - even she realized it was all meaningless: her job, the restaurants, the day-to-day decisions based solely on accumulation and conformity. Kari's dilemma was not about retreating to her former life. Her major trepidation was where should she go next? What if there was no place for her? Anxiety swirled about Kari's aura as she placed each stone, until the fear consumed her completely.

The next morning, when Owl From Heaven raised a single brick off the wall, Kari knew exactly what he was going to say before the words spilled out.

"How long do you think a wall constructed out of doubt and fear will last? Replacing one self-destructive emotion with another is not progress."

"No," Kari pleaded. But it was too late. The Grand Master continuously swiped at the wall with his staff and was gone. Fuming inside, Kari scooped up one of the bricks and held it over her head. She was consumed by an impetuous desire to smash it to smithereens. Actually, what she really wanted to do was throw it at Owl From Heaven, but since he had conveniently disappeared, she had to waylay her vengeful longing.

Kari resigned herself to rebuilding one more time, but that was it: If this effort proved futile, if it didn't meet his "beyond perfection" standards, Kari was going to terminate this sham of a test. She felt as if she was a character in a comedy of errors: All of nature was her audience, cruelly laughing at her foibles. As the day wore on, Kari grew more incensed. How dare he waste her time like this! Kari set each brick into place with a seething fury. Fueled by her anger, she was compelled to finish the wall, but doing so kept her up the entire night.

At sunrise, Kari positioned herself in front of Owl From Heaven to stave off his next attempt to pulverize the wall.

"Can we talk about this?" she asked. "I know what you're going to say, I was a little angry, I know, but..."

"A little?"

"All right, I was furious, but can't we work on that? Aren't there some exercises we can do? Please don't make me build that wall again," she begged.

He remained steadfast, watching her.

"Okay, fine! If you knock it down again, I'm leaving!"

Sidestepping Kari, Owl From Heaven methodically destroyed her house of bricks. Kari's mind reflected on a childhood story she had once read: The Three Little Pigs. Except in that anecdote the Big Bad Wolf wasn't able to blow down the pig's house of brick because it was too strong. Kari thought she had built her brick house with the same attention to detail, but ironically in her life it was the "Big Bad Wolf" who was invincible, not the house.

After callously ignoring her protests, the Grand Master left. Livid with rage, Kari lifted one of the bricks and heaved it to the ground. It crumbled into countless fragments. There was no way Kari was going to rebuild that wall! Instead, she trudged down the mountainside, jumped into her rented car and drove back to the hotel.

Feeling the need for normal human contact, Kari called Gil and apologized for her recent behavior. When she admitted that she had been under considerable duress, he offered to drive right over to attempt to lift her spirits.

When Gil arrived, to his dismay, Kari had undergone another change of heart. She kept thinking that the Grand Master was deliberately trying to get her to collapse under the strain. He would relish pushing her to the point of no return - which was where Kari believed herself to be. No, Kari speculated, I won't cave, give up, or quit! He will not win this test of wills! Then she considered: What would she be quitting to anyway? Every time Kari thought about returning to her former life, it held no interest to her. That life had been an empty shell. But an afterthought struck her: At least she was familiar with every nook and cranny within its hollow substance.

Impulsively, Kari decided to check out of the hotel and return her car to the rental place. This path, no matter how treacherous, and at times, incomprehensible, was for keeps.

Gil volunteered to drop her back off at Fay Canyon. During their drive, he implored Kari to get in touch with him if she encountered any further trouble. He even suggested she take a cellular phone with her.

"Oh, I'm sure that would go over real well," she replied.

"So all you're going to take with you is the clothes on your back?"

"Gil, will you stop worrying about me? I'll be fine."

"So how long do you think you'll be?"

"I have no idea, but trust me, as soon as this is over, I'll be in touch."

"Good luck," he offered as Kari went off to build yet another brick wall.

Gil continued to watch until Kari had disappeared from sight. As he drove away he peered over his right shoulder into the back seat and stared momentarily at Kari's suitcase which he had agreed to keep for her. A rush of melancholy swept over him. This was the first woman in a long time that he had taken an avid interest in. Kit was right - it was a delight to be around her. It made Gil more determined than ever to follow his own spiritual yearnings.

* * * *

When Kari resumed her work, it was with renewed determination. Unfortunately her fortitude waffled midway through the day. Kari's thoughts about her own life kept surfacing: Had she trapped herself? While Kari had no interest in returning to the emptiness of the material world, what other options did she have? What if she failed this test with the Grand Master? Where would she go from here? Kari was living her life in limbo and felt very unsettled. Why couldn't she fathom existing the way others did: Content to live their lives caught up in their careers or family - concerning themselves with the mundane responsibilities of going to the market, mall, post office and bank - necessities, that for some reason Kari simply couldn't relate to anymore? She sensed changes were occurring everywhere she looked. Not just in people - many leading lives to extremes, controlled by violence and addictions - but with the planet as well. Time seemed to be collapsing onto itself. There was a quickening going on. The saying: Reaping what you sow, seemed more immediate. Harsh and erratic weather conditions were on the upswing. Kari sensed something was going to happen, but what? Whatever destiny would unfold at this time, Kari felt a profound desire and innate need to help in some way - help people to wake up and understand that their lives are much more than they could ever imagine. Yet, who would believe her when she had no idea where she was going in her own life? On the one hand she was certain of impending chaos; on the other, she was a confused mess. She couldn't go back to merely existing like one of many in an uninformed flock of sheep, but she had no idea what to do next. Self-pitying thoughts usurped her mind, draining her energy until she barely had enough left to complete the house. She ended the day wallowing in her sadness.

Pink streaks of light marbled the pale blue sky. Dawn arrived, along with Owl From Heaven. He exhibited no emotion, but plenty of energy, as he leveled her latest creation that had been built upon sorrow. When he advised her to try still one more time, instead of arguing, Kari grew contemplative. Several minutes after he left, she suddenly smiled to herself: Eureka! Kari had come to a realization. Not only was she no longer sad, but she finally felt as if she understood the process. All the emotions that had ravished her these past days were gone. They had been exorcised from her spirit every time Owl From Heaven destroyed the brick wall - all the low-level emotions that had plagued her evaporated as the rampart came crashing down. Kari recognized that this arduous set of trials had been established by the Grand Master out of love. A profound sense of joy enveloped her. Now, finally, Kari felt as if she had comprehended everything that had transpired between them. Unfortunately, Kari's test was taking an inordinate amount of time because she had so many controlling emotions that needed to be eliminated.

Elated at her discovery, Kari couldn't wait to see the Grand Master again. Infused with emotions of total happiness, she spent her time singing while energetically building. By the end of the day, she could practically taste the bliss emanating from her own spirit.

Eagerly she confronted Owl From Heaven the next morning, exclaiming that she finally understood his methods and intentions. When he ignored her revelation, Kari's enthusiasm was dashed once again.

"What's wrong with it now?" she shouted, as he began his ritualistic act of devastation.

"You built a wall of happiness," he said calmly.

"Yes! Exactly. I finally figured out what this test was about and it made me happy. Isn't happiness what everyone is seeking?" Kari asked, a bit embarrassed as well as puzzled by this latest turn of events.

"Your happiness is not real. It came from external circumstances, not true joy from within your being."

"And life is nothing, I know," Kari said quietly.

"You were still building with emotion," he continued.

"Happiness is an emotion. You need to eliminate that emotion too."

"So that's what this has been about? Eliminating all of my emotions?"

"In this country they don't have a word for this

process. But in Korea they call it Jigam. Ji, meaning to stop or eliminate, and gam referring to emotion."

Kari's mind instantly flashed to her stay in Korea and her interaction with Kang Hoon. Was Kang Hoon also the Native American Grand Master standing before her now? She quickly dismissed her own question, realizing that even if he was, what did it matter?

"Okay, I get it. I can't be happy, angry, sad, greedy, fearful, impatient, or anything. I have to build with no emotion whatsoever. I can do that."

"Be my guest," Owl From Heaven said.

While a part of Kari still felt like questioning, she realized the issue was moot. Turning her attention to the work, Kari detached herself from all emotion; at times she felt like a zombie. When she was finished, Kari didn't even look at her creation; it held no meaning to her.

Obviously it held little meaning to Owl From Heaven either. He quickly demolished the walls just after sunrise.

"You've got to be kidding," Kari protested. "I did exactly what you said. I built this wall with absolutely no emotion. I thought you would be proud of me."

"There is no vitality of life in your creation," he stated.

"Easy for you to say."

"Yes, you built with no emotion, but by doing so, you succumbed to still another attachment - an attachment to nothingness."

"How can you have an attachment to that?"

"Think about it," he suggested before walking away. More than anything else, Kari was emotionally drained. What Owl From Heaven was inflicting on her, she concluded, was a peculiar but distinct form of abuse. It was getting infinitely harder to summon up the requisite physical strength to complete the wall. Her nerves were frazzled and her body was depleted, fortified solely by the fresh fruit the Grand Master delivered each morning.

But Kari tried again and as the day wore on, she became acutely aware of every symptom her body fell prey to. Not only were her hands scratched and bleeding, but every muscle ached. Through her pain, Kari thought about what she was supposed to be learning: not to harbor any more attachments. This notion had been practically beaten into Kari's raw body, a body that had become a tortured prisoner of exhaustion. She knew she had reached the end of the line. She couldn't even imagine building the house again. In fact, she felt she would be incapable of such a feat.

In lieu of a jacuzzi which her body desperately craved, Kari lay prone on the ground, elevating her knees slightly to lessen her lower back pain. Wanting only to unwind and relax, Kari was exasperated when an all-too-familiar refrain popped into her head: "Life is nothing." Not again, she pleaded, but before she relented to outright dismay, a new voice enjoined her attention. The voice(was it her unconscious?) issued a somewhat divergent message: "I am everything," it stated confidently. Naturally Kari felt the timing couldn't have been more opportune. Pondering the proclamation, Kari concluded that maybe there is a power beyond her own ego. This was her final thought before sleep rescued her from her discomfort and fatigue.

When Owl From Heaven appeared in the morning he spent a considerable amount of time inspecting Kari's work. When he nodded with approval, Kari issued a huge sigh of relief. Finally, she murmured to herself, he's satisfied.

"You did good work," Owl From Heaven said. "You are on the right track, but it's still not enough," he added as he began his daily act of obliteration. When he was finished, Kari meekly asked, "What am I supposed to do differently?"

"You'll know when you do it," he answered, leaving Kari to reflect on his statement. She did little else for the better part of the morning. Too tired to begin anew, Kari sat in the midst of the rubble. Because she had no physical energy, she was content to wile away the day in that manner.

After several hours, overcome by boredom, Kari stood up and listlessly began stacking a few of the bricks. Conscious of the fact that she was just going through the motions, Kari was about to stop the exercise in futility, when suddenly, her hands literally sprang to life. At the same time Kari felt a ground swell of energy surge and circulate throughout her body. It was as if her hands were dancing to some distant music, gracefully and briskly, laying each stone in its proper position. Left with no choice, Kari continued building the brick house, more rapidly than ever, but still with careful attention to detail.

As Kari adjusted to this bizarre, wonderful, yet overwhelming feeling, she quickly surmised that this was not her own will at work: It was universal energy working through her. Her mind was at peace when Kari finally realized the true meaning of: "Life is nothing." Nothing is not a negative. She had been interpreting it too literally. Nothing really meant everything. When a person was burdened by their ego, life is nothing. Only by eliminating ego does a person become what they in essence really are - everything, without limitation. Naturally, the ego stubbornly creates barriers to keep one from understanding this truth.

Having completed the brick enclosure, Kari continued to feel the surge of power within her. "Where is this coming from?" she wondered to herself. A moment later the Grand Master appeared from behind the bricks.

"The energy working through you is not yours. It comes from source, the same place that the creation of the entire universe began."

"Why did it come to me?"

"Because you are finally ready."

Kari breathed deeply as the energy continued to circulate throughout her body.

"You have finally tapped into the purest energy source. There's a Korean word for this too: Chun Ji Ki Woon. It means the combination of heaven, earth, energy and circulation. With that energy you built a house that will last. It will be protected by the divine."

Kari took a long look at her creation and nodded. To her it was no longer just a wall - but instead represented the nine steps of elimination and then profound rebuilding of her ego.

"Follow me," Owl From Heaven said, shattering her

reverie. "I have one more challenge for you."

"What?" Kari asked in disbelief. "What now?"

"You will see."

Owl From Heaven led Kari up a treacherous path, leading to some cliffs. He pointed to the top of an arch and motioned for her to climb the rest of the way alone. As Kari ascended she used the naturally-formed grooves in the rock to support her feet. When she reached her destination, Kari peered back down and saw Owl From Heaven staring up at her.

"If you trust me, you will allow your body to fall from there."

"What?" Kari exclaimed.

"Turn around," he instructed, "move your body to the edge of the rock and let yourself drop backwards."

There was no hesitation. Kari trusted the Grand Master completely and inched her body to the edge of the plateau.

Without another word, Kari closed her eyes and eased her body off the ledge. During the initial drop, Kari never felt faint. Her consciousness remained peaceful and un-shaken. The immediate falling sensation quickly trans-formed into a floating feeling, as Kari's body stopped its rapid free fall and hovered midway between the ledge and Owl From Heaven.

"You did it!" he exclaimed. "You eliminated your ego completely. I am satisfied - you are my disciple."

Unbeknownst to Kari, Owl From Heaven had created an energy beam that was able to support the weight of her body. This is incredible, Kari realized, as she wafted gracefully upon the magic carpet of energy.

Maintaining his focus on the energy, Owl From Heaven steadily guided Kari towards the ground where he stood. As she slowly descended, she knew how blessed she was to have this man for a teacher.

After hiking back down to the Native American ruin, Owl From Heaven engaged Kari in a meditation exercise. She sat directly across from him in a half-lotus position and, moments after Owl From Heaven directed Kari to look him in the eyes, she experienced a spontaneous influx of energy. What she was feeling was his Kundalini sweeping through her own body.

"You and I are one. You and I are one," he repeated several times. "You are me. I am you. My energy will flow into you; however you must trust that you and I are one. This is the first message of the Manuscript," he stated firmly.

As the Grand Master's energy flowed inside her, she accepted his presence. She knew she was not alone. He was a part of her. They were one. While she felt absolute peace, Kari suddenly burst into tears. It dawned on her that all human troubles stemmed from the lack of unity between people. The conflicts between husbands and wives, or parents and children, could be resolved if only people understood this. But now, this understanding was not merely on an intellectual level - Kari felt it within. "This is it," she thought, "this is the source of all human dynamics."

"When I said I would take you on as my disciple, I didn't mean follower," Owl From Heaven began. "This is not a religious affiliation. Most people involved with a religion don't trust the holy thing within themselves. They expect their problems to be solved by someone else: Jesus, Buddha, a priest or a rabbi. But they never solve their problems from within. They praise God when things go right but they also blame the same God when things go wrong. That's not what I want from you. You must believe that you have the power to create your reality using the holy thing inside of you. There are three laws of obedience for you to abide by. First, obedience to the holy thing within you. Second, obedience to your Teacher. You must have total faith and trust in me. And third, you will adhere to the principles of the ancient Manuscript. Can you do that?"

Kari nodded. "Yes."

"Good. We begin tomorrow morning. I will see you then."

With that, the Grand Master turned on his heels, and a moment later he was gone. He left Kari both anxious and excited about beginning the next phase of her journey.

Chapter 7

In anticipation of what lay ahead, Kari struggled to fall asleep. Her dreams were peaceful but vivid. She found herself floating in the middle of an ocean; her body moved fluidly in conjunction with the waves. As she gazed directly above, a few stars scintillated across the inky night sky. One star, the most luminescent Kari had ever witnessed firsthand, descended towards her. As the expansive glow approached, it beamed even brighter, until it splayed in front of Kari's face, washing her skin in radiant light. Suddenly, the light dispersed, shattering into millions of tiny incandescent particles, which floated above and around Kari like a swarm of fireflies. The entire breadth of sky shimmered. Overcome with a swelling fervor, Kari experienced an immediate infusion of love and warmth. The fever intensified, and Kari felt as if her body was on fire. She allowed herself to submerge beneath the water. Moments after she did, Kari awakened. She sat upright and couldn't help noticing that from head to toe, her body remained suffused with heat.

When Owl From Heaven didn't show up in the morning, Kari went searching for him. An hour elapsed, and Kari finally spotted him squatting under a thicket of branches, munching on a raw potato. He gestured for her to join him.

"Have you eaten yet?"

Kari shook her head and Owl From Heaven offered her a sliver of the potato.

"You'll be eating small quantities of raw food during your training," he explained. "Potatoes, beans, nuts, sesame seeds, and pine needle juice."

"Well, I'm used to eating practically nothing so I think I can manage," Kari answered.

"Still have a little of that ego, don't you?"

"I didn't mean..."

"It's okay. Once you're living out here you'll begin to feel more connected to everything and then you'll quickly realize that who you think you are is not very important."

At that moment, Kari decided she would cease talking altogether and just listen. But as the day progressed she realized that Owl From Heaven rarely spoke - only when he had something relevant to say. He wasn't as nurturing as Master Songwha - his demeanor was more dignified and authoritative. As a result, Kari felt more intimidated. But maybe, she thought, that's precisely the way he wanted it.

The Grand Master left Kari alone a substantial portion of the day to assimilate herself with the environment. As Kari meditated, she began to experience all the different types of energy that existed around her.

When her eyes closed, the curtain was raised. The canyon walls became a concert hall; the plant life, trees, rocks and animals were the orchestra. Kari was encapsulated by myriad energy wavelengths, all vibrating at various levels of sound, color, light and motion. Her mind's eye captured the symphony of pulsating auras and diverse resonance of nature's vast existence, and was able to recognize the incredible harmony at work. The universal conductor of all matter had positioned everything in its proper place. It guided the energy masses with its own hand, aided by the windswept pages of music and illuminated in part by the great sun and ever-changing moon.

That night, adhering to Owl From Heaven's advice, Kari slept inside the old Native American ruin once again. She studied the bricks of red earth which she herself had stacked several times to form walls at the edge of the plateau. If those walls could only speak, Kari pondered, perhaps they would provide clues to a previous way of life that had existed on that very spot before she had ever arrived.

Her sleep was erratic; she felt troubled, and at times, frightened. But why? Had she lived there before? Resigning herself to gazing up at the stars, Kari's mind drifted back to childhood arts and crafts projects during her current lifetime in which she decorated construction paper with handfuls of glitter.

Kari's musing was interrupted when Owl From Heaven suddenly appeared. "Native American spirits are often present here and they can make sleep difficult," he told her.

"I guess I'm not going to get much sleep then," Kari replied.

"Sleep is not your priority now," he stated.

Owl From Heaven began Kari's Chi training at the crack of dawn. "You must do these exercises daily and with full concentration. It will help you to understand the Manuscript," he explained.

While the exercises were repetitive, Kari began to feel the keen distinction between the physical and spiritual world. In the physical world everything seemed dissimilar - but that was only an illusion. By tuning in to her spiritual instincts, Kari realized that everything was really the same; everything in the energy world was interconnected, nothing was separate.

The Grand Master intuited that Kari had been the recipient of the proper message. To Kari's surprise and delight, he complimented her.

"This is wonderful," he said. "You got the point I was trying to make."

Kari's happiness spilled over into a wide grin. For the first time she felt like she was truly connecting with her new teacher. However, a part of her was still impatient, questioning their motives for repeating the same mundane exercises.

After two more days replete with identical energy

work, the Grand Master explained to Kari one of the fundamental concepts of the Manuscript. "There are three distinct worlds: the physical world, the energy world and the truth world," he stated. "In the physical world, everything is visible, but separate. And except on a superficial basis, real communication is not possible. But in the energy world, you feel more connected to everything. The Chi training that we've been doing will help you become part of the energy world. You realize the connection, but there is still some separation and total communication does not exist. Only in the truth world, a world you have yet to experience, will you find fulfillment. In this world you will discover the true principles of the universe. The truth world is the only world that is permanent. The physical world is temporary and the energy world, although flexible, is unstable. The truth world is intangible and invisible; that's why you need help from the energy world - it is the intermediary between the physical realm and the truth. The more you tune into the energy world, the sooner you will be prepared for the truth. It is almost impossible for a beginner to enter the truth world directly."

Kari realized that everything around her communicated on an energy level. As she began feeling a profound connection to her surroundings, the Grand Master continued to enlighten her with still more information regarding the eighty-one sacred symbols.

"Many of the symbols are numbers which all possess their own significant meaning. Numbers one through five are all part of the physical world," he explained. "Number six is termed 'the gate' of energy which opens onto the bridge that leads to truth. Numbers seven and eight signify that you've reached the complete energy world. Finally, number nine is truth."

"What about ten?" Kari asked.

"Ten is the same as one. You return to the beginning, only you start at a new level. But be aware that human beings are only capable of reaching the number nine. To reach ten you would have to leave your physical body behind. Ten is the number of God."

"So what level am I at now?" Kari questioned.

"Six. The exercises you've been doing will allow you to reach numbers seven and eight. Only by continued repetition are we able to bring out the genetic coding stored within your body."

"Excuse me?"

"Everyone is capable of self realization. It's genetically programmed inside us. Unfortunately, social conditioning within our current society isn't designed to encourage this type of learning. Instead, it's geared to leave us mired in fear and the status quo. Thus, we suppress our true natures and choose to live in ignorance. If all people began this training when they were younger, it wouldn't be as difficult. But with patience, persistence and dedication, everyone can ultimately reach total enlightenment."

Encouraged by his promise, Kari continued with many of the same activities she had participated in at the Ascension Center under Master Songwha's direction. The Grand Master guided Kari through the Lotus Flower exercise, in which it took a full thirty minutes for her to raise both arms into the air. Now, fully in touch with the energy world, Kari's entire body vibrated, and as her hands reached skyward, her palms literally shook. For a brief instant, Kari was in control of the entire energy world. With no limit to her sudden powers, she felt as if she could direct the energy within all of Sedona.

When the exercise was over Kari related her experience to the Grand Master, who nodded in recognition. "You are making progress," he said. "Try to experience more of these sensations. Walk around, wherever your mood takes you, and continue to tune into the energy world surrounding you. You'll be amazed at what you can discover."

Still reeling from the experience, her senses keen and alert, Kari did as she was instructed. After a few minutes, she heard a distinct rattling sound. Whirling around, Kari found herself staring at a small rock formation. Before she could turn back, she spotted a full-sized rattlesnake; its lithe body slithered through a jagged opening between the stone. Exhibiting no fear, Kari waited for the sinuous serpent to inch closer. She viewed its colorful and patterned scales, which resembled a mosaic of beautifully inlaid tile, and tuned her mind to the energy of the reptile, which was now directly beneath her. Only warm, loving feelings emanated from this much-maligned creature. Kari transmitted her thoughts to him telepathically. "What are you doing?" she asked.

"I have been watching you," the snake replied, regarding her with his eyes, which glowed yellow in the sunlight. "You are learning very much and I know you will accomplish your goal. All the animals in the canyon are sending you positive, loving energy."

Overcome with joy, warm tears spilled down Kari's cheeks.

"I wish more people were like you," the snake added. "Please know I am here for you if you need me." With that , the rattlesnake slid beneath some bushes, leaving Kari to ponder their encounter. As the day went on, more animals greeted her: a grey wolf, a scraggly coyote, a speckled lizard - all exhibited loving energy.

"According to the Manuscript," the Grand Master told Kari later, "only human beings are on the same level as God. Instinctively, animals recognize the presence of a divine spirit in human beings. When this spirit is pure, and in accordance with universal law, animals will gravitate towards it and willingly protect it. Only when humans allow their spirits to be tarnished by violence or an unwieldy ego, do animals wish to maintain a safe distance. While every creature has its own spirit, only human beings have a soul within them; a soul capable of connecting with God. In other words, a human body is absolutely necessary to start the journey towards total enlightenment."

That night Kari prayed. Not only for all the animals she had personally encountered, but for all the multifarious creatures living in the canyon. She prayed that in their next lifetime they would become human beings, and thus be able to embark upon this unique training.

The next morning, Kari was greeted by a squirrel, who pranced right up to her prone body and offered her a nut. Kari looked into the squirrel's eyes; they were watery. Tears of joy were being released. The squirrel had received Kari's prayers.

"Animals seem like such wonderful, innocent creatures," Kari said to the Grand Master. "Why don't they have the same potential we do?"

"In many ways animals are more spiritual than most people. They live in the moment, they are connected to the energy flow around them, and they are never consumed by ego. But only human beings have the presence of the holy thing or heaven within them."

"Heaven is within us?" Kari queried.

"According to the Manuscript, the Trinity of heaven, earth and human beings exists together within us all. When we feel one with the earth, we feel one with heaven, and this combination results in the realization that we are all part of the God Force. Human beings are holy creatures. In a sense, they are more powerful than God, because they possess a body and a soul. Humans can blame God and be forgiven, but they can't blame other humans and receive the same forgiveness. This is because God is beyond judgement and human beings are not. The Manuscript states that the holy thing within us shines like the great sun. It's represented within the series of symbols as the number one in the physical dimension. Its function is love. Thus, scolding and hugging are the same, because God is represented by the number ten and love is number one - in essence, one and ten are the same - both beyond the polarity of good or evil. Do you understand?"

Overwhelmed by the feeling that there was so much

information to absorb, Kari merely nodded. But Owl From Heaven knew she was making great progress.

* * * *

Kari had already begun to lose all track of time when the Grand Master ordered her to stop sleeping altogether. Before this, she had been sleeping approximately four hours a night. Now, he insisted that she remain awake at all times. "By doing this," he emphasized, "you will be able to feel the truth of the Manuscript."

The first night without sleep was relatively easy. Kari nearly nodded off once or twice, but each time the Grand Master appeared to jar her back to an awakened state of consciousness. Daytime was much easier. As Kari continued the arduous exercises and meditations, the Grand Master insisted that she attempt to feel the presence of her soul.

"When you go without sleep," he explained, "you begin to feel isolated. The more isolated you are from your physical body, the better the chances of feeling your soul."

It didn't take long for Kari to prove the Grand Master's theory. As she meditated on a ledge one hundred feet above the canyon, she experienced a distinct floating sensation. Kari felt lighter, as the feelings swept through her entire body. "This is my soul!" she exclaimed. She stood up and jubilantly shouted, "I felt my soul!" allowing her words to echo within the surrounding rock walls.

After three days of sleep deprivation, Kari began experiencing the repercussions. There were bouts with dizziness, and her mind was bombarded with illusions:

enticing mirages that rushed in, clearly uninvited, but obviously designed to disrupt her peaceful state. As the images wove through Kari's consciousness, her physical senses were jolted into action, prompting her to savor and enjoy what she was witnessing.

The initial images were of delectable food. Graphic visualizations of Kari's favorite desserts flooded through her mind: white chocolate raspberry truffle cheesecake, homemade brownies with walnuts, luscious custards, and vanilla cream mousses laced with ribbons of caramel.

A parade of handsome men followed the tempting food imagery - some in three piece suits, some clad only in underwear, and still others frolicking stark naked. They surrounded Kari, wanting to please and satisfy her every whim; all beckoning her to make a choice. Their voices were soothing and inviting. "If you accept us, we will protect you. Choose one of us and you will have everything you want," they urged.

Kari's mind battled these inner voices, as the promises became more enticing. But were they too good to be true? A part of Kari craved excitement and change. She felt confident that the men beseeching her would be able to provide that.

Naturally, the Grand Master monitored Kari's every thought, knowing that deep down everybody possessed the same corrupting influences. "The key," he told Kari, "is to divorce yourself from these gnawing desires and not sanction their domination over you."

The images kept coming, assaulting Kari's mind like a relentless interrogation. As they grew even more elaborate and seductive, her resistance weakened. Suddenly, beautiful, radiant angels encircled her. After successfully grabbing Kari's undivided attention, the beings unveiled a majestic celestial garden. Inhabiting the lush, well-tended utopia, were an assortment of animals and a bevy of servants waiting to please her. A handsome gentleman stood beside a fountain, and summoned for Kari to join him. After one of the angels gracefully positioned a crown atop Kari's head, Kari finally succumbed to her greedy desires. Moments before she was about to enter the glorious garden, the Grand Master's voice severed her fantasy.

"Kari!" he shouted, causing the images to grow fuzzy.

"Stop encouraging these false desires!"

"I'm not doing anything," Kari protested.

"You need to give them up. You have to separate yourself from them."

"That's a lot easier said than done."

"They are illusions! They're not permanent. Don't allow yourself to be deceived by that world."

Stubbornly resistant, Kari continued her dissent.

"Look, this is a world I created, not you. Maybe you should let me decide."

"It's already decided. We're going to alter your method of training."

By now, the mirages had completely faded, becoming nothing more than a distant, fond memory. Kari looked closely at the Grand Master. "What now?"

"We're going to move our location. Perhaps all you need is a change."

"Where are we going?"

"To Wilson Mountain. It's a few miles north of here. When we get there I have a surprise for you."

"Surprise?" Kari asked, but judging by the Grand Master's impassive expression, she didn't harbor any illusions about what was in store for her.

The hike to Wilson Mountain consumed over two hours. On the way, the Grand Master maintained his distance from Kari, whose mind reeled with thoughts of what lay ahead.

* * * *

As the setting sun flushed streaking red streams across the peak of Wilson Mountain, the Grand Master led Kari to an isolated, wooded area. After instructing her to climb onto a protruding tree branch above, he proceeded to strap Kari's ankles tightly to it, causing her to literally hang upside down.

"You will remain like this overnight," he said.

"And what is the purpose of this?" Kari inquired.

"You shall see," he replied, before disappearing into the surrounding brush.

Feeling the blood rushing into her head, Kari struggled to control her breathing. Only with intense concentration was she able to maintain an adequate intake of oxygen. Fortunately for Kari, her weeks of training in Korea had prepared her for the physical demands of this particular exercise.

When night fell, and only the moon and stars lit the sky, Kari had a disturbing thought: She was all alone in the middle of nowhere, and couldn't release herself without assistance. What if the Grand Master didn't return? The shrieking howls of coyotes in the distance mocked her fears.

Though her anxieties had subsided, by the middle of the night, Kari was exhausted. Just as she was about to drift off to sleep, Kari felt the tree branch swinging out-of-control.

"Who is that?" she shouted, knowing full well, despite no visible evidence, that it was the Grand Master.

After regaining her composure, Kari conjured up vivid pictures in her mind. While foods no longer held the same appeal, Kari couldn't deny an attraction to one intense image that manifested in front of her: a young man, with long flowing hair, compassionate, yet fiery eyes, and a smooth, naked chest that glistened in the moonlight. Like an Adonis, he was Kari's ideal mate - pure perfection. Despite being captivated by his presence, Kari, assuming that this was yet another test, attempted to suppress her earthly desires. Once she achieved that end, he would disappear, Kari concluded.

But he didn't. Instead, Kari felt the warmth of his energy as his arms began caressing her. His touch was wonderful, and she reached out to embrace him. Kari's "Adonis" proceeded to rub his impeccable body against hers, all the while massaging her shoulders and buttocks. By this time, each of her nerve endings tingled - aching for more of his expert touch. Finally, his lips met hers and they kissed passionately. When she looked into his eyes, he smiled; a moment later he entered her. Kari's body shivered and shuddered; she lost all control as an intense, vibrating sensation swept through her entire being. It was the type of orgasm Kari had only fantasized about; now she eagerly surrendered to the exquisite pleasure. She thought it might last forever, until the Grand Master's voice once again resounded through her head, interrupting her rapture.

"What are you doing?" he demanded.

Desperately wanting to return to her inner world of ecstasy, where fantasy surpassed reality, Kari was frustrated.

"It's just an illusion," he told her.

Though Kari tried to adhere to the Grand Master's words, she quickly succumbed to her world of pleasure. Within seconds, the energy surged once again in Kari's second chakra, and her body shook out-of-control. But the moment was fleeting.

"Stop that!" the Grand Master scolded. "You're acting like a sex maniac! Don't allow these illusions to control you. They are not real. I promise you, there's a more incredible world than this. But first you must pass this test."

"What if I can't?" As Kari spoke, her body tingled with raw, sexual pleasure. Still enmeshed in her reverie, she tried to listen to the Grand Master, but to no avail. Finally, he untied her legs. When her body crashed to the ground with a loud thud, the impact instantly propelled her back to reality.

"Come with me," he ordered. "You've proved that you can't handle a simple test."

"You have no idea what I was feeling."

"Your desires are still controlling you."

* * * *

They arrived at the entrance to Slide Rock Park, as the sun slowly crept up from the horizon and introduced the fresh light of dawn onto the surrounding red earth. Kari trailed the Grand Master down a winding path, through a dense thicket of bushes and tangled knots of tree branches, until they came upon a scenic spot overlooking a flowing waterfall. The Grand Master paused a moment, then motioned for Kari to follow him down a steep embankment. When they reached the bottom, they cautiously crossed a bridge of rocks that led to an area directly beneath the flow of water.

"Take off your clothes," the Grand Master ordered.

"You're to stand directly under the waterfall and remain there for the next three days."

Although stupefied by his bizarre request, Kari complied with his wishes and began to disrobe.

"Can I leave these on?" Kari asked, pointing to her underwear.

"That's okay," he replied. "Now move to where you'll feel the full thrust of the water."

Knee deep in the creek, Kari edged her body out farther, until she was completely beneath the cascading water. The chill was instant, yet invigorating; Kari immediately felt the thumping pressure from the rushing liquid atop her bare back. It reminded her of therapeutic massage - like deep acupressure on her shoulders, it was intense, powerful and a little painful. As Kari adjusted the position of her body, she felt the water streaming onto her head, soothing and activating her crown chakra.

Fully aware of the powerful sensations Kari was experiencing, the Grand Master remained by her side. After a couple of hours had elapsed, Kari lost all sense of time. The relentless pounding of water immunized her to all other sounds. The next thing to disappear was Kari's conception of light. With absolute clarity, she was aware that everything in the physical world was just an illusion, all created from light and shadow. But what happens when that light disappears? Then everything is empty. Kari had entered that void, a vacuum in which she was directly linked to source. It was a euphoric, and for Kari, an unprecedented feeling. All five senses: light, sound, smell, taste, touch (including sexual desire), ceased to exist. There was no more inner struggle - Kari was cut off from all disturbances - both from outside and within.

Having fully obliterated any connection to her ego, Kari concluded that her body was not relevant any longer - it wasn't who she really was. Since she was only inhabiting it temporarily, Kari acknowledged that it made little difference which body she used. Her true identity had nothing to do with her physical form.

By the end of the day, after being beaten by the incessant barrage of water, Kari's skin commenced breathing.

"You must pass the waterfall test," he told her. "There's a Korean word for it - Kum Chok. Your twelve meridians and 365 acupressure points are opening completely. This will prepare you to receive heaven and earth energy. These numbers are no accident. Time and space consists of twelve months and 365 days. The human body is a microcosm for the universe of time and space, with its twelve meridians and 365 acupressure points. When you open these, you are fully ready to become one with God. God is completely neutral - God never emphasizes one day or one month. God is all; God is peace. The reason why God is impartial is because God exists in the shape of truth. However, God moves and acts through energy. When you are tense, you are out of sync with God; you're staying away from the laws of God. This causes a disturbance in your body energy which can trigger disease. By opening up your meridians and acupressure points, you can heal yourself."

After allowing Kari time to absorb the information, the Grand Master initiated the vertical circulation exercises. It took approximately an hour for Kari's energy to fully flow through her body. Repeating the exercise, Kari accomplished the same circuit in thirty minutes; now her energy streamed rapidly on its own. By the third repetition, it took only five minutes and after that, it transpired in the blink of an eye.

During most of the second day, the Grand Master left Kari alone. She seemed at peace under the waterfall. But by the start of the third day, the Grand Master prodded Kari to attempt something she had never done before: astral travel. When the suggestion was first broached, she was reluctant. Despite her relaxed state, Kari's ego momentarily asserted itself.

"What if I don't return?" she asked.

"Trust me. That could never happen."

"Besides, how would I get past this waterfall?"

"Even one of nature's wonders is only an illusion. Your spirit can go anywhere, through anything."

His assurances slowly assuaged Kari's doubts.

"Where should I go?" she inquired.

"Anywhere you'd like."

"I know. I'll visit Master Songwha in Korea."

Concentrating, Kari visualized herself there. After hearing a prolonged whooshing sound, she soared out of her body. In a matter of moments, her spirit floated high above the Ascension Center. It was the middle of the day, but Kari didn't recognize anyone outside until Kang Hoon suddenly appeared, standing directly beneath her. He peered skyward at Kari, as if he were aware of her presence. At that precise moment, Kari was ecstatic: She had traveled across all normal boundaries of time and space.

All it took was a thought, one thought, and in an instant, Kari returned to her body. The Grand Master nodded his approval at her accomplishment.

"Now don't you see, your spirit is free - to go anywhere you want, anytime you wish."

"It's like I'm suddenly becoming aware of everything I'm capable of," Kari exclaimed.

"You're like a baby chick learning to walk. But you must be careful. Just as the eagle can attack and kill the chick, there are negative energies ready to discourage and frighten you."

"What are you talking about?" Kari fearlessly replied.

"You just said I can go anywhere I want, anytime."

Without waiting for a retort, Kari zipped out of her body once again. This time she zoomed over her father's house in California and watched him in his backyard as he prepared the barbecue pit. She sent loving messages, hoping they would prompt him to think about her.

As she was about to return, Kari suddenly felt a heavy thickness in the atmosphere around her. Moments later, she found herself wreathed in a miasma of foggy mist. Kari couldn't see a thing until the filmy haze began to evaporate. A hideous face appeared out of the shadows; it snarled at a terrified Kari. The face belonged to a gargantuan monster. Fortunately, the Grand Master's voice soothed Kari's spirit.

"Kari," he commanded. "Remember, you are always protected. What you're seeing is merely an illusion, trying to make you afraid. Like all illusions, it can't hurt you if you don't let it. Surround yourself with loving thoughts - imagine white light encapsulating you, and the images will fade away."

The minute Kari visualized a radiant white light around her, the hideous being vanished. Quickly, Kari returned to her body.

"I guess I owe you an apology," she said.

"I was trying to warn you, but you took off too quickly," he replied.

"This is incredible," Kari exclaimed. "There are no limits anymore."

"You'll have plenty of time to explore. Right now I think you are ready for your final lesson."

"Really?"

"We'll return to where you initially found me in Fay Canyon. The energy there is ideal for this type of training."

"But I don't want to leave here. I love this place."

"You don't have to be here to achieve what you've just experienced. You can be anywhere."

She knew he was right. Knowing full well that this place would indelibly remain in her memory, Kari took one last wistful look around, then followed the Grand Master, as he ambled along the winding pathway.

When they arrived back at Fay Canyon, Owl From Heaven instructed Kari to find a spot she would feel most comfortable in. But after roaming around for over an hour, Kari realized that what the Grand Master had told her earlier was true. It didn't matter where they performed the exercise.

When she confessed this to the Grand Master, he smiled.

"Then I'll decide," he said quietly, before escorting Kari to a grassy knoll under a formidable red rock formation.

"I'm going to direct a meditation in which you will interact with the Cosmos. This is the final gate. We'll begin by circulating your energy and re-opening all your meridian points."

After assuming a relaxed position, it didn't take long for Kari's energy to flow freely. As her Kundalini moved rapidly within, she experienced her body opening itself up to energy encircling her from the outside: universal energy. She was merging with everything around her. Kari felt a purity of love that she had never before experienced - that love was directed towards the Grand Master.

As the feelings consumed her, Kari wanted him to know how much she loved him. Her thoughts soon merged with his; they were suddenly able to communicate without words. Kari wept because she knew Owl From Heaven reciprocated her feelings. What he had never been able to verbally articulate before, he more than made up for with this consummate communication of love. Owl From Heaven sent Kari a profound message with his energy: He would always love her. At that moment Kari knew she would do anything for him, even die, if necessary.

Comfortable with her newfound intimacy with the Grand Master, Kari tuned in to his thoughts.

"Try to find yourself inside," he said. "Discover your real self - the one that was created at the beginning of time, at the inception of the cosmos."

Kari struggled to decipher his meaning, which he thankfully repeated. He told her that hidden gates, one at the top of her head and one at the bottom of her feet, were now opening.

"Allow them to open wide," he added. "Visualize a huge opening at the top of your head, and then imagine an opening on the soles of your feet."

Assured that she was now in sync with him, Owl From Heaven continued. "Let's start with your crown chakra. Visualize the open space expanding even more. Something wants to enter it. Do you see it? It's a beautiful Pegasus that has been sent from heaven."

As Kari experienced an infusion of energy at the top of her head, she imagined the Pegasus. A silky coat adorned its body which radiated a glinting luster from the sun. Graceful wings enabled it to float in the air above her.

"Do you see it?" the Grand Master repeated. This time Kari nodded. "Shift your concentration to the soles of your feet. Feel the energy there. Do you see what is about to enter?"

Focusing all her attention on her feet, Kari saw a cloud of smoke. Out of the haze emerged a majestic-looking creature - a Golden Dragon. This gigantic reptile with scaly skin, razor-sharp claws and a serpentine tail, ejected a burst of fire from its mouth that scalded the air.

"It's a dragon," Kari exclaimed, momentarily startled.

"Try to picture both the Pegasus and the Dragon," he said. "They are destined to meet in the center of your body, around your Dahn Jon."

Kari experienced a dramatic energy shift in her body, and was keenly aware of an implosion taking place within, as the Pegasus spilled forth into her crown, while the dragon simultaneously streamed upwards through the soles of her feet.

"What's happening?" she asked.

"Look inside your Dahn Jon. Tell me what you see," Owl From Heaven instructed.

When Kari visualized her lower abdomen region, to her amazement, she saw the genesis of life. Kari was able to witness the miracle of birth - her birth, as she physically manifested in the form of a baby girl.

"It's a baby," Kari said, tears brimming her eyes.

When she studied the image further, she noted that a golden aura encircled the precious infant. Kari stared into its eyes, which were flooded with absolute joy, and gasped, "It's me."

"Do you realize what you just did?" Owl From Heaven asked. "You created yourself."

A soothing warmth washed over Kari, as she continued to stare at the baby's face, utterly transfixed. Suddenly, a bright star magically appeared over Kari. It travelled through her crown, down towards her Dahn Jon, and landed on top of the infant's head. This extremely bright, rainbow-colored light, quickly dissolved into the baby's crown - dispersing golden light energy throughout the infant's body.

"Keep watching the star," Owl From Heaven commanded. "Look inside the baby. Do you see where it landed?"

Kari nodded.

"The star will remain permanently within the baby's Dahn Jon. That star is your connection to the universe. Heaven is now inside you."

Kari didn't know how to respond. While she felt lighter and profoundly different, she was in a state of absolute awe.

"Look at yourself. Try to see who you really are."

"Who am I?" Kari said out loud. But when she turned and looked for the Grand Master he was already gone. Following his instruction, she attempted to look at herself, but it was uncommonly bright, almost blinding. For a long time she remained sitting, absorbing everything that had just occurred. The universe was indeed within her; the inner cosmos resided in her Dahn Jon, while the outer cosmos was the galaxy surrounding her.

"I can't feel myself," she exclaimed.

Although Kari was able to see her body, she physically couldn't feel it. Even though her body was still there, there was no more "her" in the world. Kari's spirit had merged into source completely. Like a river, it had temporarily existed on its own. But as a river eventually flows back into the ocean, indeed, so had Kari's spirit returned to its origin.

At that exact moment, the Grand Master reappeared, smiling in recognition. Kari had passed the final test. By not being able to look at herself she had achieved enlightenment.

Waves of total gratitude and appreciation washed through Kari's entire being, prompting her to turn reverently towards Owl From Heaven. She spontaneously bowed before him, fully to the ground, three times.

At that moment, he swelled with pride. "Ah, I have completed my mission."

Kari noticed how radiant his face became and knew in that moment, that he had chosen to stay with God.

Owl From Heaven proudly watched as Kari assumed the lotus position and began meditating. By monitoring her thoughts, he knew Kari was no longer part of the physical world. Knowing it was all an illusion, she had completely eliminated her former attachments. What Kari felt now was a profound, consummate connection to the universe.

Kari remained locked in her meditative state the remainder of the day. Night turned to dawn, but it didn't matter: Kari had lost all sense of time. She no longer wanted to eat; she had no need for sleep. Instead, Kari only wanted to savor her blissful thoughts.

After three full days, her mind still connected to the energy of the universe, Kari received a message that originated deep within the recesses of her mind. It was a message from God. The voice was full of love. "I have loved you like I love everything in the world. Do you care about the world like I do?" the voice asked.

When Kari didn't answer, the voice commenced. "Do you know how many spirits have helped you reach this point? You are in debt to them. Of course you are under no obligation, but think of all the people who need your help."

"What am I supposed to do?" Kari inquired.

"You have a choice. You can ascend and never come back to this physical dimension or you can return and help others."

As waves of gratitude carried her to thoughts of service, Kari didn't hesitate. "I want to return," she instinctively said. "Definitely, I want to return."

Moments after making her declaration, Owl From Heaven appeared. Sensing his presence, Kari opened her eyes to face him. He brandished a proud smile.

"You are finally ready to receive your mission from God."

"How?" Kari asked.

"You are following in the footsteps of all the sages throughout history. Just like Jesus and Buddha - when they reached enlightenment, they knew they had to receive a message. Both went off to fast for long periods of time. For you I would recommend going to the Bak Du mountain which borders China and North Korea. That's where the Manuscript first appeared. And that is where you shall receive your message from God."

"Will you come with me?"

"You don't need my guidance anymore. You are now on the same level as me."

Instinctively, Kari knew he was right. And, if she needed to return to Korea to receive her message, she would go immediately. Nothing else mattered in her life.

Mt. Bak Du

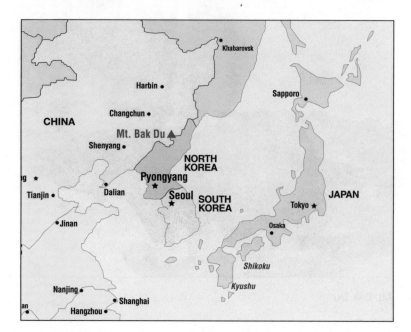

Mt. Bak Du

Mt. Bak Du is the tallest mountain in the Korean peninsula. Its summit elevation is 9,003 feet above sea level. 'Bak Du' means 'White Head'. It was named 'Mt. Bak Du' because its top is covered by white ash from volcanic eruption. It has been a spiritual and holy place for Koreans. There is a huge lake named 'Chon Ji' ('Heaven Lake') at the top of the mountain. 'Chon Ji' is 1,260 feet deep at its deepest point and 8.95 miles around. The lake contains 1,950,000,000 tons of water.

Chapter **8**

While she knew she would dearly miss Owl From Heaven, Kari's sense of loss was obviated by her desire to discover her destiny. On the long trek out of Fay Canyon leading into West Sedona, Kari reflected back on recent events. She deliberated on how quickly a person's life can undergo a radical transformation - how it can happen when you least expect it.

After scooping up a quarter from the side of the road, Kari called Gil the moment she arrived back into town. Delighted to hear from her, Gil raced over to pick her up.

After she climbed into the seat across from him, Gil stared directly at her. "It's good to see you," he finally said. "You look different."

"What do you mean?" Kari asked.

"I don't know how to describe it, other than to say it's

like you're glowing - more so than usual," he replied with a grin.

Kari smiled. On the drive out to Kit's ranch, she briefly encapsulated her experiences, leading up to her need to travel to China immediately.

"What's over there?" Gil asked.

"Hopefully some answers."

"Wait, you just spent over three weeks out there with the Grand Master and you're still looking for answers?"

"Since I started this adventure, I've gone wherever I've needed to go. I'm not about to stop now."

At the ranch, Kit greeted Kari with a strong embrace; it was almost as if he didn't want to let go. Taking the initiative, Kari slowly eased out of his arms.

"You're vibrating at such a high level," he commented. "I feel elevated just standing here next to you. Please come in and tell me all about this Grand Master who helped you achieve this state."

"I will," Kari said, "but first I have to make a reservation."

After Kari contacted a local travel agent to secure a flight out the following morning, Gil graciously offered to drive her to the Phoenix airport.

"Thank you," Kari said.

"Hey, it's my pleasure."

Kari studied Gil's face and smiled mysteriously, as if she tuned into something - a secret that couldn't be revealed at that exact moment.

* * * *

That night Kari regaled Kit and Gil with elaborate descriptions of her adventures. By the end of the evening, Kit addressed Kari with a reverence that surprised even Gil.

"It takes a very special person to accomplish what you're doing. I've seen many people flock into Sedona seeking enlightenment. Virtually all of them fail because of their wayward attachments and negativity."

"I was lucky to have the Grand Master," Kari modestly interjected.

"He was also lucky to have such a great student. He fulfilled his dharma by helping you. Now it's time for you to discover yours. I envy the experiences you're going to have."

"Anybody could do what I'm doing," Kari said.

"In theory that's true, but very few can pass the necessary tests. I never thought I would live to actually spend time in the presence of a genuine Master. Kari, I have no doubt you will complete your journey. When you do, my one request is that you tell me what you discover when you get there."

"I will," Kari responded, "I promise."

* * * *

Kari's flight to Bejing, China consumed almost an entire day. Fortunately, she was able to spend most of the trip in a state of deep meditation, causing her to feel relaxed and invigorated once she arrived.

After passing through customs, Kari made arrangements to take a commuter plane for the short flight to Yun Byun, which was located near the base of Bak Du mountain. By the time she arrived it was nightfall, so Kari checked into a modest motel, where she spent the night in a cozy log cabin.

In the morning, after obtaining directions, Kari headed out with one clear goal: to get to the very apex of the Bak Du mountain, which bordered North Korea and China. There she would not only find the highest lake on earth (everybody called it "Heaven Lake"), but also the sacred location where the Manuscript was first discovered.

By not stopping to rest, it took Kari half a day to reach the mountain area. The closer she got, the more she quickened her pace; it was as if she was being drawn by an invisible force. The force manifested as a mysterious, sacred energy that Kari felt all around her body.

Gazing at the crest of the mountain ramparts, Kari instinctively knew that this mountain was robust and holy. "The healthiest mountain in the world," is how Owl From Heaven had described it to her. What insured that heartiness was the powerful, ubiquitous water energy that permeated the mountain; having water energy on top is the ideal situation in nature. This perfectly balances the fire energy below. Similarly, the human body ideally should pose the same balance - cool water energy flowing through the head, while fire energy remained in the body.

Using her newfound powers, Kari projected her spirit outside her flesh, allowing it to float high above the peak of the mountain. Peering downward, Kari instantly felt like she was at the very center of the earth. Continuing to stare down at the mountaintop, Kari permitted her spirit to travel into the distant past - back 15 million years - to a time when this particular mountain was the highest in the world.

* * * *

Returning to the present, Kari solemnly knelt down before the mountain and closed her eyes. Pressing her hands together, she earnestly prayed to the mountain and to all the spirits that had gathered around her. Kari's supplication was interrupted when she felt a distinct presence looming over her. Standing up, Kari found herself staring at an unusual-looking, older man. Dressed in a white tunic, he had snow-white hair, a white beard, and carried an oak walking stick. What distinguished this gentleman was his face: a peach-colored tint, with rosy cheeks, that radiated sprightly bubbling energy, more akin to that of a teenager.

Speaking telepathically, in a voice laced with joy, he greeted Kari. "Oh, you finally came," he said.

"Who are you?" she asked.

"I am the guardian spirit of this mountain," he replied. "And who are you?"

"My name is Kari. I was sent here by my Native American Master in Sedona. His name is..."

But before Kari could complete her statement, the man asked, "Owl From Heaven?"

"How did you know?"

"Owl From Heaven first came here one hundred years ago. That's when he received his mission from heaven and chose to serve in the United States."

"One hundred years ago?"

"We all appear younger than we are," he said with a smile.

"Owl From Heaven predicted long ago that the United States would be a colossal world power, but he also knew it was a country that would eventually reach spiritual awakening," he continued. "So every ten years he visits here to get inspired. It was during his last visit that he predicted your appearance here today. I have been waiting for you."

Kari was touched by this man's genuine warmth towards her, and not the least bit surprised that these predictions had been made. Indeed, she suddenly felt that Owl From Heaven was a part of her, surrounding her in spirit, and existing within her as a shining, radiant light.

"Well, I'm glad I made it," Kari exclaimed. "The energy around here is very powerful."

"Why don't I direct you to the waterfall? That's where you will find the portal."

"Portal?" Kari asked.

"Owl From Heaven didn't mention that? Well, he probably knew I would show you the way."

"What exactly is a portal?"

"It's a gateway to another dimension. And while there are portals all over the world, in my opinion, this gate allows the easiest access."

"Really?" Kari said, intrigued.

"Trust me, it's where you'll find the answers you're looking for," he said, before pointing down a steep path that led through a ravine in the mountain.

"Why don't you come with me?" Kari offered.

"No, this is something you must discover yourself. When you get to the waterfall, trust your instincts, and you will find Dae boo Jeon."

"What is that?" Kari asked.

"Oh, that's Korean for the Holy Place. When you get there you will quickly discover why it was given that name."

"Well, what am I waiting for?" she responded. "Thank you for the information. Maybe we'll speak again."

"I would like that. Please know that I am praying for you."

Kari headed down the path that snaked through the ravine. It didn't take long for her to hear the crashing of water. Continuing in the direction of the flowing, plummeting sounds, Kari reached a ledge overlooking the waterfall. As she followed it, Kari realized it led directly behind the cascading water. Staring into the glistening stream, she felt the presence of the guardian spirit. His voice commanded her attention. "Kari, you need to enter the waterfall. Walk right through it. Don't be afraid."

Almost hypnotized by his rapturous voice, Kari took a few steps into the wall of water. When the ledge ended abruptly, she began a free fall. Moments after her descent began, Kari magically passed through what felt like a shift in energy - the portal - and found herself inside a vast cave.

She was standing, though on what she couldn't say. An amethyst mist swirled and roiled about her feet. Kari gazed around with wonderment. It was like she had landed on another planet - or perhaps, arrived in heaven. Pleasant smells triggered her to breath in the pristine air. Bright, colorful flowers dotted a luscious green landscape, that seemed to float around her like an island amidst clouds. Roaming through this peaceful "Garden of Eden" was an assortment of animals: tigers, white cranes, lions, peacocks, horses. Mingling freely with the animals were people, all of them dressed in white clothing. Many of them telepathically greeted Kari, who noticed that she too was clad in a white tunic. "This must be the Holy Place," Kari thought to herself.

All communication was simultaneous and pure. Kari could hear everyone at the same time. The instant one person had a thought, the others joined in the process; everybody was connected. A loving, warm feeling caressed Kari as she realized that they were all her friends.

Meandering around, Kari quietly observed what the beings were doing. She discovered that at this level many of them spent a good part of their time responding to people's prayers. Was everyone here an angel? Kari mused. She noticed that some of the beings were sending UFOs back to earth. With absolute clarity it dawned on her: Alien beings were nothing more than people, like herself, from another dimension or time. What was being projected were simply light and sound waves - this was the reason most UFOs were perceived as bright lights!

Kari spent most of the day observing the diverse

activities. While she freely tuned in to everyone's thoughts, no one pressed her to participate. When a large, white tiger approached, Kari felt only pure love emanating from this glorious animal, which playfully nuzzled against her. She sat beneath a tree, whose leaves glowed like emeralds; the tiger fell asleep in her lap. She observed the rhythmic, peaceful breathing of the majestic creature, as she ran her fingers through its silky coat.

Once the tiger awakened, Kari interacted with the other animals. A white crane made eye contact with her, and Kari followed the long-legged creature, until it gracefully lofted itself into the air. It led Kari to the entrance of a marble structure that resembled a divine palace. Clearly the bird was giving Kari a message: "This is where you are meant to go."

The crane flew beyond the silvery clouds and Kari shifted her gaze back to the palatial structure. It was surrounded by a scintillating pond which possessed the clarity and shine of a flawless diamond. Something inside Kari erupted with recognition: "This is my home," she thought, while climbing the stone steps leading inside.

Once she entered, Kari experienced a moment of absolute bliss. The atmosphere consisted of pure energy - the walls and ceiling surrounding her all vibrated to a certain wavelength. While they were visible to the eye, a person could easily pass right through them. It was as if the structure was intact, but not really - tangible, yet intangible, or perhaps something undefinable in between.

All of Kari's thoughts were suddenly focused - a clarity had come upon her within this ethereal world. She realized that her spirit required all her recent struggles; everything that had transpired within her life up until now had been necessary to enable her to arrive here - in this place and time. Knowing she was on the brink of discovering her mission, Kari felt only unadulterated joy.

Twirling around, she noticed there were beings everywhere. Many indulged themselves with lavish platters of food and flowing beverages. Others played various games, like cards, chess and checkers. All seemed entrenched in a state of permanent, all-encompassing peace. While some invited Kari to join them, still others motioned for her to enter another room, down at the back of a long, marble hallway.

Messages splayed through Kari's consciousness. She sifted through them and concluded there were two distinct groups of people here: One planned to remain in this palace permanently, while the other was here temporarily to receive their divine message before returning to earth to fulfill their spiritual missions. Intuitively, recognizing she was part of the latter group, Kari proceeded along the magnificent corridor leading into the back room. It was there that she began a process of reorientation.

Everybody around her was ardently preparing for their return to earth. Some, who had recently died knew they would be reborn as babies; they were in the process of selecting their future parents. Others, like Kari, had entered this place through one of the many portals scattered throughout the world. They were here for enlightenment purposes only. After they received their divine message, they would return to their former bodies.

Assimilating herself into that group, Kari quickly became aware of the meticulous way everyone was fortifying themselves for their departure. Primarily, they were vicariously experiencing the gamut of mankind's emotions. Only by tuning in to the burdens of human beings could one comprehend the imminent need for a spiritual renaissance. By acutely sensing the dearth of spirituality in current society, these beings were motivated to attempt utter salvation.

This was an education that Jesus, Buddha, Socrates and other sages had undergone before they formulated their own individual insights. Many of their spirits hovered about, allowing Kari to become aware of their prominent achievements. As each sage appeared in front of Kari, for the first time, she fathomed why their messages were so profound.

When Kari confronted the radiant spirit of Jesus, she understood why he preached that the primary responsibility of all people was unconditional love. Jesus emphasized the need to love thy neighbor, forgive all transgressions, and attempt to live a pure life.

Next, Buddha's spirit manifested itself. Kari realized that Buddha's lasting achievement was to make mankind aware of the holy thing that exists within everyone.

Finally, Socrates appeared. He had clashed with the ancient Greeks because they thought the source of the cosmos was outside of man - residing in the elements: wind, fire, water and earth. But Socrates, despite widespread incredulity, had emphasized man's significance; only human beings were responsible for their spiritual lives.

For a few minutes, the spirits of these prominent sages remained in close proximity. Kari felt their energies vibrating; she sensed they would always be a part of her. After the sages departed, she realized they had left her with a legacy of spiritual understanding. They paved the way for other sages to be recognized: Three prominent Korean ancestors introduced themselves to Kari, before explaining their role in history.

Initially, Hanin appeared. He was the first person to receive messages from the old Manuscript. The divine message came from heaven, which means it originated from within his own brain cells. Even at that time, Hanin concluded that heaven is the part of the brain that man doesn't use.

Next came Han Woong, a Korean who established a holy village of approximately 3,000 people, all of whom diligently adhered to the tenets of the Manuscript. The first rainbow family, they lived a utopian life in an area near Bak Du mountain.

Finally, Dahn Gun appeared to Kari. In his time he was a renowned teacher and lawmaker for the tribes living on the Korean Peninsula. Inspired by the Manuscript, Dahn Gun established the first true democracy on Earth. His reign ended in the year 2240 BC.

All these men communicated one profound message to Kari: Live by the Manuscript. Before they departed, they infused her with feelings of love. These ancestors had all been praying for someone like Kari to resurrect the true meaning of the Manuscript.

As Kari reflected on her encounters, she realized the

significance of her role. The Earth's soul was screaming out for people to change their way of life. To assist in that process, there was a dire need for sages to cooperate in bringing about widespread enlightenment.

It suddenly dawned on Kari why entire civilizations - like the Mayans - had suddenly disappeared from Earth years ago. While the Mayans were living in accordance with the Manuscript, everybody around them was succumbing to greedy desires and physical needs. To escape the encroaching materialism, the entire Mayan group had ascended; now they were living harmoniously in this divine world - this palace that Kari had recently discovered. Fortunately, many of them, acknowledging the grave need on Earth, were preparing to return and assist in the necessary transformation of man's consciousness.

Not wanting to waste another moment, Kari decided that she longed to return to earth so she could serve. After following the corridor back into the main room, she exited the marble building, and passed through some lush foliage to an area where the white crane seemed to be waiting for her.

It studied Kari's face, before making a beeline for a small cave. Feeling a strong energy force beckoning her, Kari followed the crane inside the enclosure. She was abruptly pulled forward; sucked into the magnetic core of the portal. Within seconds, Kari stood on a plateau, peering back at the magical waterfall.

Still charged with divine energy, Kari instinctively began to climb higher. Though it was getting dark and a blustery wind pummeled her, Kari was determined to reach the top of the mountain. It was there, Kari knew, that she would finally receive her mission.

When she arrived at her destination, Kari stood tall, gazing out upon Heaven Lake below. A light mist rose in the air; through the haze, Kari felt the presence of guardian spirits all around her. She was unaware that angels flock to be present when a soul is on the verge of reaching its full awakening. The presence of these celestial beings caused feelings of awe to stir within Kari, and she bowed her head. Two angels lifted her up and escorted her to a protruding stone. It was shaped like a circular satellite dish and served as a platform that faced Heaven Lake. After easing her onto its glistening surface, the angels disappeared.

Feeling a stillness in the air, Kari tuned in to the energy around her. A humming sound commenced, slowly increasing in tone until the vibration was palpable.

Transfixed by the sound, Kari only peripherally noticed the appearance of four colossal, crystal pillars, which magically descended from the sky. Sent to protect Kari, they lodged themselves into the ground, encircling her.

Surrounded by these lofty, gleaming monoliths, Kari continued to be mesmerized by the vibrational sounds that kept increasing in magnitude. Locked into a trance-like state, she didn't notice when eight more crystal pillars appeared. Falling to the earth, they formed a circle around the first four pillars.

Moments after they wedged themselves into the

ground, the humming sounds ceased. All was silent. The angels who originally accompanied Kari remained at a safe distance behind the pillars - it was forbidden for them to enter this newly created sacred space. They could only observe and pray.

As Kari looked at the surface of the lake before her, she recognized it as the Second Gate - the "Heaven Palace."

Entering the waterfall had only been the First Gate. That was merely preparation for what was to come.

Kari was in a state of absolute peace and tranquility when she observed flames shoot up from the glassy surface of Heaven Lake. Fiery lines appeared in definite arrangements, clearly depicting the symbols of the ancient Manuscript. As the flames shimmered and reflected off the glossy swells of water, Kari's body experienced the distinct vibrational sounds of the Manuscript. The vibrations were so powerful, they pierced her body, prompting their movement into every cell. Like the crescendo of an orchestra, the deafening sounds overwhelmed Kari, until she literally became them. The first four symbols of the Manuscript were now prominently illuminated before Kari's eyes. All around her, enlightened souls were unilaterally chanting. The chants finally abated when the voice of God began to speak.

"There is no beginning. No end. Every creature came from one. There is no end and no beginning. The source is nothing but human consciousness, whose original brightness is that of the sun."

As more symbols rose up from the water in dancing flames, the message continued. But Kari was barely hearing the words. Instead, her entire body felt the message, deeply, at the core of her soul.

"From one there is three. Three is heaven, earth and the human being. The origin of three is from eternal source. You never die,"

As Kari's body vibrated, the following words resounded within her: "You are God. You are God. My purpose, my mind is Love. You are God. God is inside you. God is Love. You are love."

A divine presence swept through Kari's body. Images flashed through her mind, as if a movie were playing. She saw the national flag of Israel, then harrowing visions of violence assaulted her consciousness.

"The country of Israel was established and based upon my will," God said. "But it didn't last. I had great expectations, but people lost their way. This makes me sad."

After that Kari witnessed the birth of the United States; the words from the Declaration of Independence sifted through her head.

"In the United States, over two hundred years ago, they formed a country based on democracy. They had the right idea, but man soon corrupted the original intent. In the process, they decimated the Native Americans in an attempt to expand their country. Despite a constitution espousing the equality of all mankind, a Civil War was fought because some people felt they were better than others by the sheer illusion of the color of their skin. But the major problem was that people wouldn't allow divine source to guide them. They let their egos control everything. This makes me so sad."

More images of countries flooded into Kari's mind: Japan, Korea, England. "In Japan, they misused my name," God continued. "Their top leader is called Heaven King, but they are using my name in vain. In Korea, they still carry the legacy of the original Manuscript, but no one treats it with the proper reverence. They denigrate it, and therefore, they deny my will, because my will is the Manuscript. This makes me sad. England once used my name to conquer half the earth, killing countless innocent people in the process. Invoking my name, they fought many battles, but they never abided by my wishes. This too makes me sad. All the nations of the world have done terrible things in the name of God. It seems that religion is only a source of great conflict between people and nations. Why do people do such horrible things in my name? I am love. There is no conflict inside of me. Can you see that?"

After listening with rapt attention, Kari succumbed to feelings of melancholy herself. But she knew God was not looking for her sympathy; he only wanted her to understand his immense disappointment in mankind.

"Through the ages, I have sent many sages and phi-losophers to spread my word - Jesus, Moses, Buddha, Mohammed, Socrates and Thoreau. All of them have made a difference, but many of their messages have been distorted. People ignore what they don't feel comfortable with. Now it is your turn Kari - it is time for a woman to understand the essence of my teaching and spread my word. Females have always been under a lot of pressure and conflict, trying to maintain equal standing in a world dominated by man and patriarchal religions. You, having chosen to express in this lifetime as a woman, already understand how difficult things are. But that cannot stop you. It is time for everyone - female and male - to realize my will. There is no difference between you - all females and all males are my children. It doesn't matter what race you are: white, black, red, yellow. Remember that you are all my children. All I ask is that you never corrupt my will. Never! My will is love. Love for everyone. There is no race, no sex, no nation - no separation, only love. This is your mission, Kari. You must let all human beings know my will. Can you do that?"

"Yes, I will!" Kari stated emphatically.

"I am confident you will succeed where others have not," God continued. "It is time for me to show you what the future holds for mankind. Would you like to see that?"

"Yes."

"This is an optimistic future, but it's one you can help bring about. The first thing to consider is the ideal family. Parents must become spiritual parents, which will make it easier for them to understand and raise their children. In today's world, parents lack the necessary enlightenment to truly love their children. This is why most children lose respect for their parents as they grow older. They are seeking that love, that energy, which can only come from enlightened souls. That is why you have so much drug use and rampant sex among your youth. They are searching for love - true love, that can only be found within themselves and their connection with source. But they don't know that because there's no one who can teach them. Their parents never learned that simple truth either. That's why you have high divorce rates, sexual indiscretions and affairs, workaholics, alcoholics, drug abusers and overeaters. People are terribly confused and lost. The way to solve this is to educate this generation of parents. When all parents have gone through the necessary spiritual enlightenment, they will begin to raise their children with a deeper, more nourishing love and understanding of truth. Once those energy cravings are understood and fulfilled, the youth of the world will respect their parents and elders, instead of rebelling against them out of disillusionment. Parents will no longer feel that they own their children. Instead, they will realize that their children are beings just like they are; in many cases, a child's spirit may even be older and wiser than that of its parents. No matter, all beings chose which parents they want to incarnate through, depending on which path they need to take - which lessons need learning or teaching."

In Kari's mind, she saw families living in perfect harmony. There was an absence of conflict and hostility; no longer was the dysfunctional path the most popular option. It all starts with love: Spiritual parents who love themselves are more readily able to garner their children's respect and love. This begins a positive cycle.

Next, Kari was treated to depictions of future politicians. People were no longer motivated by the talons of power; instead, politicians were driven by love, not ego. They governed their countries with compassion. Their primary goal was to manifest God's will.

In conjunction with this, Kari imagined a future where religions no longer divided people. Instead of stubbornly clinging to their individual faiths, people arrived at the stark realization that all religions had one core aspect in common: the Truth. This Truth dictated that all people have the same divine essence: the holy thing within.

"The future also holds a place where people must return to a pure love for sports. Through time, sports have been corrupted by money and violence. Once sports were used by man to express their love for God. Now, people either don't participate, or, they have ulterior motives. They get in shape primarily to satisfy their own egos. Their physical bodies, and their energy, have become corrupted. People need sports to express my will, my love. Physical exercise is necessary every day for people to balance their spiritual nature," God proclaimed.

"Finally, there are the future artists," God continued.

"They will help spread the word by expressing my divine nature in their work. Artists will return to a pure love of their craft. There is no reason all mankind cannot participate in different kinds of art. Art purifies the soul."

As Kari envisioned this future, she saw the most exquisite paintings, she heard the most beautiful music, and she felt the sheer joy of the participants. Art was for everyone! Moreover, Kari concluded, it helped inspire man to understand the Truth.

Kari saw what education would be like in the future. She observed teachers cheerfully enlightening students about their divine nature. Only by acknowledging their spiritual side, would future students be ready to contribute in a positive manner to society.

"Now you have seen the future," God stated. "This is the world I desire, and I hope it is one you want as well. Remember, my energy is your energy. My will is your will. My mind is your mind. There is no difference between you and me. Now, do you understand your mission?"

"Yes!" Kari shouted. "I am ready."

"Remember, I will always be here for you, to protect you and guide you. But it is your time now. You must enlighten people to this message. Please meditate on everything I have told you today. If you need more guidance, I will be here. But now it is time for me to go."

"Where are you?" Kari suddenly asked.

"I am everywhere. I am inside you, in the vast oceans, in the mountains, in the stars. I am everywhere."

"Who are you?"

"I am heaven and earth energy."

It wasn't just the words that affected Kari; it was their vibration. The instant she grasped their full meaning, Kari understood on a profound level that she too was heaven and earth energy. Kari had reached the end of her spiritual odyssey.

As this message settled in, an explosive sound erupted around her and reverberated inside her head. Instinctively, Kari realized she was experiencing the birth of the universe - the "Big Bang" - and as the powerful sounds slowly abated, they gave way to a chorus of blaring trumpets. The sky overhead opened up, releasing scores of lotus flowers. Flocks of angels danced amidst the

raining blossoms, which, reflecting off an expansive rainbow, glowed myriad colors. As Kari savored these sights,
a congregation of holy animals arrived. They came from all
four directions: a turtle from the north; a dragon from the
east, a white tiger from the west, and a red pegasus from
the south.

Within moments, all sages throughout time arrived to
witness this event and congratulate Kari. After their tele-
pathic messages streamed into her mind, Kari knew she
would never be alone again - she would always have their
protection and support.

An enormous expanse of bright light, two to three
miles in width, swept over Kari, encircling her. After she
incubated within the radiant light for a few moments, it
disappeared.

As strikingly vivid and powerful as the images por-
trayed in a Michelangelo painting, a melange of beings,
animals, plants and angels formed a circle around Kari.
Simultaneously, they bowed to her, displaying their total
respect for what she had achieved. Even some fallen angels
appeared because what Kari had accomplished was
beyond the duality of good and evil. This holy gathering
symbolized and celebrated the culmination of a spirit discovering heaven within.

Kari basked in this sea of joy and love until a distinct
stillness penetrated the air, as all that had assembled
disappeared. The crystal pillars vanished. No more flames
licked at the water; the lake looked calm.

Kari thought about climbing back down the mountain,
but quickly dismissed that notion. She needed time to

reflect on the message she had just received. Assuming the lotus posture, Kari began meditating. Still feeling a keen connection with God, she felt anything was possible.

Her spirit eased out of her body and began traveling all over the planet. But this wasn't enough. Kari soon realized that she had the capacity to navigate her spirit into other dimensions. The time line of past, present and future had been destroyed. There were no limits to where Kari could travel; no boundaries to the universe. Floating through space, she lost all sense of time. She realized how easy it would be to merge her spirit with the universal energy, to dissolve herself back into source. But knowing that this would not help to achieve her ultimate purpose, she returned back to her body.

Kari focused her concentration on the world she used to be a part of. Instead of a paradise, she realized that it was a civilization spiraling toward self-destruction. Her thoughts brought tears to her eyes, and her crying continued, unabated, for the rest of the day. She understood that enlightenment was the seed of tears; these tears were necessary for purging her soul.

But the sorrow soon turned to bliss, as Kari grew determined to fulfill her destiny. She spent the next couple days visualizing the future that God had laid out for her, fixating those very images in her mind. Her goal was to do everything in her power to achieve that ideal world.

Chapter 9

After climbing down from Bak Du mountain, Kari began germinating a cocoon of determination inside her soul - as the released butterfly invites people to appreciate its beauty, Kari would invite everyone to enter the heaven that existed within themselves. Still, she knew it wouldn't be easy for one primary reason: All over the world people steadfastly clung to old belief systems. However, Kari wouldn't let anything deter her. For the first time, she knew what she would be doing for the rest of her life; Kari finally acknowledged a divine purpose to her existence.

On the flight back to the United States, Kari had graphic dreams of Sedona. At one point she soared out of her body, hovering high above the sacred land; without warning, she was swept into the distant past where she observed Native Americans performing an elaborate fertility ceremony. Momentarily distracted, one Native American chief peered skyward in Kari's direction; their eyes locked. Knowingly, he lofted a blessing towards her that was felt as an adrenaline rush through Kari's entire body: He was praying for her success in the future.

Kari made the decision to return immediately to Sedona where both Gil and Kit were delighted to welcome her back. When he first laid eyes on her, Kit was speechless; finally, visibly touched by the efflux of her energy, he smiled.

"Gil, I hope you're aware that what you're witnessing is a miracle. For someone from our culture to undergo such a radical spiritual transformation, in such a short time, is truly astonishing," he said.

Into the wee hours of the night, both Kit and Gil listened to Kari's stories. She vividly recreated everything that had occurred, culminating with her message from God.

"You became Source, didn't you?" Kit asked.

"Yes, and it was wonderful."

"I've always wondered." Kit speculated, "that if someone were to truly reach that state of nirvana, what would be their incentive to return to the physical dimension?"

"That's easy," she began. "There is only one reason - to serve mankind. I can't imagine a greater joy in life."

"When will you start? What will you do?" Gil asked.

"I've already begun," Kari stated, "and who better to be my first student, than you," she continued with a smile.

"Knowing Gil like I do, you've got your work cut out for you," Kit joked.

"I don't see it as work. It would be my pleasure," Kari added, before turning back to Gil. "Why don't you get some sleep so you'll be fresh in the morning?"

Truly touched, Gil embraced Kari before heading off to bed. While he slept, Kari slipped outside to gaze up at the sky. She focused on one prominent star which notably flickered, blinking rainbow colors, before darting away. Realizing this light had undoubtedly been sent from the First Gate, Kari prayed that more of those spirits would soon return to Earth to join her. She implored those beings to stop their interdimensional games and begin the process of utilizing their time and energy to help enlighten others.

* * * *

The next morning, Kari and Gil climbed to the top of Bell Rock. Kari ascended gracefully. Released from all her former fears and insecurities, it was as if she were gliding up the side of the formation. For the first time, Kari noticed a distinct healing energy emanating from its surface. As Gil struggled beside her, Kari analyzed his energy. While he had a generous, compassionate nature, Gil's aura was riddled with holes. But Kari knew that Gil, like everyone else, had the potential to travel the same journey she had. All he needed was the necessary motivation, which she believed existed, and guidance from the proper teacher.

When they reached the summit, Kari engaged Gil in a meditation exercise. After easing him into a relaxed state, she used her fingertips to infuse his body with her divine energy. As a warmth encapsulated Gil, Kari knew he was experiencing the sensation of universal energy for the first time.

Later, when he opened his eyes, Gil was euphoric.

"That was unbelievable," he exclaimed.

"So you'll be my first student?" Kari asked, already knowing his answer.

"Are you kidding? I kinda feel that's why we met."

Kari smiled at him.

"Together, we're going to save the world, aren't we?" Gil asked.

"We're going to try," Kari responded.

Moving to the edge of the plateau that overlooked Sedona, Kari's thoughts turned optimistic. She knew that one highly vibrating person had the capability to enlighten the masses. "Yes," she shouted, "one person can trigger the awakening process for all. One individual can indeed make a profound difference!"

Grateful that she had been chosen for this mission, Kari inwardly smiled: She knew her bliss would soon be shared by all.

THE END

Appendix

Chon Bu Kyong
(The Scripture of Heavenly Code)

Dahnhak Exercise

CHON BU KYONG
THE SCRIPTURE OF HEAVENLY CODE

天符經

一始無始一析三極無
盡本天一一地一二人
一三一積十鉅無匱化
三天二三地二三人二
三大三合六生七八九
運三四成環五七一妙
衍萬往萬來用變不動
本本心本太陽昂明人
中天地一一終無終一

INTRODUCTION

Chon Bu Kyong, The Scripture of Heavenly Code, is the oldest Korean scripture. This scripture teaches Han, the ultimate oneness, its basic trinity, Heaven, Earth and Human, and the relationship among them. It includes the basic principles of the Cosmos, Creation, Evolution, Growth, Consummation and the principle of human completion.

No agreement has been reached about the meaning of the scripture. However, most scholars who study it agree that it has a fundamental truth which all philosophies, sciences and religions seek to explain. The scripture is composed of 81 characters. It is unique in that it contains no explanatory or descriptive comment. Not unlike a puzzle, the main part of the scripture consists of numbers that express the principles of the Cosmos.

ORIGIN

The origin of the scripture has a long, mysterious history. Over 9000 years ago, it was passed by word-of-mouth. The divine king of ancient Korea who built the City of Light 6000 years ago ordered it to be recorded in Nokdo letters. Nokdo is one of the ancient writing systems in which each letter resembles the footprint of a deer. Nokdo was the first written form of the scripture. From the wisdom gained through the scripture, the king taught his people the ultimate truths of the Cosmos, thereby bringing the civilization of ancient Korea to enlightenment.

TRANSLATION OF THE SCRIPTURE

The first translation of the scripture from Nokdo letters to Chinese characters was done by Choi, Chi Won(scholar, A.D. 857~?)[1]. Choi found the scripture on a tombstone, and after translating it, wrote it into a small book.

---

1) Choi, Chi Won (A.D. 857~?)
Scholar, writer and government official. Author of <u>KYE WON PIL KYONG</u>

THE SCRIPTURE TODAY

The scripture was the foundation on which the government and education of ancient Korea were built, but this background was supplanted over time. Eventually, the scripture was forgotten by almost all Korean people. It has been kept alive in a few historical texts.

In 1911, Kye, Yon Su(historian, ?~A.D. 1920)[2], who collected ancient Korean history books, wrote HAN DAHN KO KI, a book that includes the history and contents of the scripture in its entirety. Despite censorship by the Japanese occupying forces during the occupation of Korea by Japan (1910~1945), HAN DAHN KO KI was read and kept alive by a few people who studied ancient Korean history. The book was republished in 1979 and widely distributed.

Since the publication of HAN DAHN KO KI twenty years ago, the scripture has become widely available again. Scholarly and historical treatises have followed, although many questions remain unresolved. Since the scripture is still being decoded, scholars agree that the scripture contains the highest level of instruction on important principles of religion, philosophy and science.

---

2) Kye, Yon Su(?-A.D. 1920)
Historian. Author of HAN DAHN KO KI, collection of five Korean ancient hi
one of which includes the Scripture of Heavenly Code.

PHONETIC PRESENTATION OF
THE SCRIPTURE OF HEAVENLY CODE

天 符 經

Chon Bu Kyong

一	始	無	始	一	析	三	極	無
il	shi	mu	shi	il	sok	sahm	guk	mu
盡	本	天	一	一	地	一	二	人
jin	bon	chon	il	il	ji	il	yi	ihn
一	三	一	積	十	鉅	無	匱	化
il	sahm	il	jok	sihp	guh	mu	gwe	hwa
三	天	二	三	地	二	三	人	二
sahm	chon	yi	sahm	ji	yi	sahm	ihn	yi
三	大	三	合	六	生	七	八	九
sahm	dae	sahm	hahp	yuk	saeng	chil	pahl	gu
運	三	四	成	環	五	七	一	妙
woon	sahm	sah	sohng	hwan	oh	chil	il	myo
本	本	心	本	太	陽	昂	明	人
bon	bon	shim	bon	tae	yahng	ahng	myong	ihn
中	天	地	一	一	終	無	終	一
jung	chon	ji	il	il	jong	mu	jong	il

Read left to right, up to down.

SCRIPTURE OF HEAVENLY CODE

One Begins unmoved moving, that has No Beginning

One Parts to Three Crowns, while staying a Limit-less Mover

Heaven is the One that comes First

Earth is the One that comes Second

Human is the One that comes Third

One Gathers to Build Ten, and Infinite Forms Become Triads

Heaven gains Two to make Three

Earth gains Two to make Three

Human gains Two to make Three

Three Triads Make Six, and they Create Seven, and Eight

Nine comes there, and there comes a Turning

Three and Four Making a Circle

Five with Seven make One whole

Way-less is the way All Comes and All Goes

Features are Changing, and Change-less is the Maker

Divine Mind Is the Eternal Light, Looking toward celestial Light

Human Bears Heaven and Earth, and the three make One

One is the End of all, and No Ending has the One

WHAT CHON BU KYONG MEANS

The scripture teaches the principle of the creation and evolution of the Cosmos and the principle of human completion. Through these principles, the scripture teaches us about our identity and the life path we are meant to live, to which we are asked to return for our survival in the new millennium.

The translation of the scripture follows below. The first element in each sentence contains the letter-for-letter translation of the Chinese characters, followed by the common, or most apparent contextual meaning of the entire sentence.

The Principle of the Creation and Evolution of the Cosmos

一始無始
One / Begin / No(thing) / Begin
One Begins unmoved moving, that has No Beginning.

"One" is the ultimate reality commonly mentioned as the origin of all beings in most religious or metaphysical philosophies.

一析三極無盡本
One/ Part / Three / Crown / No(thing) / Exhaustion / Origin

One Parts to Three Crowns, while staying a Limit-less
Mover.

"One," the ultimate reality, separates to become three,
representing three different dimensions of existence. The
origin of these three dimensions, however, remains one
and the same, from beginning to end.

天一一地一二人一三
Heaven / One / First / Earth / One / Second / Human
/ One / Third
Heaven is the One that comes First.
Earth is the One that comes Second.
Human is the One that comes Third.

"Heaven"refers to the spiritual dimension of existence.
"Earth"symbolizes the material dimension of existence.
"Human"stands for every form of life and the energy, or
vitality, which animates all life forms.

一積十鉅無匱化三
One / Gather / Ten / Huge / No(thing) / Limit /
Become / Three
One Gathers to Build Ten, and Infinite Forms Become
Triads.

"One," the ultimate reality, individuates into beings that
gather, or merge, and re-form into higher beings.
Throughout the process of individuation and gathering, or

merging, each being, while developing unique traits, contains within itself the original three basic elements of Heaven, Earth and Human.

天二三地二三人二三
Heaven / Two / Three / Earth / Two / Three / Human / Two / Three
Heaven gains Two to make Three.
Earth gains Two to make Three.
Human gains Two to make Three.

Heaven gains earth and human to become a triad which is composed of heavenly heaven, heavenly human and heavenly earth. The same combining principle applies to Earth and Human. Earth, for example, gains Earthly heaven and Earthly human to become the triad of Earthly Earth, and so forth. All the triads form nine different dimensions, or categories of existence, from Earthly Earth to Heavenly Heaven.

大三合六生七八九運
Big / Three / Unite / Six / Seven / Eight / Nine / Circulation
Three Triads make Six, and they Create Seven, and Eight. Nine comes there, and there comes a Turning.

As heaven, earth and human move around in an integrative trinity, the Cosmos grows and evolves into a big circulation. This circulation becomes the life and death cycle for individual living beings, the rise and fall for countries and nations, and the expansion and constriction cycle for the Cosmos.

The Principle of Human Completion

三四成環五七一

Three / Four / Form / Circle / Five / Seven / One
Three and Four Making a Circle
Five with Seven make One whole.

When Three internal Dahn-jons (energy centers in a human body) and Four external Dahn-jons form to create an integrated circulatory system, and when Five Elements of Energy flow through this circulatory system composed of the Seven Dahn-jons, the energy mechanism of the human body becomes complete.

Dahn-jon refers to the energy centers located along the meridian system. They concentrate and enhance the flow of Ki-energy. There are seven Dahn-jons in the human body, three internal Dahn-jons and four external Dahn-jons. The three internal Dahn-jons are divided into the Lower, Middle and Upper Dahn-jon (see illustration on opposite page).

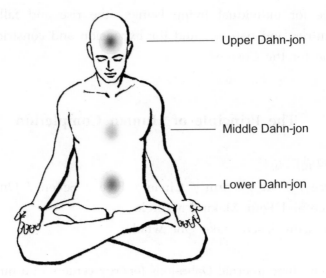

Upper Dahn-jon

Middle Dahn-jon

Lower Dahn-jon

As the three internal Dahn-jons develop, a human being grows from physical health to enlightenment. The first step to enlightenment is the completion of the Lower Dahn-jon. In this stage, the human being's vital energy is strengthened and his physical condition improves remarkably. The next step involves the maturity of the Middle Dahn-jon, during which the human being expresses spontaneous love as his heart opens and expands. Finally, the Upper Dahn-jon is fully awakened and enlightened when the human being grasps, or recovers, the integration of the trinity. When this completion of the Upper Dahn-jon is achieved, the human becomes perfect.

妙衍萬往萬來用變不動本
Mystic / Wide / All / Go / All / Come / Feature / Change / Not / Move / Origin

Way-less is the way All Comes and All Goes
Features are Changing, and Change-less is the Maker

All things change, but the Origin, despite changes in its appearance, remains eternally unchanged.

本心本太陽昂明
The original / Mind / The original / Big / Light / Look / Light
Divine Mind Is the Eternal Light, Looking toward celestial Light

The original divinity remains unchanged, shining like the sun. It looks toward its own origin, the celestial, eternal light.

人中天地一
Human / In the Middle / Heaven / Earth / One
Human Bears Heaven and Earth, and the three make One

Human bears, or carries, Heaven and Earth inside, and Heaven, Earth and Human make an integrated whole.

The Principle of the Cosmic Completion and Eternity

一終無終一
One / end / No(thing) / End / One
One is the End of all, and No Ending has the One

All ends in "One," but "One," the ultimate reality itself, never ends. Likewise, a human being, when completed, becomes one with the "One" in its eternal NOW, beyond any distinction of life/death and existence/non-existence.

HARBINGER OF
COLLECTIVE TRANSFORMATION
FOR THE EARTH'S NEW MILLENNIUM

"I've studied ancient Korean history for years. I discovered Chon Bu Kyong (The Scripture of Heavenly Code) in the late 1970's at the library of Ehwa Women's University. Since then, I've studied it continually. My conclusion is that Chon Bu Kyong is one of the best scriptures expressing the truth of the cosmos and nature as numbers. The scripture came from an enlightened Korean man 9000 years ago. It is a very rare scripture, representing the truth of the creation and evolution of the cosmos and human completion through the simple 81 characters."

-Lee, Jung Jae (1931~)
Historian and President of the Korean Ancient History Academy

"I found Chon Bu Kyong at the U.S. Library of Congress in the early 1980's. Since then, I've studied it and realized that it has more profound cosmic truth than any other scriptures. I believe that Chon Bu Kyong has a remarkable message that can attract the attention of the people of the world, both presently and in the 21st century. I think that many people will realize the truth of the cosmos and of human beings from the scripture."

-Kim, Kwan Tae (1947~)
Ex-professor at the Huntington Career College, U.S.A. (1992~1995)

DAHNHAK EXCERCISE

Do-In Exercise (Meridian Gym)

Do-In is an integrative stretching exercise. It activates the meridian channels and restores their functions. It also eliminates the physical blockages of the meridian channels to facilitate mind/ body communication. It relaxes and prepares the body and mind for Dahn-jon Breathing (Meditative Breath work) and other Dahnhak exercises.

See p.115

Hang-Gong (Meditative Breath work)

Hang-Gong is meditative breath work with postures that are designed to facilitate deep Dahn-jon breathing. It activates the Dahn-jon system and improves the circulation of Ki-energy through the meridian channels. Each posture maximizes Ki-energy in various parts of the body. Hang-Gong fortifies the meridian system and increases the natural healing power of the body by strengthening the immune system and supporting organ function.

See p.116

Un-Ki-Shim-Gong (Conscious Control of Ki-energy)

Un-Ki-Shim-Gong is a gentle, dynamic meditation focusing on the rhythmic flow of Ki-energy. The exercise focuses on extremely slow and relaxed movements of the arms and hands, called "the motionless-motion." The movements are like clouds floating in the sky, or the slow, persistent blooming of a flower. This exercise helps one learn how to control and utilize the Ki-energy and brings one peace, joy, and a positive view of life and the world.

See p.135

Ji-Ki-Gong (Communication with Nature)

Ji-Ki-Gong is an exercise designed for effective energy exchange between humans and nature. It helps one learn to receive the energy of nature and circulate it through one's whole body. This exercise is composed of various motions: light as a bird, elegant as a crane or strong as a tiger. Through these different motions, one feels the great joy of communicating with nature as well as training one's body.

See p.141

Chon Bu Exercise (Chon Bu Kyong Practice)

Chon Bu exercise expresses the unique meaning and energy of each character of Chon Bu Kyong (The Scripture of Heavenly Code) as a motion. When one practices this exercise, one feels the highest level of pure energy embracing one's entire body. Chon Bu exercise recovers the energy circulation of the body and restores, or returns, the body and mind to the original state.

See p.208

Where to Experience Heaven Within

Sedona Dahn Retreat Center
3500 Bill Gray Road Sedona, AZ 86336
Mailing : P.O.Box 2283 Sedona, AZ 86339
Tel. 520-282-4300 / Fax 520-300-0962
Website : http://www.sedonaretreat.com

CGI Holistic Fitness Club
111 Homans Ave. Closter, NJ 07624
Tel. 201-784-5575 / Fax 201-784-2466

Irvine Dahn Center
(Representative of Western U.S. Division)
4940 Irvine Blvd. #109 Irvine, CA 92620
Tel. 714-669-8330 / Fax 714-669-8328

Flushing Dahn Center
(Representative of Eastern U.S. Division)
136-73 Roosevelt Ave. Flushing, NY 11354
Tel. 718-762-6373 / Fax 718-539-7286

This experience is available at any Dahn Center in the U.S.A